Chloe Adams is the perfect heroine f... has ever wished they could step out of the... ... and do it with daring, verve, and a sense of humor. Chloe is a heroine who approac... evastating personal expe... ...ves ... ...ng, and even laugh about it!

Siri Mitchell,
author of Kissing Adrien *and* The Cubicle Next Door

Chloe had me in stitches from page one, and sighing in satisfaction at the end—she made me want to be daring too!

Camy Tang,
author of Sushi for One? *and* Only Uni

Daring Chloe is an engaging, entertaining story! Turning the pages, I felt like I was a real part of the well-traveled Getaway Girls gang, a happy participant in every one of their exciting adventures.

Annette Smith,
author of A Bigger Life *and* A Crooked Path

Also by Laura Jensen Walker

Dreaming in Black and White

Dreaming in Technicolor

Reconstructing Natalie
(Women of Faith Novel of the Year, 2006)

Miss Invisible

A GETAWAY GIRLS NOVEL

Daring Chloe

Book One

Laura Jensen Walker

ZONDERVAN®

ZONDERVAN.com/
AUTHORTRACKER
follow your favorite authors

■ ZONDERVAN®

Daring Chloe
Copyright © 2008 by Laura Jensen Walker

Requests for information should be addressed to:

Zondervan, *Grand Rapids, Michigan* 49530

Library of Congress Cataloging-in-Publication Data

Walker, Laura Jensen.
    Daring Chloe : a Getaway Girls novel / Laura Jensen Walker.
      p. cm.
    ISBN 978-0-310-27696-8 (pbk.)
     1. Self-actualization (Psychology)—Fiction. I. Title.
PS3623.A3595D37 2008
813'.6—dc22

                         2007047709

Published in association with the literary agency of Alive Communications, Inc., 7680 Goddard Street, Suite 200, Colorado Springs, CO 80920.

Interior design by Christine Orejuela-Winkelman

Interior illustration by Ruth Pettis

Printed in the United States of America

---

08 09 10 11 12 13 • 23 22 21 20 19 18 17 16 15 14 13 12 11 10 9 8 7 6 5 4 3 2 1

For my sister Lisa, who shares my
reading obsession, with much love.

(Trixie Belden rocks!)

And for my Book Ends book club: Betty Jo,
Carol, Cheryl, Gabriela, Jamie, Janelle, Jennie, Lisa,
Michele S., Michelle W., Sarah, and Sheri.

Although I've poached a couple of the books
from our club, rest assured, none of the
Paperback Girls are based on you.

*I do thank God for my books with
every fiber of my being.*

Oswald Chambers

He that loves reading has
everything within his reach.

William Godwin

Part 1

january

*L*ittle Women

> Customs of courtship vary greatly in different times and places, but the way the thing happens to be done here and now always seems the only natural way to do it.
>
> *Marjorie Morningstar*

At 1:33 a.m., nine hours and twenty-seven minutes before my wedding ceremony, my fiancé dumped me. By text message.

The "Going to the Chapel" ringtone woke me, and I grabbed my phone off the guestroom nightstand before it woke my sister, Julia, asleep in the twin bed next to me. I opened one eye, fumbled for my glasses, and peered at the luminous green numbers on the digital clock radio.

Poor baby. Probably too keyed up over the excitement of the big day to sleep. I smiled and snuggled under the covers to enjoy a romantic text message. Chris had been a little stressed and distracted at the rehearsal dinner earlier, but that was to be expected. Wedding preparations were definitely stressful. Thankfully, tomorrow—today—it would all be over, and we could at last start our happily ever after.

I read his text, eager to see what sweet, tender things he had to say.

SORRY, CLO. CAN'T DO IT. TOO MUCH. GOTTA GET AWAY. PEACE.

"Ryan?" My fingers flew over my phone. NOT FUNNY. JUST A FEW HOURS AWAY, CHRIS. LOVE YOU!

Ryan Chandler was Chris's best man and roommate. This kind of stunt didn't seem like him, but it had to be. Right? But Chris didn't answer my text. His battery must be low. I called him on his landline and got his answering machine: "Hey, it's Chris O'Neil. I'm not around right now, but I'll return your call when I get back, so leave a message."

He'd changed his greeting. Gone were the sarcastic comments about picking out flowers and schmoozing extended family members. His voice sounded odd. Strained and strange. Not the excited tone of a man about to leave on his honeymoon. I shoved the covers off as I tried his cell. It went straight to voice mail. I texted again: WHAT'S GOING ON? YOU OK?

No reply.

Concerned, I pulled up Ryan's number and dialed. He picked it up on the first ring. "Hi, Chloe." There was no reassuring laugh in his voice.

"What's going on?" I whispered, not wanting to wake Julia. "Where's Chris? Is he okay?"

"He's fine. Physically fine." Ryan gave a heavy sigh. "Look, Chloe, there's no easy way to say this. The wedding's off. Chris doesn't want to get married. I know the timing really sucks, but—"

I dropped the phone. It slid off the comforter and clattered to the hardwood floor between the beds, waking my sister.

"Chloe? What's wrong?"

I couldn't answer. I couldn't breathe.

In my daze, it dimly registered that Julia leaned down and

picked up the phone. "Who is this?" she demanded. "Oh, I see. Okay. Thank you."

Julia flipped the phone shut and looked at me, her gorgeous tawny eyes wet and filled with pity. "I'm so, so sorry." She flung the covers off and moved toward me, her silky nightgown swishing around her. She stopped when I raised my hand.

The hand with my engagement ring.

I let out a sob and sank back on the bed, gasping as my eyes gushed and my nose ran, snot mixed with tears falling on my oversized T-shirt that was beginning to fray at the hem.

"What's going on?" My parents appeared in the doorway, my dad's skimpy hair sticking up every which way.

I looked up at them through blurry eyes, unable to say the words.

"There's not going to be a wedding," Julia informed them.

"Not going to be a wedding?" My aunt Tess, champion and surrogate mother, strode into the room behind my parents and enfolded me in her wiry arms.

I laid my head against her chenille-robed chest and cried. And cried.

And wondered if it was possible to text message a kick in the groin.

As I approached the kitchen the next morning, I could hear my twin cousins, Timmy and Tommy, Tess's sixteen-year-old sons, plotting revenge.

"We'll give Chris something to think about."

"Oh yeah. And then some."

"Now boys—" my mother started, but broke off when she saw me in the doorway. "How are you feeling this morning, dear?" she asked.

"Just great. Especially for someone who just got dumped. It's not every day a girl gets left at the altar. We should celebrate."

Mom flushed and turned her attention back to frying bacon. Julia looked down at her lap.

"Take it easy, Chloe." My dad squeezed my shoulder as he set down a cup of coffee in front of me. "Sniping at your mother won't make things any better."

"You're right." I gulped the French roast and scalded my tongue. "Sorry, Mom."

Mom, who is all sweetness and light, content to cook and clean for her family, sew costumes for church, do crafts, and volunteer in the nursery, is completely my opposite. I'm the undomestic, uncrafty daughter with perpetually bad hair who hates sewing, cooking, cleaning, and especially nursery work. Mom reads *Better Homes and Gardens*; I read John Grisham. Mom reads the *Reader's Digest* condensed version, and I read the unabridged, uncut, unsterilized version. And as such, our relationship is often about miscues and miscommunication.

Julia the Perfect is, of course, Mom's clone.

When I got engaged, though, Mom was suddenly in my world and in her element, helping clueless me pick out flowers, bridesmaid dresses, the cake, everything. Now, with one late-night text message, that was all gone.

I looked at the kitchen clock — 8:25 — and wondered how I was going to get through the next couple of minutes, much less hours. I stared at the second hand as it made its agonizingly slow sweep around the numbers. Five seconds. Ten seconds. Twelve. How could time be so interminable? So painful? Each sweep of the hand taking me closer to the scheduled time of my walk down the aisle was like a butcher knife through my heart. I wanted to scream, kick, and tear my hair. But that wasn't my style. Instead, I pushed my messy hair behind my ears and glanced across the breakfast table to my redheaded cousins who'd stayed over last night along with Tess for the wedding.

The wedding that was no more.

"I heard the phone ring," I said casually. "Was it Chris? Did you guys talk to him?" I tried to still the hopeful flutter in my breast.

"I'm sorry, honey, it was Ryan," Tess said. "He called to let us know that no one would be able to reach Chris. He was heading out on a backpacking trip so he could get away and—" she made quote marks with her hands—"'think.' Ryan also said he'd contacted the pastor and told all Chris's friends and family what happened."

"Didn't waste any time, did he?" I slapped my mug on the table, sloshing the muddy brown liquid over the top. I'd actually known Ryan before Chris. We were friends in the same singles Sunday school class at church, and it was at a singles event—a hike along the Pacific Crest Trail—where Ryan had introduced me to his new roommate, Chris. One look into Chris's gorgeous hazel eyes flecked with gold and I was gone.

Hiking wasn't really my thing. A little too heavy on the bugs, lizards, and exertion. Plus, there was always the prospect of mountain lions waiting to pounce on unsuspecting city-girl me. No thanks. I'd rather stay home curled up with a good book. On that particular day, however, Shannon, a friend of sorts from the singles group who was nursing a major crush on Ryan, had pleaded with me to go along. "C'mon, Chloe, you don't even really have to hike," she cajoled, knowing full well my aversion to the great outdoors. "I know where they're stopping for a picnic lunch, and we can park nearby and just walk in a little ways to meet up with them at the site."

Shannon sweetened the deal. "I'm bringing my triple-fudge brownies."

"With chocolate chips?"

"You got it."

"Let me find my tennis shoes."

Her hopes of getting together with Ryan hadn't worked out—he saw her as just a buddy. But Chris didn't look at me through buddy eyes. We both fell hard and fast, which didn't sit well with Ryan. He thought we were infatuated and needed to take our time and really get to know each other. Looks like he may have been right.

Julia mopped up my spilled coffee with a paper towel. "Remember, Chris loves you. He probably just got scared. Lots of men get cold feet. I'm sure you'll hear from him soon."

"Riiiiiggghht." I laid my head down on the table. Some stray sugar granules dug into my cheek.

Tommy—or was it Timmy?—gave my back a couple of awkward pats. I heard his brother say with a Tony Soprano swagger, "Whaddya say, Uncle Jim? Let's find this guy and teach him not to mess with our family."

"Family?" My head popped up like a jack-in-the-box. "Oh, no. Everybody's coming o—"

The back door slammed. "Where's our poor darling girl?" Aunt Gabby burst into the kitchen. "You poor, poor thing. How awful!" She swept me into her arms, her titanic chest heaving with indignation beneath her Hawaiian-print polyester muumuu. I appreciated the comfort, but come on: she was dressed in a Hawaiian-print polyester muumuu for my *wedding* ceremony.

An unearthly shriek pierced the air. "But I wanna wear my flower-girl dress and throw roses on the ground. You promised!"

Aunt Gabby released me to comfort her six-year-old Nellie Oleson spawn who'd followed her in. "Now, Erica, sweetheart, remember what Mommy and Daddy told you," she soothed.

"There's not going to be a wedding, so you can't wear your dress today. But you can wear it to church tomorrow instead."

"That's right, angel." Middle-aged Uncle Bud squatted down in front of his daughter from the netherworld. "You can wear your pretty dress tomorrow and throw flower petals in the backyard after church."

Uncle Bud and Aunt Gabby, my dad's sister, never thought they'd have kids. They married in their mid-thirties and started trying right away, but to no avail. Then Aunt Gabby received an unexpected gift for her fortieth birthday; a blue line on her at-home pregnancy test. Seven-and-a-half months later, Erica, the light of their lives—and the bane of the rest of the family's—arrived.

"Noooo!" Erica glared at me and then dropped to the kitchen floor, flailing her arms and kicking her legs. "Wanna wear it today, wanna wear it today!"

I love my family, but it was too much. They were too much. I fled upstairs.

Tess—she'd asked me to drop the *Aunt* prefix on my six-teenth birthday—followed me to my old bedroom that my parents had made into a guest room after I'd moved out.

I pulled on jeans, a T-shirt, and my favorite blue fleece hoodie after yanking my flyaway bed-head hair through a po-nytail holder. "I have to get out of here."

"I'm with ya. Let's blow this popsicle stand. Just give me two seconds to change," she said. "I'll drive."

And drive she did, hard and fast, in her old MG convert-ible. We didn't talk. There was no need. It was impossible for Tess to hear me with the top and windows down anyway. Which was just as well. I don't think my aunt had ever heard those particular kinds of words come out of my mouth.

I inserted my iPod ear buds, shut my eyes, and leaned back against the leather seat, lost in Rosemary land. Most of my friends had never heard of Rosemary Clooney, or if they had, only as gorgeous George's aunt. But Tess had introduced me to her when I was a little girl. I pumped up the volume on the torch song Rosemary sang in *White Christmas*, "Love, You Didn't Do Right By Me."

Fifteen minutes later, my eyes flew open as the bottom of the MG scraped on a steep driveway. "Dunkeld's? You picked Dunkeld's Bookstore?"

"They have the best lattes around. You've said so yourself." She picked up her purse with the pen-and-ink caricatured faces of famous women writers on the front. "I vote for a couple of medicinal lattes to take the sting out. And I have a craving for their cranberry scones."

"I'll just wait out here."

"No you won't. You didn't do anything wrong. You have no reason to hide. It's Chris who needs to keep his sorry self out of sight."

Which is why he went backpacking. I shuddered at the thought of bugs, mice, and not even porta-potties in the remote wilderness areas where my fiancé—ex-fiancé—liked to hike. He knew I wouldn't follow him there.

"Now come on. I need caffeine."

"Okay. But put that thing on your other shoulder. Sylvia Plath is giving me the evil eye again."

"She's just wishing she could rethink that whole oven thing."

Tess slung her bookish bag over her scrawny shoulder as we entered our favorite bookstore and headed straight to the café. "Two tall skinny lattes with a double shot, one with foam, one no-foam," she ordered.

"Make mine a triple. And I'd like a chocolate-chocolate-chip cookie too. Tess?"

"A cranberry scone, please."

Beethoven's Fifth Symphony sounded, and Tess fumbled in her purse beneath Virginia Woolf's elongated nose. She flipped open her cell. "Hi, Julia." Her eyes flicked to mine. "She's fine. Oh, she must have had her phone off. We went for a drive and stopped to get a latte. Did you want to talk to her?"

I frowned and shook my head no.

"Oh, sorry. I think she just went into the ladies room. But we'll be back soon, don't worry. And tell your mom not to worry either. See you in a bit."

"Thanks." The last thing I wanted was to talk to Julia the Perfect. I grabbed my latte and cookie, hunching my shoulders in an attempt to hide the neon sign on my chest flashing, "Jilted bride, jilted bride," and hurried to the farthest corner table before I blinded everyone in sight.

"Feel better?"

I nodded. But I was lying.

"Okay, so the first thing is to get you the heck out of Dodge. The last thing you need is to hang around here and face everyone's pity and platitudes when your heart has just been ripped from your chest. Plenty of time for that later." Tess sent me a speculative look from behind her red rectangle glasses. "Know what I think you should do?"

"What?"

"Go on that cruise to Mexico anyway."

I stared at her. "My *honeymoon* cruise? Are you kidding?"

"You need to get away. Besides, you paid for the tickets, right?"

"I put them on my credit card so Chris wouldn't max his out." Defending my fiancé to my family had become a way of life. They were always criticizing him—his "lack of responsibility," his "flakiness," his "immaturity."

All except for Tess.

Only now it looked like she might be joining the anti–Chris

O'Neil chorus. But she knew better. Especially on my almost wedding day.

I looked at my watch. "In an hour and twenty-four minutes I'm supposed to be walking down the aisle to the man of my dreams." Tears started to prick my eyelids again, but I forced them down. "Man of my dreams—hah! Who does he think he is to do this to me?"

"Now you're talking." Tess slapped my knee in girl-power solidarity.

"Ow!"

"Sorry. Don't know my own strength."

"I'll say. For a little woman, you pack a lot of power."

"You know what they say—good things come in small packages." Tess, who usually avoided clichés like the plague—unlike me, who thinks they have a time and a place, like here—waggled her reddish-brown eyebrows over the top of her skinny red glasses.

"Chloe?"

I knew I should have stayed in the car. I braced myself, pasted on a smile, and turned to face the force of nature that was Becca Daniels.

"I'm so *sorry!*" Becca, one of my bridesmaids, flung her arms around me in typical fierce fashion. "I've been trying to call you all morning, and when you didn't answer, I stopped by your parents' house and they told me you and Tess had gone out. Are you okay? You must be devastated. That jerk!"

Heads swiveled our way.

"Why don't we sit down?" Tess suggested.

"Sorry." Becca's olive skin reddened beneath her inky pixie-cut bangs. "Was I being too loud?"

"You?" Tess lifted an eyebrow.

"So, what happened?" Becca whispered as we sat down at the laminate bistro table.

"I-I don't know."

"I'm so sorry. What can I do? Just tell me. Anything. Whatever you need."

"Well, you could—oh, no. I don't believe it."

"What?" Becca and Tess said in chorus.

"Ryan."

I'd forgotten that he often grabbed his Saturday breakfast here. Clearly a little thing like a cancelled wedding wasn't going to stop his stomach. "He's coming this way. I'll die if he sees me." Grabbing an oversized Picasso art book from the closest table, I scrunched my head down behind it.

Tess also hid her head by ducking it under the table on the pretext that she'd dropped something. But Becca shot up from her chair. Unable to see anything but *Don Quixote*, I listened to her Birkenstock clogs clunk away then stop.

"Becca? What are you doing here?" Ryan's voice carried easily to our table.

"I work here."

"I know. But I thought you took off for the wedding."

"You mean the wedding that wasn't? The wedding where the Cowardly Lion groom bailed at the last minute?"

I cringed behind my book camouflage.

"You don't know the whole story."

"I know that your cold-footed *friend* didn't even have the guts to give Chloe a heads-up that something was wrong."

"He tried, but he didn't know how. But I agree. If it were me, I'd have handled it differently."

"Yeah? How's that?"

"I'd never have let things get this far if I was having doubts. I'd have definitely shared my concerns with my fiancée earlier and not waited until the last minute."

A brief silence ensued.

"But," Ryan continued, "I think Chris did the right thing."

It was all I could do not to pop my head up from behind my book and say, *What?*

Becca had my back. *"What?* Leaving his bride at the altar on her wedding day?"

"He didn't leave her at the altar—he let her know the night before."

"Big of him."

"It was the best he could do. He didn't want to embarrass her in front of the entire church."

"And you think he didn't, just because he wasn't in the actual *building?*"

"Would you rather they'd gotten married and it wound up in divorce? At least they hadn't taken their vows," Ryan said. "I have to give Chris props for that. It was a really hard thing for him to do, but ultimately it was the right thing."

"Yeah, maybe for him, but what about Chloe?"

My nose began to itch, but I knew I didn't dare scratch it. The last thing I wanted was to draw attention to our table. Apparently Tess decided crawling around on the floor any longer would do precisely that, as she surfaced to huddle beside me behind the book.

"For Chloe, too," Ryan said, his tone gentling. "Which I think she'll see in the long run. Chloe wasn't ready for marriage. And if you're honest, you'll admit it. Beating your sister to the altar isn't a good enough reason to get married."

I gasped. So much for not drawing attention. I tried to cover the gasp with a cough, sneaking in a nose scratch beneath my glasses at the same time, all while still hidden behind my oversized art book.

Ryan backtracked. "Maybe that was a little harsh. But did you really see them as a good match? They're so different.

Chris is an adventure guy, a risk taker, a daredevil. And Chloe's so ... well ... not."

"But differences are what make a relationship interesting," Becca argued. "If they were exactly alike, it would be boring."

The B-word hung heavy in the air like a wet sheet on a clothesline.

"Maybe it's best if we let them sort it out."

"Yeah if the Cowardly Lion ever returns from the wild."

"He will. He just needed some alone time." Ryan paused. "Please tell Chloe when you see her—tell her I'm sorry for the way this all went down and that I'll be praying for her."

I peered around Picasso and watched Ryan's blue Chuck Taylors vanish through the door.

"You forgot your breakfast," Becca called after him, but he was already gone.

Slamming the art book shut, I sprang from my seat. "He'll be praying for *me*? He'd better pray for his risk-taking, dare-devil friend, 'cause when I find him, I'm gonna *kill* him. Bet he won't find *that* boring."

Tess grabbed her literary purse. "Come on, Chloe. You're going on your honeymoon. And I'm coming with you, so let's go buy a bikini. I'm thinking red thong."

2

"Can't keep still all day, and, not being a pussy-cat,
I don't like to doze by the fire. I like adventures, and I'm
going to find some."

Little Women

"Now that's what I'm talkin' about!" Becca's excited voice
pierced the salty air.

Refusing to be left behind while Tess and I had fun in the
sun, Becca told her boss she was finally going to take those
days off he'd been bugging her about, and Monday morning
we were on our way.

Good thing Tess is a travel agent.

She managed to pull the right strings to get Becca last-
minute cheap tickets on our five-day Mexican cruise and also
save me penalties from switching Chris's reservation to Tess's
name and trading in the queen-size honeymoon bed for two
singles.

Tess and I had a great room with a balcony and ocean
view—which I kept imagining Chris and I sharing—while

Becca was squashed into not much more than a closet with no view. But she didn't care. She was hardly ever in her room anyway, only to sleep and change. She was always dragging us off to some new shipboard activity — tennis, trivia games, karaoke, even salsa dancing, where Tess surprised both of us with her fancy footwork.

"You need to go on one of those ballroom-dancing TV shows," I said to my aunt later that night while she was brushing her teeth before bed. "You'd blow everyone else out of the water."

She rinsed and spit. "Nah, I'm too old. But I could see Becca doing it."

"What wouldn't Becca do?"

I thought back to the first time we'd met Becca. There was a booksigning at Dunkeld's for a local, not-well-known-yet author, who had written a spy thriller in which the hero donned many disguises — including a clown suit — in his pursuit of the bad guys. And as Tess and I joined the others in the sparse audience to listen to the author and get our books signed, suddenly the *Mission Impossible* theme blared from the speakers, and a clown clad in a baggy, lime green polka-dot costume, fake red nose, and frizzy orange wig, came racing through the bookstore toward us.

A curious crowd followed on his heels.

The frenzied clown zigzagged between the rows of now-filling chairs in time to the frenetic spy music. And when he got to the middle aisle between the chairs, he promptly dropped to the ground and rolled in a trio of somersaults to the podium, ending his journey with the splits, which prompted a round of enthusiastic applause.

The clown jumped up, bowed, and moved behind the podium where he yanked off his wig and fake nose, revealing a grinning, elfin, and very obviously female face.

"Welcome to Dunkeld's," the lady clown said, reaching up to ruffle her inky black flattened hair back into short, spiky position. "My name's Becca, and I'm happy to introduce you to our local author Peter Lincoln, who's going to give Tom Clancy a run for his money with his latest spy novel, *The Hunt for Norville Blake.*"

After the successful signing, Tess and I went up and introduced ourselves to Becca, who, we learned, was a clerk at Dunkeld's and fellow bookaholic like us. She'd recently graduated from college with an English degree, and invited us to join a women's book club she was just beginning.

That was nearly two years ago, and since then, Becca had also invited me to join her on several of her wild-and-crazy escapades — bungee-jumping, paintball wars, snowboarding, and speed-dating.

I always decline politely. The book club is enough.

Today, Becca the Adventurous had managed to talk me — dare me, actually — into snorkeling off Cabo San Lucas while our ship was docked for the day.

Me, the girl who's scared of water.

Not all water, though. I have no problem with the pool at my parents', and I linger in the tub for my Saturday night soak. But the ocean's a completely different animal. Not the least is all the creepy-crawly creatures and animals of the deep. Fish I don't mind so much. Actually, I love fish — a little sea bass or grilled salmon and especially fresh-cracked Alaskan King crab with drawn butter.

"C'mon, Chloe. You'll love it!" Becca urged. "There's nothing like snorkeling. Wait'll you see all the gorgeous fish. The colors will take your breath away."

"What will really take my breath away is when I see sharks. Big old hungry sharks looking for a little lunch." I hummed the music from *Jaws.* That movie terrified me when I saw it as a kid — as it would have anyone in her right mind — and left me with a lingering fear of the sea. And especially sharks.

"That was Hollywood. And that was also a great white. Not even a real one. It was a goofy mechanical shark they built for the movie. You won't see any great whites around here."

"So you're promising me that if we go snorkeling, we won't see any sharks?"

"Nah."

Tess looked at her.

"Probably not," Becca amended. "Not that close to the surface. And if we do, it would only be harmless, cute little nurse sharks. What we'll most likely see are beautiful colorful fish, maybe some coral, and, if we're lucky, sea turtles."

Colorful fish worked for me. But it was the sea turtles that really did the trick.

I've always had a thing for turtles. I had a couple when I was little and always loved to watch them poke their heads out of their shells and meander slowly across my bedroom carpet. To get up close and personal with a huge sea turtle in its natural habitat would beat the childhood carpet races and then some. "Okay, nature girl. Lead the way."

Tess plopped a straw hat over her wispy auburn hair. "While you two do your Jacques Cousteau thing, I'll be checking out the shops. Let's meet at Cabo Wabo's for lunch around twelve thirty. I hear they have great seafood and fabulous margaritas. See you in a few hours." She waggled her fingers at us as she strode away.

I was tempted to follow her. Was I really ready to do this deep-sea adventure? Who knew what frightening things lurked in the deep? But then, who knew that I'd be spending my honeymoon with two girlfriends rather than with the man I loved? Not exactly what I'd dreamed of when Chris and I had planned our romantic cruise. He'd had to calm my water fears as well. "Don't worry, babe, I'll protect you," he'd promised, pulling me close, when I'd shared my deep-sea reservations with him.

Yeah right. Just another one of the promises he'd broken. Had he ever meant anything he said? Or was it all just a big lie? And if so, how could I have been so deceived? So stupid.

Or maybe just intentionally blind?

Not going there. Not now. I can't. This was supposed to be my *honeymoon*. I shoved my hand beneath my glasses and dashed away the wetness, focusing my attention back to Becca and what she was saying.

She assured me we wouldn't go too far from shore. Becca also said that I could rent a wetsuit, which would keep me warm and give me extra buoyancy in the water. But no way was I going to wriggle into one of those rubber torture devices and squash all my butt-and-thigh cellulite together into a giant piece of Swiss cheese for the whole world to see. Especially when I noticed a couple of women close to my size walk past in the black rubber suits with a big *L* on the front.

Yeah right. Let me just announce to the whole world that I'm a loser. And a large one at that. Almost as bad as a scarlet *A*. Almost.

Becca led me to the rental shack where we picked up our snorkeling gear. I stuck my feet into the ungainly, oversized flippers and took a few tentative steps. Can you say duck out of water?

Daisy Duck had nothing on me.

I removed my glasses, placed them in the pocket of my shorts and carefully rolled my clothes into a towel which Becca said would be safe left on the beach.

She snapped my mask into place, but everything remained blurry.

"Hey, I can't see."

"My bad. I forgot you need a prescription one. Come on." She removed the offending goggles and hurried off to exchange them while I waddled behind her in my awkward footwear.

Forget Daisy Duck. I was Bozo the Clown. All that was missing was the red hair and red nose, but a couple hours in the sun would take care of the latter.

We exchanged the mask for one that allowed me to actually see, and Becca showed me how to insert my mouthpiece and use the snorkel. I could tell she was impatient to get going.

I followed her into the ocean and instantly regretted my decision to nix the wetsuit. That water was seriously cold! I warmed up, though, after we swam and splashed around for a few minutes, which also helped me get used to the flippers, which worked so much better in water.

Becca inserted her mouthpiece and motioned for me to do the same. Then she gave me a thumbs up and submerged her head. I took a deep breath, stretched out so I was floating on my stomach, clutching a pink foam noodle, and stuck my face beneath the water's surface.

Wow.

Finding Nemo didn't do justice to the glorious water world laid out before me. It was like swimming in a Jackson Pollock painting.

I looked over at Becca and could see her eyes crackling with excitement behind her mask. I returned her thumbs up as I drank in the amazing sights passing before me.

A school of electric-blue-and-yellow angel fish swam past, followed by a mass of vivid orange fish with big dark eyes and a fan-like thing on their backs. They soon darted off, except for one little guy who straggled behind and swam right up to my goggles, checking out this strange creature invading his watery space. I lowered my hand to pet him/her — how can you tell if fish are male or female?—but he was too fast. In an instant he was gone.

Becca waved, and then dove down like a mermaid, checking everything out farther below. Not me. I was a happy girl just floating on top of the water and looking down on the myriad sea life.

All at once, something brushed against my ankle. My heart dynamited from my chest, but when I glanced at my feet, I saw it was another school of little yellow fish darting past.

Aw, they're so cute. I made funny faces at them from behind my mask. Then I caught a glimpse of a big dark shadow moving a little farther below. Definitely not cute little fishies.

Something else.

Something big.

Something terrifying.

I knew it. Certain death was circling below me. Soon the water would be a frothing, thrashing scene of unspeakable carnage, and whatever remained of me would be shipped home in a small Tupperware container. I spit out my mouthpiece and ended up taking a huge gulp of salty water. I jerked my head out of the water and started to hyperventilate and wave my arms.

Becca, alarmed by my frantic flailing, popped up beside me and removed her mouthpiece. "Are you okay? What happened?"

"Dark! Big! Shadow!" I sputtered.

"That was just a stingray."

"A stingray?" I continued to cough. "As in huge flapping winged demon with poisonous tail?"

"Only if you get too close. They're more afraid of you than you are of them. If you don't bother them, which, clearly, you won't, they won't bother you. Trust me. Ready to go back?"

"Becca! What if we see a shark next?"

"That would be so cool!"

"Yeah? In what universe?"

"Aw, don't be a baby. If we did see one, it'd be deeper below anyway and probably just a cute little nurse shark. I've always wanted to pet one."

"You're certifiable."

"People tell me that all the time. But it keeps life interesting, don't you think?" She winked. "Here's the thing: the rule of thumb with sharks is to assess them like a dog. Some are aggressive, so you stay away. And some are passive and will let you get close enough to touch them. That's the kind I'm looking for."

"*Looking* for? Are you nuts? Who in their right mind would look for a shark? We need to go back *now*."

"No way. This was expensive and we haven't even seen anything yet. This is the chance of a lifetime. We're staying."

"You may be staying, but I'm leaving."

"I don't think you want to do that," Becca said. "A lone swimmer is much more attractive to a shark. And they can sense fear. Given the amount of fear you're exuding, I'd give you about ten yards before you're fish food."

"Are you being serious or just trying to scare me so I stick with your insane adventure?"

Becca simply smiled, stuck her mouthpiece back in, and submerged beneath the water. Clearly the woman I thought was my friend had been abducted by hostile aliens and replaced with the Creature from the Black Lagoon.

I had no choice. Hesitantly, I followed her but stuck to the surface.

Within seconds, another cluster of fish — electric blue with a yellow stripe down their backs — swam by.

Gorgeous. Absolutely gorgeous. Maybe the ocean's not so bad after all. I gently kicked my flippered feet as I glided smoothly along the surface of the giant tropical fish tank, enjoying the marine life all around me. Farther off and a little deeper, I noticed a dark oval shape slowly moving my way. I strained to see through my mask, which was starting to fog up, and then caught my breath as a large sea turtle swam closer. Although he didn't possess the flamboyance of the tropical fish, his spotted legs and arms captivated me. I stared at his dark, heavy shell as he paddled by—a shell that protects him from sharks and stingrays.

Even I would swim in the deep if I had that kind of shield from danger.

I watched in wonder until my beautiful turtle was out of sight, and then I turned to catch Becca's eye and give her a major thumbs up.

Only Becca was entranced with her own marine life farther below. I squinted, trying to make out what she was holding. It was a baby Jaws, and not only was Becca holding it, she was petting its belly.

Any minute now the enraged mother shark would emerge from the deep and turn Becca into a modern-day Jonah, swallowing my friend whole. Or not so whole, since it was, after all, a *shark.*

Spitting my mouthpiece out again—the least of my worries now was gulping salt water—I set a new Olympic speed record as I splashed to shore. A few minutes later, Becca caught up with me on the beach, where I was struggling out of my flippers. "How'd you like your first snorkeling experience?"

"First and last you mean."

"What? Why?"

"Because you're crazy. Petting a Mini-Me Jaws! Who do you think you are—some sort of aqueous X-Men mutant?"

"Chill. It wasn't any big deal."

"It was to me. You totally freaked me out."

Becca's mouth said I'm sorry, but her eyes were still spar-kling from the experience.

My turtle had put the same sparkle in my eyes, but a turtle is a far cry from a *shark*. I shook my head to clear it of the scary movie theme music and my saltwater-drenched pony-tail smacked my cheek. The next time Becca tried to talk me into one of her dangerous adventures, I was bringing along reinforcements.

If I'd been with Chris, this wouldn't have happened, right? Like Becca, my beloved—*former* beloved—was also a thrill seeker. He'd have had me in that water in nothing flat. And although I'd have protested all the way, I'd have done it.

For him.

My shoulders slumped. What had happened to make Chris bail at the last minute? What did I do?

Or was it what I didn't do?

We showered at one of the outdoor cabanas, changed into shorts and tanks, and met Tess at Cabo Wabo's, where she was already tasting the Wabo-Rita. She nodded to her glass and held up two fingers to the approaching waiter.

I reminded my aunt that I was a Diet Coke girl.

"I know. But this is a special occasion. You're on vaca-tion. Time to live a little. Besides, one margarita's not going to hurt you. Trust your Aunt Tess." She waved a glossy brochure. "Guess where we're going this afternoon?"

"If you say scuba-diving, I'm going to throw up."

Becca's eyes brightened.

"Not to worry. You need lessons for that, anyway. No, I had something else in mind." Tess paused, and then said in a sonorous tone, "Call me Ishmael."

Moby Dick had been one of our classics last year in book club. Most of us found it too long and boring to get through. But not Tess. She loved it.

Every interminable page.

I gaped at her. "You want us to go whale hunting? Isn't that illegal?"

"Yes, but whale watching isn't." She read excitedly from the brochure. "Making the longest migration of any mammal, these whales migrate some 6,000 miles south from Alaskan and Siberian waters to winter in the warm waters of Baja California and the Sea of Cortez. Here they find shelter and food and give birth to their young." Tess looked at us with shining eyes. "Just imagine. We might see a baby whale being born!"

"You already have." I patted my hips. "Ten pounds, three ounces."

"Can I continue?"

"Sorry. Go on."

"Gray whales can weigh up to 73,000 pounds," she recited. "With long snouts and double blowholes on top of their heads, grays have a hump with dorsal ridges running to their tail in place of a dorsal fin. On a whale watching excursion, you'll see spouting, breaching, and sounding (showing their flukes), all spectacular sights."

Tess held up three tickets. "So let's hurry up and eat, because our boat leaves in forty minutes."

"No way! Really?" Becca grabbed one of the tickets. "Um, how much were they? My landlord just raised the rent, so things are a little tight. Time to find a new place to live."

"Don't worry about it. My treat."

Becca lived paycheck to paycheck, which was why I was so surprised she was able to join us on the cruise—especially at the last minute. "That's what plastic is for," she'd said, brandishing her Visa. "Life's too short to let a little thing like money stop you from doing what you want."

Chris had felt the same way about money, but my responsible self blanched at the notion of spending so recklessly. I'd been a saver ever since I got my first savings account at ten, and I'd been adding to it ever since, only withdrawing from it when absolutely necessary—like when my car needed a new transmission. At the rate I was going, by the end of the year I'd have enough money saved to put a hefty down payment on a nice little house. A house I'd planned to share with Chris and eventually our family.

I took a deep breath of sea air to clear my head of those happily-ever-after thoughts and focused in on the here and now instead. Just in time.

We gasped in unison as a massive gray whale leapt out of the water and splashed back down. Wow. Chris would have loved that. He's seen whales in Monterey and said it was something he'd never forget.

What's he doing right now? I thought. Is he still backpacking? Is he thinking about me? Maybe he's rethinking his decision … I know guys get cold feet. And things did move pretty fast—less than three months from the proposal to the wedding.

My fingers slid to my shorts pocket and touched my cell.

No, I'm not going to check to see if he's called. Probably can't get a signal out here anyway. I refuse to think about Chris anymore. I'm just going to have a good time with the girls.

"This honeymoon without a husband thing's really workin' for me." I stretched out in my chaise lounge on deck the next day, sipping a pink tropical drink and basking in the sun in my navy one-piece. (I'd nixed the thong bikini idea.)

"Me too." From her matching chaise lounge next to mine, Tess stole a look over her sunglasses at four tanned beach boys with great abs playing water volleyball in the nearby pool.

"Down, girl."

"Nothing wrong with looking."

Yes there was. If I looked at their toned chests and six-pack abs, I'd be reminded of Chris's strong, comforting chest, which I should have been cozying up to this very minute on our honeymoon.

I buried my nose further in my book, but the wind made my flyaway hair obscure some of the words. I sighed and yanked my hair back yet again into my one-size-fits-all ponytail.

"Hey guys, I have a great idea!" Becca plopped down on a nearby deck chair, today wearing her sleek orange one-piece that resembled the old *Baywatch* babes' swimsuits—minus the jiggle. Becca was lean and lithe.

"For book club," she continued, "instead of just *talking* about the books we read every month, why don't we live out some of the adventures in the books? Wouldn't that be cool?"

Tess gave Becca her Lauren Bacall half-lidded look. "You want us to cut off our hair like Jo and sell it so Marmee has enough money to visit Father in the hospital?"

"Oh." Becca did that little moue thing with her mouth. "I forgot *Little Women* is our next book."

"Which means you haven't even started reading it yet." I held up my dog-eared copy. "How do you plan to have it finished by next week?"

"No prob. I'm a fast reader. I already read it years ago, so I just need to give it a quick skim."

"Sacrilege!" I clasped my hand over my heart. "You can't give Jo a quick skim. Or Beth. Or—"

"Amy," Tess said. "Especially Amy. She wouldn't like it at all."

"All right already. Calm down. I promise to give the March girls my undivided attention later if you'll give me yours now." Becca scooted closer. "Don't you think it'd be great? I got the idea yesterday when we were whale watching, Tess, and you said, 'Now I know how Captain Ahab felt.' That stuck in my mind and I started thinking how fun it would be if we could actually live out some of the same adventures the characters in our books do. How exciting is that?"

She snapped her fingers. "I know! We could read *Into Thin Air* and go mountain climbing!"

"Isn't that the one where all those people died on Mount Everest?"

"They didn't *all* die. The author didn't. And it's a great book." Becca got a far-off look in her eyes as she looked out to sea. "Or, we could read *A Perfect Storm* and go fishing on a boat."

"No way. I saw the movie, and they *all* died."

"But that was in the Atlantic Ocean, not the Pacific, which is more peaceful. The name even means that."

"Name-schmame, it can still capsize a boat during a storm," I said. "Can't you come up with something a little less hazardous?"

"Like what? *Sense and Sensibility*? *Pride and Prejudice*?"

"Careful now," Tess said. "Don't be dissin' my Jane Austen."

"Sorry. I was just looking for a little more action — something to liven up the book club and maybe attract more members."

"Speaking of attracting . . ." Tess lowered her voice. "You're attracting a couple admirers."

We glanced at the pool. Two of the fab-ab boys smiled and waved.

Becca turned her back to them. "Not interested. Surfer dudes aren't my style. I like a guy with more intellect, less testosterone."

"I'll take both," Tess said. "Might as well go for the brass ring. And you never know. One of those guys could be a nuclear physicist."

Becca snorted. "They probably can't even spell nuclear physicist."

"N-u-c-l-e-a-r p-h-y-s-i-c-i-s-t." A bronzed, dripping Adonis appeared behind Becca. She had the grace to blush. But by now he'd turned his attention to me.

"Great book. Jo's my favorite." The sun bounced off his pearly whites. "I'm Ben. Would you like to get together later and debate whether Meg should have married Mr. Brooke or held out for a rich guy?"

I didn't care how good-looking he was or how much he loved Jo, the last thing I was in the market for right now was a man.

"No, thanks. I'm actually on my honeymoon."

3

Her daughter enjoyed a most uncommon degree of
popularity for a woman neither young, handsome, rich, nor
married.

Emma

"Did you have a nice time, dear?"

I set my suitcase down and raised an eyebrow at my
mother, who blushed and began to stammer. "I mean I know
the hon-uh, trip wasn't what you'd planned, but I was hoping
you had some fun. You usually do with your aunt Tess."

Was that a hint of jealousy I detected? Nah. Mom had
Julia the Perfect to bond with over sewing and Sunday school.
Tess and I had always shared the books connection, ever since
she began reading bedtime stories to me when I was little.

Her eyes flicked to the bare arms I was releasing from my
sweater. "I see you got a nice tan."

"I went snorkeling with Becca."

"In the ocean? You?"

I bit back a sarcastic reply. Mom was trying. Clumsily, but still. She, more than most, knew my track record with water.

"It was great. Amazing, in fact. Until Becca started playing with a shark."

"A shark?" She paled. "You were in the water with a *shark?*"

"Not for long. I got out of there fast. And it was a pretty small shark. Becca was having fun petting its belly, but I wasn't about to go there."

"I wouldn't have either. That girl certainly is a daredevil, isn't she?"

"Yep."

My mother had a hard time understanding how Becca and I could be friends. Becca was the wild-and-crazy adventure girl, who'd lived in seven states before she was eighteen and loved to push the envelope, while I was safe, stay-at-home Chloe, who'd lived in the same town my whole life and wouldn't know how to open the envelope much less push it.

"Okay if I do a load of laundry?" I started pulling dirty clothes out of my suitcase. "I want to get all the salt water out of my clothes."

Mom scooped up the pile of clothes and fluttered past me to the garage door. "I'll do that for you. Why don't you sit down and have a cup of coffee and a piece of blueberry streusel coffee cake?"

"You don't have to do my laundry for me anymore." I followed my mother out to the two-car garage. "I'm a big girl now. I know how to separate whites from—" A stack of silver and white packages on one of the utility shelves caught my eye. "What are those?"

She hesitated. "Some wedding presents that came in the mail. We weren't quite sure what to do with them, so we stuck them there for now."

"I'll tell you what we can do with them. Throw them in the trash." I inclined my head to the largest package. "Starting with that one."

"You can't! That's from your Great-Aunt Jenny back in Iowa. You know she's on a fixed income. She probably saved and saved to get you that gift. The least we can do is send it back so she can return it and get her money back. That's the proper etiquette when a wedding's been called off."

My mother, Emily Post.

But she was right. I didn't want my friends and relatives to have to pay for Chris's last-minute change of heart. I just didn't know if I had the heart to deal with it.

Mom gave my shoulder a tentative squeeze. "I'll return them all for you if you like."

"Thanks." Then I noticed one box that stood out from the rest. A brown moving box with an envelope taped to the top, bearing my name. I sat down abruptly on the step, recognizing the familiar handwriting.

"Chris and Ryan stopped by yesterday with some of your things," Mom said gently.

Back-to-reality slap.

Hard.

In the face.

I pushed my glasses up over my forehead and rubbed my eyes.

"I'm afraid your father gave Chris a piece of his mind, and so did I."

"You did?" I dropped my glasses back down to stare through them at my placid, Proverbs 31 mother. "What did you say?"

"I don't remember exactly." She gave an embarrassed shrug. "I may have used the words *jerk* and *wimp* though."

Who'd have thought? Words like that weren't in her usual vocabulary. But then, this wasn't a usual occurrence.

My eyes were drawn back to the envelope. I wonder what the jerk has to say. Although … was he really a jerk? Just a week ago he was the love of my life. Funny how things can change in a heartbeat. Maybe he was going to say it was all a mistake. That he was sorry and he'd just gotten cold feet and was begging my forgiveness.

As if.

"Mother?" Julia's voice wafted out to us from the direction of the kitchen. "Where are you?"

That's all I need. Julia the Perfect with her flashing two-carat, emerald-cut engagement ring. Although my wedding had derailed, nothing would get my organized sister's off the tracks. Her wedding—with my domestic queen mother's help—would be a smooth ride from start to finish. I rubbed my finger where up until last week, my tiny diamond had occupied a place of honor. It was lying in a saucer upstairs on the guest room dresser where I'd left it. I still hadn't decided what to do with the symbol of my broken dreams.

Give it back, I guess. That is, *if* the engagement was still off. Maybe Chris had had a change of heart while I was gone. They say absence makes the heart grow fonder. My fingers itched to open his letter.

"Just a minute," Mom called in to my sister. She gave my knee an awkward pat as she moved past. "Take your time, dear. If you need me, I'll be right inside." The door shut behind her, and I could hear her and Julia's muted voices in the kitchen. Discussing Julia's wedding, no doubt.

I rushed over to the box and snatched the letter from the top, ripping it open with shaking hands.

Dear Chloe,

I'm sorry for running out on you just before the wedding. I know it was messed up. More than a few people have told me it was the coward's way out — like Ryan, people at church, my parents, your parents.... But I haven't been feeling good about the wedding for a while now, only I just didn't know how to tell you. You were so excited, and I didn't want to bring you down.

Seriously? Everything happened so fast it kind of blew my mind and I just couldn't deal. The new job, the wedding, the condo ...

It's not you; it's me. I've realized I'm so not ready to settle down. My gypsy blood, I guess. I went backpacking to clear my head and to pray and think things through and to see if it was just cold feet. But it's not. I'm just not ready to get married. To anyone.

And I'm not trying to be harsh or anything, but you're not who I thought you were. Remember when we first met, when you were hiking the Pacific Crest Trail with your girlfriend? It wasn't until later that I discovered you'd only hiked in about fifty feet. Truth is, you're pretty much allergic to nature unless it's in books. Where everything's safe.

And I'm an outdoor guy. I need to be outside. Which is why that new nine-to-five job wasn't working for me. I'm more of a free spirit, as you know. So I'm taking off for San Diego tonight. I have a couple buddies who said I could crash with them, so I'm going to just chill and surf and take it day by day.

You're a special girl, Chloe, and I know you'll find the right guy someday. You've got some great things going for you, but we just weren't a good match.

Peace and love,

Chris

P.S. Here's some of your stuff you left at my place. Oh, and I'm giving you the cappuccino machine.

He's giving *me* the cappuccino machine? The machine

I bought? Big of him. I tore the letter in half and in half again and threw it in the trash.

My family was right about my fiancé. Ex-fiancé. He was an immature, irresponsible jerk. Guess that's what I get for falling for a younger guy—Chris always said our age difference didn't matter, that it was just a number. And I believed that. Or tried to. A five-year age gap in your thirties, forties, or even fifties is no big deal.

I'm sure there are some mature twenty-three-year-olds out there.

He just wasn't one of them. I thought back to the myriad burping and loogie contests he'd have with his old high school buddies on a regular basis, the all-night Game Boy marathons, and how he always unscrewed the lids on the salt and pepper shakers when we left Johnny Rockets, leaving a mess for the waitress.

And don't even get me started on his financial irresponsibility.

I'd ignored all those juvenile things because when I was with Chris, he made me feel like the most beautiful woman in the world. And when you grow up in the shadow of the gorgeous Julia, that's pretty heady stuff.

There were times, however, when I felt more like Chris's mom than his girlfriend. Which is why from now on, I'm only dating guys over thirty. *When* I start dating again, that is. Which probably won't be for a long, long time.

I opened the box. Inside was my *Chronicles of Narnia* I'd loaned him when I discovered he'd never read it. He still hadn't. The red ribbon I'd used to tie them together bore the same taut bow I'd made when I handed it to him. Rustling through a stack of CDs, I was happy to see my fave Rosemary Clooney and Sandi Patty. Chris never could get into my music. He preferred hard rock and the blues. I pulled out several relationship books I'd left at the duplex he rented with Ryan in hopes that he'd read them sometime, including *Men Are from Mars, Women Are from Venus,* and *The Five Love Languages.*

In my dreams.

I'd tried to explain to Chris how these books would help us understand each other better and learn how to communicate successfully, but he wasn't *feelin' it.*

Guess I should have seen that little red flag.

Of course Julia and Justin, her perfect intended, read the books together and discussed them afterward. Justin even filled out all the answers in his workbook.

I thumbed through Chris's copy of the premarital workbook our pastor had suggested we fill out independently. Not one pen or pencil mark on any of the pages. He'd clearly checked out of the relationship ages ago. I'd been a little annoyed and embarrassed when he showed up for our counseling meetings with no answers or comments in the workbook, but now the blank space seemed so much more significant. And sinister.

Call me clueless.

At least I had a few of my favorite things back. Just no raindrops on roses. A couple of weekends before the wedding that wasn't, I'd had a garage sale and gotten rid of a lot of "extra" stuff since Chris and I would be combining households and he preferred a spare, less-is-more, casual look. My tastes leaned more toward the cozy and cottagey—some would say cluttered—with antiques, knick-knacks, floral quilts, and books. Tons of books. Everywhere.

I should have seen the writing on the wall. But I wanted to make my husband—soon-to-be-husband—happy. So I did a clean sweep of my apartment and got rid of lots and lots of stuff before I moved into our new condo. Chris said he was allergic to dust, so he was particularly keen that I lose most of my books—especially the old ones. "What do you need all these books for, anyway?" he'd grumbled. "You read too much. You need to actually get out and live life more instead of just reading about it."

How do you explain to a nonreader that books aren't just things but treasured friends? Companions?

I tried hard to purge my library and did manage to get rid of a couple dozen paperbacks that I'd already read and didn't plan to read again. But others, like the complete boxed set of *Little House on the Prairie* and my whole *Babysitters Club* collection, I just couldn't part with.

They wouldn't go in my pared-down marriage condo, yet I couldn't say good-bye to them either. I figured when we had kids in a couple years, clutter would become a part of our daily lives and Chris wouldn't mind as much. So I separated all my books into stacks: best friends, old friends, classic friends, new friends, and casual acquaintances I hadn't had the time to get to know yet. Then I packed them all in boxes that I stored in my parents' attic. I kept out a few novels I hadn't read yet and some oversized hardbacks and art books that would look good placed here and there amidst Chris's rocks, driftwood, and sports stuff on our new bookcases.

Aside from all my books, the hardest thing for me to let go of had been my Grandma Chloe's antique cherry wood secretary desk with the drop-down top, where I'd spent many happy little-girl hours reading and writing. She left me the beautiful desk when she died. Chris hated it.

"It's so old-fashioned," he said.

I couldn't bring myself to sell Grandma's secretary though. It was a family heirloom. Instead, I gave it to Julia, who had coveted it forever. It had been a real wrench to watch her and Justin carry it out of my old apartment and down the stairs to his waiting pick-up.

"Are you sure you want to part with this, Chloe?" Julia had asked, a worried frown puckering her porcelain forehead. "I know how much you've always loved it."

"We're making a fresh start, aren't we, babe?" Chris hugged me to him. "Out with the old and in with the new."

"I have always loved it, Jules, but Chris is right. We're making a new start together, and we want everything to be fresh and new. Besides, we're going for a more contemporary look."

"Well, if you're sure ..."

I had been sure. Sure of Chris and sure of our love and our new life together.

How could I have gotten it so wrong?

I knew we had some communication issues — which is why I wanted him to read those relationship books — but all couples do, right? It's that whole male/female differences thing. Wasn't it?

Those differences extended to the more contemporary look that Chris liked and I was trying to, which was evident in our new high-rise apartment downtown that I'd moved into the week before the almost wedding.

At Chris's urging, I'd given up my old, much-loved one-bedroom apartment in midtown and signed a one-year lease with an option to buy on a new two-bedroom condominium downtown that would give us more room. Chris's credit wasn't good, so it had to be my name on the lease. Our eleventh-floor condo was located in the heart of downtown, just three blocks from my work and less than a mile from Chris's.

"We can walk or bike to work every day and spare the environment," he said when we first checked out the high-rise condo. He slapped me playfully on the rear. "And it will be good exercise too."

The week before the wedding, we moved most of our

combined possessions into our new place, which had a fabulous view of the Sacramento River and the mustard-colored Tower Bridge that was a Sacramento landmark. Chris had tried to coax me into letting him move in with me before the wedding. "Aw, c'mon," he wheedled. "We're getting married in less than a week."

But on this issue I held firm. I may have given in to him in a lot of other areas, but not this. "It will be worth the wait," I promised.

"I'm counting on it."

Yeah, right. I'd been counting on it too. Counting down the weeks, days, hours even, until we'd be one. It had been really hard to wait, and I'd taken ribbing from some of my friends about holding out until the wedding night. Call me old-fashioned — everyone does — but my wedding gift to my husband was going to be my virginity. But that was the last thing I wanted to think about now. I kept repeating to myself Philippians 4:8: *"whatever is true, whatever is noble, whatever is right, whatever is pure, whatever is lovely, whatever is admirable … think about such things."*

I wonder if Chris might have stayed if we'd made love.

Whatever is true . . .

Yanking the rubberband off my too-tight ponytail, I turned my mind to more practical matters. Like our — correction, my — new condo, where I'd only spent one night so far. There were so many last-minute things to do before the wedding, and the condo was so far from my parents' house in the suburbs, that I'd stayed with them the last couple of nights before the ceremony.

At least, that's what I told myself.

Truth is, the condo felt a little too cold and hard to me in all its shiny newness. But once Chris moved in, I knew we'd warm it up. And though the rent was nearly double what I'd paid for my cute one-bedroom, with my upcoming raise and Chris's new job, we could swing it.

Except now there was no Chris.

No new job.

And a one-year signed lease.

I groaned and laid my head in my hands, my set-free-from-its-ponytail-prison hair doing its standard static electricity thing. How would I ever be able to afford the high rent on the high-rise I hated?

It's not like I didn't earn a good salary at my analyst job with the State of California. I did. Much better, in fact, than a lot of friends my age who were still working at entry-level jobs while they tried to find themselves.

I'd found myself in the fifth grade.

Even way back then I knew that I wanted to get a good, steady job with benefits, including a great retirement and a healthy savings account. Grandma Chloe always told me it was good for a woman to be able to make her own way in the world and not to have to be financially dependent on a man. She'd seen too many instances of women whose husbands had died or divorced them and they'd been left helpless and totally unprepared to take care of themselves, not even knowing how to balance a checkbook.

Not me. I wasn't my Grandma's namesake for nothing.

That's why I had an automatic deposit from my paycheck into my savings account for a down payment on a house. Grandma Chloe had also taught me that real estate was the best investment a girl could make. And like Virginia Woolf, I wanted a room of my own.

Only not just a room. A whole house. Preferably a cute little bungalow in an older part of town. And if I kept saving the way I had been, before the year was out, I'd have enough for a substantial down payment—provided of course that I didn't dip into savings to make my new rent payment.

I groaned again.

Then I recalled what Becca had said on the cruise about needing to find a new place to live.

Could I handle a roommate though? I've lived on my own for the past five years, and I liked my solitude. I blew out a wistful sigh as I thought back to the darling midtown apartment I'd given up for Chris. I'd been willing to trade in my solitude and the cozy apartment for happily-ever-after bliss with Chris.

Don't go there. Focus on the here and now and the immediate need: a roommate.

My college roommate had been such a bad experience—she liked to ingest all kinds of strange and unusual substances, including oregano—and not in spaghetti—that I'd sworn never to have a roommate again unless it was my husband. And Becca can be a little irresponsible, a little wild and crazy.

Like that whole shark thing.

Pushing the underwater incident out of my mind, I took a deep breath. Desperate times call for desperate measures. I punched in her number.

"Becca, have I got a deal for you."

4

"It's so dreadful to be poor!" sighed Meg, looking down at her old dress.

"I don't think it's fair for some girls to have plenty of pretty things, and other girls nothing at all," added Amy, with an injured sniff.

"We've got father and mother and each other," said Beth contentedly, from her corner.

Little Women

Two hours later, with Becca by my side and a basket of clean laundry in my hands, I turned the key in the lock to my new home.

"Whoa. Can you say industrial?"

"I know."

As Becca checked out the fresh-from-the-factory condo, I saw the living space through her eyes: the gray stamped concrete floor, new black leather sectional that took up much of the great room, glass coffee table, narrow black bookcases — with very few books—and my wedding present to my groom—the huge flat-screen TV dominating one wall.

She whistled. "That sucker's huge."

"Uh-huh. Chris loved to watch sports on the big screen. I'm sure he hated leaving my gift behind, but since it was mounted to the wall, he couldn't really take it with him." I looked around. "Of course, that didn't stop him from taking the rest of his stuff."

Chris had cut a wide swath through the place. The empty dining area had indentations in the black area rug where his exercise bike and portable basketball hoop had stood, and the new black bookcases we'd—I'd—bought from Ikea had been emptied of all his rocks, sports paraphernalia, and video games. All that remained on the shelves were my oversized art books and a few hardbacks.

"Love the bookcases; although, they're pretty empty." Becca flipped through a Grisham.

Sure they're empty. I was trying to accommodate my almost husband. In fact, most of the place was an accommodation to Chris. The big-screen TV that required some installation guy to bust into the wall, which turned it into a "permanent fixture" according to my homeowners' association and kept me from tearing it down on the spot and returning it to the store. The empty bookshelves, the glass coffee table, the gigantic couch …

I wondered if I could return or sell off anything. Maybe I could rent the condo out for big sports events. But that would fill the place with smelly jocks, salsa stains, and Dorito crumbs.

Totally not worth it.

Becca looked askance at the silver flat-screen monster ruling the living room. "Not exactly Picasso, is it?"

"What if you cover it with something?" she suggested. "I know where you can pick up a velvet Elvis cheap."

"No thanks."

And then I remembered. I shot into the master bedroom, bypassing the king-size bed with its black-and-white plaid comforter Chris had wanted. Inside the walk-in closet, I pulled down a bulky, oversized package from the top shelf and carried it back into the living room, where I began to undo the plastic covering it.

"What's that?" Becca asked as a jumble of jewel-tones hove into view.

"An antique quilt I fell in love with at a thrift shop. I wanted it on our bed, but Chris didn't like the idea of sleeping under something so old."

"Ooh, let me see." Becca helped me unfold the crazy quilt. When I bought it, the store owner told me that the scraps of velvet and satin it was made of had come from her ex-husband's great-grandmother's baby clothes. "It's beautiful."

"Isn't it? Help me lift it up. How do you think it would look hanging on the wall—covering the boob tube?"

"Sweet. It would add some color to this place."

"That's what I thought." I adjusted my glasses and examined the back of the ancient pieced-together fabric. "I'll ask my mom if she'll sew a sleeve at the top, and we could install a quilt rack thingy above the TV. Then when it's time to watch TV, we'll just slide the quilt over to one side, like a curtain."

"Perfect." Becca cast a dubious eye at the leather sectional. "You didn't pick *this* out, did you?"

"In what universe? No, Chris wanted it because it's a 'man couch.'"

"Well, since neither of us are men, what say we take it back and exchange it for something a little more comfortable?" She pointed at the glass coffee table. "And maybe trade that in for something wood while we're at it?"

Who knew Becca and I had similar furniture tastes? No glass and leather for us. "No prob. I still have the receipts, and these pieces haven't even been used, so it shouldn't be any problem exchanging them." I scuffed my foot on the contemporary concrete floor that had been a bone of contention between my beloved—ex-beloved—and me. "And I'm also going to raid my parents' attic to see if they have any old rugs they're not using."

"Just call us Ty Pennington & Company." Becca nodded to the galley kitchen with its stainless steel appliances and black granite countertops. "At least we don't have to do anything there. That kitchen rocks."

"Ya think?"

"Oh yeah."

"I don't know." I worried a hangnail on my little finger. "Seems a little stark and institutional to me."

"And you didn't think that before you signed the lease?"

"Well, yeah, but Chris really liked it."

Becca's eyes flashed. "New rule: *Stop* being a doormat and *never* suppress your own thoughts and opinions for a man again. Deal?"

"Deal." I sprinted to the kitchen, ponytail flapping, so Becca wouldn't see my flaming face. "I still think it needs a little color to—" I was stopped in my tracks by a huge gourmet food basket tucked in a corner of the counter that had been invisible from the living room.

A food basket with a card addressed to Mr. and Mrs. Chris O'Neil.

"What's up?" Becca joined me and saw the basket. And the card. She slid me a hesitant glance. "Want me to open it?"

I nodded.

Becca read aloud, grimacing as she did: "Welcome, new-lyweds. Here's a little something to keep those home fires stoked—and to save you from cooking for a couple days since we know you'll be busy with other things. Love, Sheri and the gang." She directed a quizzical glance my way. "Who's Sheri? And how come she didn't get the message that the wedd-uh, circumstances had changed?"

"Sheri's the receptionist and diehard romantic from work." I ripped open the cellophane to remove the bottle of champagne sticking out the top. "The very pregnant receptionist now on maternity leave. She probably had this all set up before she went on leave and no one else knew to cancel it."

Becca eyed the basket of bounty. I could tell she was itching to dive into it—the same way she'd dove under the sea in Cabo to explore the treasures there. "What I want to know is, does this Sheri have good taste or are we talking Cheez Whiz and Ritz crackers?"

I pulled out a package of Alaskan smoked salmon and imported English cheddar and affected a snooty British accent. "Nothing but the best from our champagne wishes and caviar dreams girl."

Becca's eyes glittered as she zeroed in on a box of pears. "Ooh, I recognize these! They're from Harry and David. We got a box at the store last Christmas from one of our authors who lives up in Ashland. They're the most amazing pears you've ever tasted."

Any second now she was going to start foaming at the mouth.

"Help yourself." I continued to rummage through the basket as she chomped into the juicy fruit. "Just try and save me one."

"Ub kors, whaddya ache me for?" she mumbled around a mouthful of pear. "Uh pig?"

"Just so you don't root through those." I set a box of truffles off to the side and continued to remove goodie after gourmet goodie from the never-ending basket: more cheese, English water crackers, fat red apples, peanut butter pretzels, a variety of breakfast breads and mountain preserves, mixed nuts, English shortbread, and something called Bing cherry chocolates.

"Those chocolate cherries are to die for!" Becca said. "Have you ever had them?"

"Nope. I don't get out much."

"Well, honey, that's about to change." She tore into the tempting chocolates package and held it beneath my nose. "Try and resist that."

I popped one into my mouth. Definitely not my mother's chocolate-covered cherries that she bought in a two-dollar box from the grocery store every Christmas. I popped in another one and chewed slowly.

"See what I mean?"

Becca's voice punctured my food ecstasy. I opened my eyes, and as I looked around the formerly stark and pristine black-and-white kitchen now a mess with the decimated remains of the basket, my eyes lit upon the red apples on the black granite countertop.

"We need to bring some color in here."

"Good thing I have a red toaster and teakettle. If you want, we could pick up a few more accents at Target." What she meant was, I could pick up a few more accents at Target. Becca wasn't going to have much more to spend on this place after rent and utilities. When I had told her what the rent was, her normally olive complexion turned cotton-ball white. "No way can I pay half of that."

I'd reassured her that since I was taking the large master bedroom and bath with a tub, shower, and huge walk-in closet, she didn't have to pay as much—she could simply pay the same amount she was paying at her studio, and chip in for utilities and groceries.

I took her on a tour of the rest of the condo, showing her the stackable washer and dryer behind an accordion door in the hallway and her smaller bedroom with its fabulous view of Tower Bridge.

"Sweet!" Becca stuck out her hand to shake mine. "Let's start turning this cell block into a home, roomie. And the first thing we need to do is rescue your books from your parents' attic."

Three hours later we sat back with a satisfied sigh, having filled the cubed black bookcases to overflowing with my books and Becca's—arranged alphabetically, by subject, of course.

My new roommate didn't work in a bookstore for nothing.

We had butted heads a couple times over the organization: Becca liked all her books arranged standing up, but I preferred to mix it up a bit with some books stacked on their side like I'd seen once on one of those designer shows I'd been pressured into watching with my mom and Julia.

"But books aren't about how they look," Becca said, horrified. "It's all about content."

"True. But why can't that content be arranged attractively too?"

The doorbell rang.

"Wonder who that is?" I stood up and brushed my book-dusty hands against my jeans.

"Maybe the condo association welcome committee? Here to make sure no one's absconded with their big-screen TV?"

I peeked through the peephole and released a loud sigh.

"Who is it?"

Turning to face Becca, I mouthed Ryan's name and then opened the door.

"Uh, sorry to disturb you," Ryan said, distinctly uncomfortable, "but Chris called and said he left his stunt kite here and asked if I'd pick it up and send it to him."

"Seems you're always picking up after him." I grudgingly waved him in.

He gave a casual nod to Becca sitting cross-legged on the floor. "Hey, what's up?"

"Just getting settled into my new place."

"You're moving in?"

"Someone had to," I interjected. "I couldn't afford the rent on my own, and there's that whole lease thing."

"Chris never told me he signed a lease."

"*He* didn't. It's called bad credit." I waved him toward the sectional. "Have a seat while I see if I can find that kite."

I checked the hall closet. Nada. Unless it was masquerading as an ironing board. I moved to the bedroom, jerked open the closet door, and began shoving clothes aside. I finally found the kite in the far corner, partly hidden by my sweaters—the rainbow kite we'd flown on a windy day in Sausalito on our second date. I remembered it well, it was a chilly fall day, and we'd been running up and down the beach trying to catch just the right wind to keep the kite soaring. I'd taken off my glasses, which had gotten wet from the tidal spray, and Chris kissed me for the first time.

Yanking out the boxed kite and tearing a corner of cellophane in the process, I stormed back to his best man. As I passed the kitchen, an apple from the decimated honeymoon basket caught my eye.

"Heads up." I threw the apple to Ryan, and he caught it neatly. "You might want to send that to Chris along with the kite since it was a gift to both of us. Of course it would probably be rotten by the time it got to San Diego, but I think that would be appropriate, don't you?"

"Chris isn't rotten, Chloe. You know that."

"No, actually, I don't. I don't know anything about Chris anymore except that he's a coward and a jerk." I pushed my glasses up—I really needed to get to that glasses place at the mall and get them adjusted. "But I know you're happy. You never wanted us to get married."

"I just thought things were moving pretty fast. And that neither of you was quite ready." Ryan met my eyes squarely. "I still think that. But I am sorry he waited until the last minute to realize that. He was afraid to hurt you."

"Looks like he got over that fear."

"I'll say." Becca strode over to me in girl-power solidarity.

"Well . . ." Ryan stuck the kite under his arm and pocketed the apple. "Guess I'll be going. Thanks, Chloe. Hope to see you at church Sunday."

Becca, who didn't have much use for church or organized religion in general, snorted. "Yeah, right."

Was I ready to go back to church and face everybody? How humiliating. But I didn't want to blame God for what Chris had done. It wasn't his fault. I couldn't blame him, right?

While I wrestled with myself, Becca's voice dimly registered through my brain fog. "Don't let the door hit you on the way out."

I blinked and Ryan was gone. I felt like Samantha on *Bewitched* (although everyone always tells me I look more like Tina Fey with the whole brown hair and glasses thing).

"Okay, stop thinking about Chris. That's the past." Becca popped open the bottle of champagne and filled two glasses. "And this is the future."

She raised her glass in a toast. "Here's to new roommates and new beginnings."

5

> "Wouldn't it be fun if all the castles in the air which
> we make could come true and we could live in them?"
>
> *Little Women*

Normally, leading the discussion at the Paperback Girls Book Club wasn't my strong suit — that's more Becca's thing — but tonight I jumped at the chance to be in charge, so I could steer it away from what I knew was on everyone's mind: my wedding that wasn't.

"So which of the four little women did you identify with the most?" I'd chosen *Little Women* as our January selection, so it was up to me to lead the book club discussion.

I'd already marked down which March girl reminded me of which Paperback Girl.

"I don't know about the rest of you," Becca said, "but I totally relate to Jo." Of course she did. They shared that same reckless, adventurous spirit, born-leader nature, and storytelling gifts.

"Now there's a surprise." Tess arched her brows. She was

another Jo, in love with words and the theater, adventurous, and unafraid to take risks. But Tess also had elements of Meg, the oldest and most practical March daughter.

"Jo was too much of a tomboy. And I can't believe she whacked off all her gorgeous hair!" Kailyn fluffed her golden mane. "Personally, I identified more with Amy." Kailyn — our youngest at twenty-three — the resident girly-girl and most beautiful of the group, with her perfect body and cascading blonde curls, was definitely Amy.

"You do what you have to," Kailyn's mother Annette said. It was a little trickier classifying Annette as one of the four March girls. She was more like Marmee, the wise, kind mother. With perhaps a trace of Meg.

Paige Kelley was another Meg, although not as pretty. Not that Paige is unattractive; she's just kind of ordinary: medium height, medium weight — plus a few extra pounds now and then — medium-length, medium-brown hair. Not anyone who would ever stand out in a crowd. Until you got her talking about movies. Then she becomes as animated as Amy.

Jenna, perpetually tan and athletic to a fault — definitely Jo all the way.

And me? I'm a combination of practical, responsible Meg and shy, stay-at-home Beth. Deep down, though, there's a part of me that longs to be Jo.

Seven very different women with a love of books in common.

Becca's Almond Joy eyes snapped, crackled, and popped. "I had this great idea for the upcoming year. I thought that instead of just sitting around stuffing our faces and discussing the books we read like every other women's book club on the planet" — she paused dramatically — "we could live out some of the adventures in the books instead!"

"Uh, I'm really not up for sucking anyone's blood." Jenna held up *Dracula*, her suggestion.

"You're not?" Tess said. "Where's your sense of adventure?"

Becca rapped her knuckles on the white board she used to keep track of our book suggestions. She'd started the Paperback Girls nearly two years ago with a dozen women, but over time the club had been whittled down to our core group of seven.

That first year, each woman got to choose a book, and we wound up with a list from all sides of the literary spectrum: Dickens and Dostoyevsky, Hemingway and Faulkner, Charlotte Brontë and Virginia Woolf, Danielle Steel and Jackie Collins, Dr. Laura and Dr. Phil.

Sarah and Lisa, the two best friends who'd selected Jackie Collins and Danielle Steel, weren't too crazy about Dickens, Dostoyevsky, or Woolf, but Faulkner was the final nail in their book club coffin. They fled, flip-flops flapping. To be honest, most of us were tempted to flee after Faulkner.

After a couple more literary defections, we decided to set up some group guidelines. We wanted to improve ourselves, but also have fun and mix it up a bit, so after much discussion and a vote, we decided to include both fiction and nonfiction. The only requirement was that all the books had to be paperback. Each Paperback Girl was asked to bring two or three choices to the planning meeting, and we had to select at least one book from each member.

"For instance." Becca held up a green paperback with a black-and-white photo of a woman, aviator glasses perched on her head.

"Is that Amelia Earhart?" Annette squinted over her reading glasses.

"Same era, wrong continent. This is Beryl Markham's

memoir, *West with the Night.* She was a pilot in Africa in the 1930s and friends with Denys Finch Hatton and the writer Isak Dinesen—"

"Dinesen and Hatton?" Movie buff Paige's eyes lit up. "Robert Redford played Hatton in *Out of Africa.* I loved that movie. *So* romantic. He could wash my hair any day."

"Any day in Africa," Tess reminded her. "And I understand they have lots of bugs there."

Becca ignored the rabbit trail and continued. "Beryl Markham was this fearless, amazing woman. She was the only female professional pilot in Africa at that time."

"You want us to go flying in Africa?" I gulped.

"I wish. I had something a little more local in mind. There's this place in Lodi where you can go gliding." Becca sent us a sly smile. "And right across the street they have skydiving."

"Not for this girl," Kailyn said.

"Or this one," her mother agreed. "No way will y'all ever catch me jumping out of a perfectly good airplane. That's what the pilots I worked with always used to say. And if a pilot in the Air Force of these here United States sees no reason to jump out of an airplane, neither do I." Fifty and strawberry-blonde, Annette originally hailed from Texas, and she still retained traces of her accent.

"I'm with you." I imagined myself hurtling to the ground and landing with a splat when my parachute didn't open. "Way too scary."

"No it's not."

Six heads swiveled to Jenna.

"I went skydiving for my twenty-fifth birthday, and I'd do it again in a heartbeat. It was the biggest rush ever."

"Yesss!" Becca pumped her fist in the air.

"Count me in," Tess said.

"Tess!"

"What?" Behind her glasses she made her eyes all wide and innocent. "I've always wanted to go skydiving, and I'm not getting any younger. I'd like to take a page from Jenna's book and do it for my birthday too. Except it would be my fiftieth."

It was hard to believe at times that Tess came from our family. None of the rest of us had her daring, adventurous spirit. Everyone else just thought she was different. I loved her for it.

"Do all the adventures have to be physical in nature?" Paige asked Becca.

"Uh, yeah," Becca said, her voice dripping with sarcasm. "What else?"

"An adventure means doing something you've never done before—taking a risk and trying something new," Tess said. "I like the idea of adding some physical adventures to get us off our couch-potato butts, but why limit ourselves? Why not expand ourselves mentally and culturally as well?" She held up her two suggestions: *Marjorie Morningstar* and *From the Mixed-Up Files of Mrs. Basil E. Frankweiler.*

"What's *Marjorie Morningstar*?" Becca frowned. "I don't recognize that."

"That's because you're young. My mother read it in the 1950s when it was first released and fell in love with it. She gave it to me when I was a teenager in the 1970s and *I* fell in love with it too," Tess said. "It's a coming-of-age story of a young woman in 1930s New York who wants to break away from the wife-and-mother expectations her parents have for her and become an actress instead."

"And the adventure aspect would be?" Becca tapped her foot.

"Going to the theater. We could see a play in town or go to San Francisco and make a whole day of it."

"Works for me as long as we don't have to see *Annie.*"

Jenna grimaced. "If I hear 'Tomorrow' one more time, I'll slit my throat. That reminds me — I'd like to offer my other suggestions."

"Let me guess." Becca prepared to add Jenna's titles to the white board. "A mystery maybe?"

Jenna was our resident horror and mystery lover, and she was always trying to drag the rest of us over to the dark side with her. In addition to *Dracula*, she suggested an Agatha Christie and Raymond Chandler's *The Big Sleep*.

"Well I think shopping's always an adventure," Kailyn said. "So I nominate *Confessions of a Shopaholic*."

Becca groaned.

"What?" Kailyn shot a pointed glance at Becca's frayed Birkenstocks. "Someone here could do with a little shopping adventure."

Kailyn also suggested the children's paperback *Heidi*, while Annette, our classics lover, nominated *Emma*, *Les Misérables*, and *Wuthering Heights*.

"Ooh, I've always wanted to read *Wuthering Heights*." Paige stared dreamily off into space. Paige was a sucker for romance, especially the tragic kind.

"I have too, but I'm leaning more toward *Emma*," Tess, our Austen aficionado said.

"I don't know what kind of adventure we're going to find in a Jane Austen," Becca grumbled. "All everyone does is sit around and talk."

"Or have picnics and talk," I said.

"Or drink tea and talk." Becca widened her eyes in mock wonder. "Although sometimes they take incredibly exciting strolls around the room. Those Austen chicks were really adventurous."

"I'm with Becca." I offered Tess an apologetic look. "*Persuasion* was a bit excruciating — although I *loved* the movie.

But I don't think I could handle another Jane Austen. Can't we go with something a little more exciting? If you really want classic, then let's do classic Grisham — *The Firm*."

"Loved the movie."

"One of Tom Cruise's better ones."

"Getting off track again. Time to vote."

Becca pouted when the majority nixed her female pilot memoir, but brightened when we all agreed on *Dove*, the true tale of Robin Graham, whose story was featured in *National Geographic*. My Grisham selection got nixed too, but the group voted for my second offering, Bill Bryson's *A Walk in the Woods*.

We also agreed that the Paperback Girl who'd chosen the book had to be the one who came up with the adventure we would reenact from its pages.

"Within reason." Kailyn shot a warning look at the more adventurous girls in the room. "Anything involving bungee jumping or polar bears is off limits."

Paige, who'd chosen the nonfiction *French Women Don't Get Fat*, offered to teach us the little she knew about French cooking, wrapping up her lesson with a five-course dinner at her home. "If you've never eaten escargot, it can be quite an adventure."

"I have an even better idea!" Becca jumped up. "Why don't we take a couple French cooking classes from an actual French chef in" — another dramatic pause — "*Paris*?"

"Paris? Are you crazy?" I stared at her.

We all did.

"Who in the world could afford to go to Paris?" Kailyn asked.

"We could — if we start saving now." Becca said, her entire body pulsing with excitement. "Since we take December off for the holidays, if we make *French Women* our last book, that would be next January. And I've seen cheap off-season fares in the paper for less than four hundred bucks from San Francisco to Paris." She looked at Tess. "Right, travel agent?"

"I found round-trip tickets for a honeymoon couple for only $299 apiece." Tess looked at me, stricken, when she realized she'd said the H-word.

"It's okay," I said with what I hoped was a wan smile. "I got my honeymoon."

There was an awkward silence that Annette hurried to fill. "You're better off without him, honey," she advised. "Better to have found out now rather than later when you're married. You wouldn't have wanted it to end in divorce."

"No you wouldn't," said Paige, who'd gone through an unwanted divorce two years earlier.

It was Annette's turn to look stricken. "I'm sorry Paige, I didn't mean—"

"I know you didn't. Don't worry about it," Paige said, turning to me with a sympathetic look. "I know how much it hurts when the man you love leaves, Chloe, and the last thing I want to do is suggest that your pain isn't as real just because you hadn't yet said 'I do.'" She rubbed her ringless finger. "I will say, though, that breaking those vows is really hard."

"But *you* didn't break them," Annette said. "*He* did when he ran off."

"Creep."

"Jerk."

"Swine." I slammed my book down. "Why are men such creeps?"

"Not all." Annette fidgeted with her wedding band.

"She's right. Mom and Dad have a great marriage," Kailyn said. "Problem is they've spoiled me for settling for anything less, which makes it hard on the dating scene."

"That's 'cause all the good ones are taken."

"Tell me about it. They're all married, in a long-term relationship, or gay."

"Not all of them," Annette said. "There are some nice guys in your singles group."

"Yeah, if you don't mind wimps who still live with their mother, guys just coming off their third divorce, or dumb jocks who never take their head out of their big-screen TV."

Becca exchanged a knowing look with me.

"We're just living in the wrong era," Paige said. "We need to go back in time when men were more romantic. Like Colin Firth in *Pride and Prejudice*. Or, be still my heart, Hugh Jackman in *Kate and Leopold*."

"Getting off track again, girls," Tess said.

"This club isn't about movie stars or Hollywood or men," Becca said. "It's about books and reading and learning and an amazing group of adventurous women who can do anything we set our minds to. Right?"

"Right!" they chorused.

"Right," I echoed faintly.

Becca asked Tess if she could get us an idea of the cost for airfare, hotel, and other expenses, including cooking lessons. "I read on the Internet where this guy surprised his wife during their anniversary trip to Paris with two days of lessons from a French chef, and it wasn't all that expensive," she said.

"*C'est fait.*"

"Huh?"

"Consider it done," Tess said. "Better check out some French language tapes, missy." She nodded at me.

"*Mais oui.*"

And don't freak out about the whole flying over the ocean thing. This is just another one of Becca's wild and crazy ideas that will probably never come to pass.

"So what's our *Emma* adventure going to be?" Becca asked.

"Going on a picnic? Dressing up and going to a ball? Sitting around making droll comments?"

Annette offered up a serene smile. "You'll just have to wait and see."

When I got home from book club that night, my answering machine was blinking.

Maybe it's Chris, and he's having second thoughts about the break-up.

I held my breath in anticipation as I pushed play. "Hi, Chloe, it's your big sister. Are you there?" There was a pause, and then Julia continued. "I just wanted to see how you were doing and to let you know that if you ever want to talk, I'm here. Also, Mom and I are hosting a craft night — Cheryl Cummings is going to teach us all how to knit, and I thought you might want to join us. I know sewing's not your thing, but knitting is completely different."

Yeah, like that's ever going to happen.

I deleted the message.

Part 2

February
*E*mma

6

Emma Woodhouse, handsome, clever, and rich, with a comfortable home and happy disposition, seemed to unite some of the best blessings of existence; and had lived nearly twenty-one years in the world with very little to distress or vex her.

Emma

A week later, Becca and I were kicked back reading on either end of the comfy, sage green couch I'd gotten for a song through Craigslist and finishing off the last of the smoked salmon from the newlywed basket.

"How are you coming on *Emma*?"

"I'm not. Talk about boring." Becca plucked some crackers from the plate on the pine coffee table we'd picked up along with the couch. I'd been able to return the glass table and sectional for a full refund, and although I stuck most of the money back into savings, I used some of it to buy the replacements, as well as a rug and two comfortably squashy chairs from my favorite thrift store.

"I'm kind of bored too." I scarfed up the last sliver of salmon before Becca could pounce on it. "Tess tells me it's because our generation has a short attention span."

"Or it could be—and I know it's sacrilege for me to utter this—but maybe Jane Austen's just a boring writer?"

"Better not let Tess hear you say that! Or your boss. She'd be appalled. The whole rest of the world can't be wrong. Her books are classics. And to be classics, by definition, means they've stood the test of time."

"Well, it's not going to take anymore of my time." Becca tossed her paperback on the coffee table. "I'm just going to order the movie from Netflix and be done with it. Life's too short to waste on books I don't like."

I flipped through my *Emma* pages. "I wonder what adventure Annette will have concocted for us from this? An afternoon tea, maybe?"

"Yeah. Like that's really adventurous."

"Have you ever been to one? The tea selections alone come from every corner of the globe and it can be quite an adventure choosing the precise one you want. And learning to crook your pinkie while holding a fragile teacup without spilling is a major acrobatic feat."

Becca stuck her nose in the air. "Under certain circumstances there are few hours in life more agreeable than the hour dedicated to the ceremony known as afternoon tea."

"Well la-di-da. Where's that from?"

"*Portrait of a Lady* by Henry James."

"Wait. You think Jane Austen is boring but not Henry James?"

"I didn't say I didn't think he was boring too—I just remember the opening line from when we studied him in class."

Most people our age quoted from movies and TV shows, but Becca was always quoting from books. Maybe by living with her, I'd soak up some of her bibliophile brilliance and be able to impress everyone at work with a new party trick.

Work was becoming a little less awkward these days, much to my relief. When I returned the first Monday after my Mexican cruise, my supervisor, Bob Jefferson, a middle-aged father of three daughters, was concerned and solicitous. As was everyone else—except a couple women from personnel who just pretended to be.

(Becca was always asking me what it was that I did exactly at my job. Everyone did. Okay, so maybe analyzing bills and regulations for the Department of Health Services wasn't the most exciting thing in the world, but it was a good, steady job with great benefits, including three weeks of paid vacation a year. How could I complain?)

I'd arrived a little early the day after the cruise so I could put my lunch in the break room fridge without being seen by the hordes of coffee drinkers who clustered around the caffeine machine at the start of the work day. But Bob was already there, filling his World's Greatest Dad cup.

"Chloe." He enfolded me in a bear hug. "How *are* you?" He released me and gave me a searching look.

"I'm fine."

Bob raised a bushy eyebrow over his bifocals.

"All right, I've been better. But I'll be fine."

"I don't doubt it for a minute. And if you don't mind my saying so, you're better off without him. You deserve someone better. I always thought so."

Then why didn't you say so? Give me a little heads-up, maybe?

As I thought back though, I remembered that Bob had diplomatically voiced concerns on one or two occasions after seeing the two of us together.

I just refused to hear.

Stubborn much?

"Oh well. Life goes on. Right?" I opened a packet of Splenda and shook a little into my coffee mug. "And so does work, so guess I'd better get back to—"

"Chloe!" Michelle, one half of the dynamic gossip duo from personnel, rushed up to me, eyes glittering in hopes of getting the full scoop. "You poor thing! You must be so devastated and humiliated. I can only imagine how you must be feeling. Would you like to talk?"

To you? In what universe?

"Sorry, Michelle. Chloe needs to get to work." Bob glanced meaningfully at the clock on the wall. "We all do."

She flushed and gave my shoulder a fake sympathy pat. "Okay, but if you want to talk or just need a shoulder to cry on, you know where to find me."

I nodded and hurried after Bob, nearly running into Carol, Michelle's other middle-aged-gossip half, on my way out.

"Oh, Chloe! How awful," Carol said. "How *are* you?"

Carol was just the second in a constant parade of concerned or curious coworkers stopping by my desk that first day, all offering up sympathy and platitudes or stories of their own.

"Chloe, I'm so sorry! Chloe, is there anything I can do? Did you know the same thing happened to my cousin? Blah, blah, blah." By the mid-morning break, I couldn't stand any more and fled to the ladies room to hide until the coast was clear.

I was in the midst of composing a mental list of one hundred and one ways to torture and humiliate Chris if he ever showed his sorry face again when from inside my metal stall, I heard the restroom door open.

Noiselessly, I pulled my leather mules up to rest on the commode.

"I chipped in ten bucks for that shower gift," Betty Jo, our department receptionist, whined. "Guess I'll never see that again."

"Tell me about it," Michelle's nasal voice joined in. "I don't know why we had to buy such expensive towels from Nordstrom anyway. Wal-Mart would have been just fine."

"Or Target," Betty Jo said. "But you know miss executive secretary who thinks she's all that had to be in charge of the whole shower. She's probably never even set foot in a Target or Wal-Mart."

"I'll bet she did when she was still a lowly peon like us," Michelle said. "Before she got her big promotion, I mean." Michelle gave a loud sniff. "And we all know how she got—"

The bathroom door squeaked open, hushing the women.

"Oh, Carol, it's just you." I could hear the relief in Michelle's voice. "We were just saying how we'd probably all be stiffed for Chloe's shower gift."

"Never mind about that." Carol giggled. "Do you know what I heard?"

"No. What?" they chorused.

Now what? How could this get any worse?

"I heard that he dumped her by text message! Can you even *imagine*?"

"No! Really? How humiliating."

"But delicious."

They all left, cackling together.

I stayed in the stall, legs still hunched in front of me, tingling with hundreds of little pin-pricks from the uncomfortable position.

One of my shoes fell off and landed on the floor with a plop.

I don't know how I made it through the rest of that day.

But on my way home I drove through McDonald's and ordered a Big Mac, a McFlurry, and a large fries.

Sometimes all a girl can do is supersize it.

Two weeks after the *Little Women* meeting, when I got home from work on a Monday evening, I pulled two thick creamy vellum envelopes from the mailbox along with the usual assortment of junk mail. One envelope had my name handwritten on the front in beautiful calligraphy, while the other was addressed to Becca, and both had Annette's return address on the back.

Eager to learn what our first book club adventure would be, I tore open my envelope in the elevator. A small piece of paper fluttered out. I caught it in mid-air and read. "Dress casual but not sloppy. Skirts, slacks, or dress jeans, neatly pressed. No baggy, faded pants with rips or tears."

I smiled. Annette's Southern, middle-aged, Air Force tendencies always reared their pressed-and-pleated head. She couldn't stand wrinkled, shredded, or torn jeans. And the baggy hip-hop gangsta-style pants with three inches of boxers peeking up over the top?

Not in her universe.

"But Mom, it's the fashion," Kailyn would patiently explain whenever her mother complained about her low-slung, ripped, or frayed jeans.

"It may be the fashion, baby girl," Annette said, "but not when you're with me."

As I let myself into the apartment, I pulled out the creamy cardstock invitation. "The honor of your presence is requested this Saturday evening at six o'clock at the home of Annette Hunt, 5927 Kensington Lane. R.S.V.P." I could hardly wait until Becca got home and saw her invitation. Maybe if we put our heads together, we could figure out what Annette had cooked up for us. I'd expected it would be some kind of formal English tea or something, but I couldn't imagine Annette allowing jeans at such an event—pressed or not.

Pulling a frozen pizza from the fridge, I popped it in the oven, then changed into sweats and settled in with *Emma* again on the couch. Now that we'd seen the movie version, I understood the book so much better and surprised myself by really liking it. Jane Austen was funny—brilliant, actually.

The front door flew open and Becca bounded in.

She dropped her bookbag on the floor with a dramatic thud and flung her coat over one of the chairs as she headed to the kitchen. "Oy! What a day I had today." I heard the refrigerator door open and close, a little rustling, and then she was back. She sank into a chair and held up a pen-shaped plastic-wrapped package. "String cheese?"

"No thanks."

Becca tore open the plastic and took such a vicious bite that if she had bitten off her own finger with it, I don't think she would have noticed. "You won't believe it! We had a book signing with this local author who was totally obnoxious. First, she shows up with six ginormous posters of herself that were obviously taken about twenty years and two facelifts ago. And she wants me to display these pictures all around the store, including in front of the restrooms." Becca jumped up, sucked in her cheeks, and fluttered her eyelashes at me. "That way we can get them both coming and going, dear," she trilled in a high falsetto.

"Then she wants to know why we hadn't ordered more than twenty copies of her *self-published* book—an awful self-published book, I might add, with about a hundred misspellings and typos per page—and why we didn't have her first book in stock to sell to the *huge* crowd that was going to materialize. Yadda-yadda." Becca shoved her hand through her spiky black hair. "Of course, nobody showed up except her mother, grandmother, and one of her neighbors. And only *one* of them bought a book. So then she blamed me for not publicizing the event more."

She dropped back down into her chair, sprawling her legs out in front of her. "Some of these authors are so high maintenance." Then she noticed the formal envelope with her name and snatched it up. "What's this?"

"Open it and see." I flapped my creamy vellum at her. "I got one too."

Becca groaned when she read the clothing instructions. "What's up with that? Why's Annette insisting we get all dressed up for this deal?"

"All dressed up? She said we could wear jeans—they just have to be pressed."

"Nuh-uh. Look." She handed me her small slip of paper.

I pushed my glasses up on my face—seriously, must go to the mall and get them adjusted—and read aloud: "Please dress dressy, but not formal. No evening gowns, but a suit or dress and heels are required. *No Birkenstocks.*" The last was underlined.

"That's weird." I looked up at my roommate. "Mine's totally different. Think Annette might have made a mistake?"

"Sergeant Etiquette? Since when?"

Becca and I pulled up in front of Annette's house at 5:58 Saturday night. Although Becca was never on time for anything, I had an inbred aversion to being late. My mother had drilled into my sister and me that lateness showed a lack of respect and consideration for others, so I adopted that rule as my own.

What can I say? I've always been a girl who follows the rules. Pretty much.

And good little rule follower that I am, I showed up in my

best dress jeans—but not pressed because, really, who irons jeans?—red sweater, and favorite black ankle boots.

Becca had chosen a green jersey dress that went great with her coloring, and low-heeled black pumps. "I don't care what Annette says," she declared as she was getting dressed. "I'm *not* wearing high heels. I'd fall and break my neck. Besides, do you know how bad those things are for your feet?" She did, however, consent to wear the soft black cashmere cardigan studded with seed pearls across the bodice that I'd snagged from my favorite vintage clothing and thrift shop. She looked fabulous except for the big scowl on her face. "I still don't see why you got to wear jeans and I had to dress up."

I pressed the doorbell. "Well, we're about to find out, so quit griping."

Kailyn, who still lived with her parents, opened the door wearing jeans, a pink hoodie layered over a white tee, and pink Skechers.

"No fair!" Becca said. "How come everyone else gets to wear jeans, and I'm in a dress and heels?"

"You call those heels?" Annette, clad in gray wool slacks and a matching sweater with a string of pearls at her throat joined us and looked askance at Becca's feet.

"You're lucky I even wore these." Becca said as we followed the dynamic mother-daughter duo inside.

Annette led us into the living room where we found Tess also in jeans, tennies, turtleneck, and a cropped denim jacket, Paige in a brown corduroy skirt and sweater, and Jenna ... Jenna was a revelation. She wore a figure-hugging black cocktail dress with tiny rhinestones twinkling at the collar, a white pashmina shawl, and four-inch stilettos.

"Wow." I whistled. "You look dressed to kill."

"Yeah, she could definitely take someone out with one of

those lethal foot weapons." Becca backed up in mock horror. "Remind me not to get on your bad side."

"Better not, Birkenstock girl."

Our hostess clapped her hands to get our attention. "Thank y'all for coming and for followin' your instructions." Annette dropped a glance to Becca's feet. "Most of you." She nodded to a tray of crystal goblets on the coffee table and instructed us to each take a glass of sparkling cider. Annette never allowed alcohol in her home. Not after growing up with a "fall-on-the-floor-drunk-every-night daddy," she said.

"Mr. Knightley, in fact," Annette recited, "was one of the few people who could see faults in Emma Woodhouse, and the only one who ever told her of them." She raised her glass. "To the Mr. Knightleys of the world."

"Here, here," Paige said. "Especially if they look like Jeremy Northam."

"I'll drink to that." Kailyn smacked her lips. "He was yummy."

"Has everyone read *Emma*?" Annette's eyes zeroed in on her daughter. "Or did you just watch the movie?" she drawled.

"Sorry." Kailyn looked sheepish. "The movie was great, though, and I watched *Clueless* too. Does that count?"

Annette closed her eyes. "Her character depends upon those she is with; but in good hands she will turn out a valuable woman."

Paige whispered to me, "I didn't know we were supposed to memorize lines from the book, did you?"

"Nope."

Jenna glanced over at Becca. "Give it up, book-quote girl. Are you in on this?"

It was Becca's turn to shake her head. We turned puzzled faces to Annette.

Annette directed her gaze to our resident Janeite. "Could you please tell us what this month's book selection was about?"

"*Emma* is a comedy of manners with a matchmaking heroine who manipulates people and circumstances to what she wants or thinks is best," Tess said, "including whom they should be with romantically. Ultimately, though, it's a celebration of the power of love."

"Exactly." Annette beamed.

"Exactly what, Mother?" Kailyn asked, frustration evident in her tone. "And how does this translate to our first adventure?"

"Chloe, what kind of heroine did Tess say Emma was?"

"Uh ... " I shot a quick glance at my aunt, whose eyes registered dawning comprehension and dismay. "A matchmaking one?" I said weakly.

"Mom! You're not playing matchmaker again!"

As one, we all turned in horror to Annette.

7

I always deserve the best treatment because I never put up with any other.

Emma

Annette plumped the pillows on the couch and adjusted the coasters on the end table before fixing us with a serene look. "And what would be so wrong with that? Y'all are always complaining that there're no good men out there, that all the good ones are taken."

Jenna crossed her long, athletic legs. "They are."

"Oh, no, they're not," Annette countered with a satisfied smile. "As you'll see in," she looked at her watch, "just a few minutes."

"What?" Kailyn squeaked. "You set us up on blind dates?"

"I'm *so* not going on a blind date with some stranger," Becca said.

"Me either."

"It's a double date," Annette said. "There's safety in

numbers, which is why I split y'all into pairs. And why you're not all dressed the same, either." She consulted her PDA. "Chloe and Paige will go out for a casual dinner; Jenna and Becca will dine at Antoine's, and Kailyn, you and Tess will go bowling."

My normally unflappable Aunt Tess threw me a look of horror.

"*Bowling?*" Kailyn screeched. "You've *got* to be kidding. I don't know how to bowl."

"I know. That's why this will be a new adventure for you."

"The last time I bowled was over twenty years ago. I dropped the ball on my husband's foot and fractured it," Tess said.

"Well, try to be more careful tonight." Annette handed each of us a slip of paper. "These are your dates' names. I've personally selected each one, and I know for a fact that none of them are married, ax murderers, or escaped convicts."

"That's comforting," Tess said.

Kailyn read the name on her paper. "Henry Meeks? What is this, freaks and geeks night? He's such a dweeb. And goofy-looking, besides."

"Remember to look beneath the surface, baby girl," her mother said.

I shot a desperate glance at the doorway, wondering if I could somehow make my escape without Annette noticing. Times like these made me wish I had my own invisibility cloak.

"James MacDonald?" Tess frowned at her slip of paper. "That name seems vaguely familiar."

"It should. You booked him on an Alaskan cruise with his kids last year a few months after his wife died," Annette said. "He said he's lookin' forward to meeting you in person, said you were very kind and understanding."

This James guy was already scoring points with me. I just hoped he was the real deal. Tess deserved a nice guy. Uncle Ted had died almost ten years ago. She'd been alone far too long. And I hoped she'd have fun bowling with him tonight. But as for me? I edged toward the door.

"Where are you going?"

"Um, I'm really not ready to start dating yet, Annette."

"I know, honey. Bless your heart. That's why this is just a fun, casual evening with friends. Don't even think of it as an actual date." She giggled. "You and Paige are going to have such fun! I almost wish I was going with you."

"So come along. If it's just a fun evening with friends, why don't you join us?"

"No can do. I've already made plans with that good-lookin' hunk of man of mine." She smiled as big as Texas.

The doorbell rang, and Annette hurried to answer it.

Jenna smoothed her skirt, Tess rifled through a magazine, Kailyn glared at her mother's retreating back, Becca scowled, and Paige and I exchanged anxious looks.

Annette ushered in an attractive, silver-haired man in jeans and a polo shirt, followed by a younger, bookish-looking guy, also in jeans, but wearing a T-shirt that proclaimed "Revenge of the Nerds."

Kailyn shot daggers at her mom.

Annette introduced James and Henry to everyone, then hurried them along with Tess and Kailyn. "Y'all don't want to be late now. I booked your lane for six thirty."

Tess winked at me as she left.

Well, all right then. This James guy definitely has promise.

Annette consulted her list. "Next up are Becca and Jenna. You have reservations for dinner at Antoine's with Michael and Thomas. And afterward you're going to see *Swan Lake*."

Becca groaned, and culture-vulture Paige quickly offered to take her place.

"Uh-uh." Annette wagged her finger at Paige. "This is supposed to be an adventure. Something you haven't done before." She gave us a sweet smile. "I've got something else planned for you two."

That something else was a sushi/karaoke bar.

Great. Raw fish and singing in public. So not two of my favorite things.

I nearly bolted from the car when our new male friends informed us of where we were going, but I didn't want to leave Paige holding the seaweed. At least Annette didn't hook me up with a young guy. Will Thompson was in his mid-thirties, decent-looking, and, I learned, a real estate agent who owned his own home. Daniel Lund, Paige's date, who worked in the same agency as Will, was a couple years older.

Both guys were pleasant enough, and I was delighted to discover that neither one was a jock, so we didn't have to spend the entire evening politely pretending to be interested in boring sports talk and statistics.

The sushi, though, was a problem. I've never been able to stomach the thought of raw fish, no matter what they call it or how they dress it up in seaweed. I stuck to teriyaki chicken.

"Come on, try it," Will urged, holding something called *sashimi* under my nose.

I bolted to the restroom.

"Chloe?" Paige's worried face appeared behind me in the mirror above the sink where I was rinsing out my mouth a few minutes later. "You okay?"

"I will be. Got any mints?"

"Altoids okay?" She offered the tin to me.

"Perfect." I popped one in my mouth, enjoying the heady peppermint rush.

"So," Paige said, "I've been thinking of what we can do to get back at Annette."

"You mean besides piercing her belly button and making her go to church in bleached and torn low-rise jeans and flip-flops?"

"The pierced belly button is a great touch!" Paige rubbed her hands and looked at me from beneath her brown bangs. "You do know we have to do the karaoke thing, don't you? It's part of the rules. We agreed to do whatever adventure each person set up."

"Were we on drugs or what?"

"No, just caught up in the Becca excitement." Paige snapped her fingers. "Hey! I know how we can get Annette back."

"How?"

"Have Becca insist she go skydiving after we read that lady pilot's memoir."

"That's a little scarier than karaoke, don't you think?"

"Not much."

"Besides, we didn't choose the flying memoir."

"Oh yeah. Well, we'll just have to think of something else. Like maybe hiding all her Paula Deen cookbooks or something."

We decided we'd better come out of hiding and rejoin our friends so they wouldn't think we'd bailed on them. And fifteen minutes later, when the karaoke night kicked off with a re-markably good Will and Daniel doing their Righteous Broth-ers impression of "You've Lost that Loving Feeling," Paige and I followed with "My Heart Will Go On" from *Titanic*.

We went for broke and sang as loudly and out-of-tune as we could, each trying to sing louder than the other, and fre-quently breaking into giggles — particularly when we thumped our chest every time we sang the word "heart," the way Céline

Dion had done at the Academy Awards. Afterward, we stumbled off the stage to our seats, laughing helplessly.

Will and Daniel high-fived us. "You girls rock! That was absolutely awful."

"Thanks. You guys weren't so bad yourselves." I blotted my forehead with a cocktail napkin.

When I looked up, a man stood by Paige's chair, studying me.

Ryan.

"Hello, Chloe. Having a nice time?" Was that disapproval in his voice? I bristled. How dare he show up here and judge me. Chris left me, not the other way around. And it's not like I was on a date.

"I hope you punched him out," Becca said later that night when I told her of Ryan's comment at the sushi bar.

"No. But I wanted to." Boy, had I wanted to. But I'd been avoiding Ryan at church and everywhere else ever since Chris dumped me. Dumped. A word I'd rather not think about.

New subject. Church? Did I really want to think about that either? Not only had I been avoiding Ryan at church, I'd been avoiding church altogether. And feeling guilty about it. I just couldn't handle all the clichés and platitudes. "God has something better for you. It just wasn't God's will. Maybe God's trying to teach you something, blah, blah, blah."

I always love the way everyone else seems to know what God is thinking. To me, it's more of a mystery.

Sitting down on the couch and shucking off my boots, I turned my attention to my roommate. "How was dinner and the ballet?"

"Good, but a little stuffy." She made a face. "I liked the food better than the ballet — too prissy for me. And way too long."

"And your date?"

"Like I said, the food was good." Becca yawned and stretched and said she was heading to bed. "Long night."

Sure was. Although I had to admit, it had been kind of fun, too. Until Ryan showed up. Who did he think he was getting all snarky with me? He's not the boss of me. Besides, I just know he had a hand in Chris's breaking up with me.

Be fair. How can you know that?

You don't think he shared any of his misgivings about our engagement and upcoming wedding with his roommate, the groom-to-be?

Maybe. Probably. Since they did live together, after all. Then again, maybe not. They are guys. They don't talk about relationships the way women do.

Whatever.

I ended my internal ping-pong match and jumped in the shower to get rid of my karaoke flop sweat. As I shampooed the lingering scent of sushi from my hair, I sang one of Rosemary's old hits, "Mambo Italiano," to get my mind off Ryan and Chris.

Chris.

I sang even louder, until Becca's voice outside the bathroom door made me jump. "Hey Sinatra, shut up, will ya? Some of us are trying to sleep here."

Finishing my shower in silence, I rinsed and toweled off, then padded quietly into my bedroom where I slipped on a comfy oversized T-shirt and slid between the sheets.

Only I couldn't sleep.

"Mambo Italiano" kept playing over and over in my head like a broken record. I tried to drown it out by humming "It's a Small World," but then I had a new broken record playing over and over in my brain.

I tried counting books. Sheep never worked for me.

Neither did books this time. Maybe if I counted up all Chris's bad qualities ...

Immature.

Sports-obsessed.

Irresponsible.

Bad with money.

Controlling.

Didn't read.

Fun.

Carefree.

Cute.

Unafraid to take risks.

Loved kids.

Told me I was prettier than Julia ...

Don't go there.

At last, knowing sleep was impossible, I picked up our next book club selection from my nightstand and lost myself in the delightful children's story of the two kids who ran away from home and hid out in the Metropolitan Museum of Art in New York City.

How fabulous would that be? To be surrounded by all that beauty 24/7?

I could think of worse things.

march
*F*rom the Mixed-up Files of
Mrs. Basil E. Frankweiler

&

APRIL
*C*oming Home

8

She didn't like discomfort. Even picnics were untidy and inconvenient: all those insects and the sun melting the icing on the cupcakes.

From the Mixed-Up Files of Mrs. Basil E. Frankweiler

I wasn't big on discomfort any more than twelve-year-old Claudia. But it was a crisp spring day over three months since my break-up, and I was feeling good. The sun was shining, the wisteria was blooming, and the Paperback Girls were headed out on another book-club adventure. This time, we were combining our March and April selections, *From the Mixed-Up Files of Mrs. Basil E. Frankweiler* and Rosamunde Pilcher's epic *Coming Home*, into a two-part, one-day adventure in San Francisco.

Paige, Becca, Tess, and I were leading the way to the City by the Bay in our two-car caravan in Paige's gas-hog but comfortable Taurus, while Jenna, Annette, and Kailyn followed behind in Jenna's sporty red Jetta.

"I'll sure be glad when next month rolls around and we can get to the outdoor stuff," Becca grumbled.

"We *are* outdoors," Tess said.

"Yeah. In a *car.* Driving to a museum."

"Have you ever been to the California Palace of the Legion of Honor?" Paige asked.

"Nope."

"Well, then it's a new adventure for you, isn't it?" Tess turned around in the passenger seat and batted her eyes at Becca.

"You'll love it. You too, Chloe." Paige met my eyes in the rearview mirror. "It's pretty amazing. And the view of the Bay is incredible."

Tess had actually taken me to the Legion of Honor for my tenth birthday, followed by lunch at the famed Cliff House afterward. And I remember liking the museum, being entranced by all the paintings, and intending to come back, but somehow I had never gotten around to it.

I was relieved, however, that Paige had offered to drive. The last time I'd driven in San Francisco had been right after college graduation when a couple of classmates and I had decided to celebrate by dancing the night away. Unfortunately, my tiny Toyota was not an automatic, and driving a stick shift through the almost-vertical streets of wild-and-crazy San Francisco must qualify as one of the top-five most terrifying things in the world.

Just behind sharks, spiders, sushi, and cheap pedicures.

I'd only been back to San Francisco a few times since — but always with someone else at the wheel, and I always made sure the car was an automatic.

Paige wove through the steep city streets and turned onto Geary heading west to Lincoln Park. Passing the remote golf course and arriving at the isolated Legion of Honor a few minutes after ten, we managed to snag the last couple of spaces in the narrow side parking lot. We piled out of both cars and followed tour guide Tess past wind-whipped cypresses that looked like a giant had squashed the greenery between his fingers.

That same wind sliced through my thin jacket as Tess led us to an opening on the high bluff overlooking San Francisco Bay and the elegant Golden Gate Bridge. I hugged myself to keep warm and sucked air in between my teeth as I drank in the remarkable sight of the shimmering Bay laid out below like a sparkling sapphire necklace.

"Oh my," Annette breathed. "Would you look at that view!"

Jenna whistled. "Now that's what I call great art."

"Check out all the sailboats!" Becca pointed to a cluster of moving white dots below. "See! We could have done our sailing adventure now instead of waiting until this summer."

"Only if we wanted to freeze our tushies off," Annette drawled.

"Um, not that I wouldn't mind the weight loss, but I'm actually freezing mine off right now." Paige shivered. "Okay if we go inside?"

Reluctantly we turned away from the gorgeous natural art and trooped across the parking lot toward the imposing white-columned structure guarded by two large stone lions. The center arch reminded me of pictures I'd seen of the Arc de Triomphe in Paris.

Paris.

It would be nice to be in Paris now, since it was April after all. I hummed a snatch of the old song.

Since we were saving up for Paris, we couldn't afford a trip to New York in the same year, so Tess decided that instead of running away to the Metropolitan Museum of Art the way Claudia and her younger brother, Jamie, had done in *From the Mixed-Up Files of Mrs. Basil E. Frankweiler*, San Francisco would do just as well. She went into travel guide teaching mode and told us that the Legion of Honor was designed as a memorial to California's World War I casualties and opened in 1924.

Annette let out a low whistle as we entered the airy courtyard dominated by a familiar imposing bronze statue. "Hey, isn't that the thinker dude?" Kailyn asked.

We circled the sculpture. "Check out those calves," Jenna said admiringly. "Great muscle definition."

"But I saw *The Thinker* in Paris years ago." Annette's penciled brows beetled together. "Was he moved here or somethin'?"

"No. The original is still in Paris." Tess checked her guidebook. "This is one of several original casts in museums around the world."

I made another slow circle around the famous statue, checking it out from every angle. It wasn't only the thinking man's calves that had great definition. His back, shoulders, powerful arms, and magnificent head, deep in thought, were carved to a glorious perfection.

Amazing. Absolutely amazing. I wonder what he's thinking.

Kailyn tugged at her mother's sleeve. "Can we go in and do the art stuff now?"

Tess beamed at Kailyn's eagerness as she led us past the white columns flanking the courtyard to the entrance, informing us that inside we'd find several more sculptures along with paintings, prints, and some decorative arts. "And there's a wonderful Renoir I think you'll especially love," she said.

"What I'd love is to have time to get in a little shopping before we go back home," Kailyn said.

"And what I'd really love is to stop by Pier 39 to visit the sea lions," Becca said, "and pick up the information for our summer sailing adventure."

Tess sighed. "You can lead a horse to water, but you can't make him drink."

We agreed to split into two groups with Jenna, Becca, and Kailyn in one, and Tess, Annette, Paige, and me in the other. Then we synchronized our watches to meet in three hours at the Ritz-Carlton for our second adventure of the day, afternoon tea.

As we wound our way through the beautiful museum, I realized I always wound up with all the older women. What was that all about? Chris said I acted even older than I was — maybe he was right. Maybe that's just part of who I am. Nothing wrong with that.

Tess led us into an immense marble gallery that resembled a cathedral, with light pouring in from the high arched windows, illuminating the bronze Rodins far below.

I sucked in my breath.

How could metal and stone look so real? So alive? As if it was going to move or speak at any moment? I lingered before a statue of John the Baptist. I could almost hear him preaching: *"I baptize you with water for repentance. But after me will come one who is more powerful than I, whose sandals I am not fit to carry."*

My sandals carried me slowly into the next room of statues. Except Rodin's work wasn't just statues or lifeless monuments. I stopped before an immense hand that seemed as if it wanted to reach out and grab mine. My fingers itched to touch it, to clasp *The Mighty Hand* in mine, but I restrained myself.

The guard in the doorway helped.

Moving on, I came to a small yellowed plaster of *Eve in Eden* encased in glass, hiding her head and covering her nakedness in shame. Then I stopped before another of Rodin's works that was nearly as famous as *The Thinker* outside — *The Kiss.* No covering their nakedness in shame for that couple. They were too in love, too caught up in their passion.

Oh, to be kissed like that. To be loved like that …

I pushed thoughts of my almost husband away (resolutely this time) and hurried past the remaining sculptures to rejoin the rest of the group. I found them in the Impressionists room, grouped around Tess's Renoir.

"No wonder you love this." Annette gazed at the painting of a mother trying to dress a happy, rosy-cheeked child who was more interested in playing with a kitten instead. "The colors are so warm and soft, with such a dreamy feeling to them. This reminds me of my sweet baby girl when she was little."

"The chubby arms or the exposed bottom and dimpled thighs?" I asked.

"All of it. The whole adorableness of the scene. And would you look at those precious curls. Isn't she darling?"

"Very. Except that she is a he," Tess said.

Paige was distracted by another painting. "Look! It's one of Monet's *Water Lilies.*"

And people call Thomas Kinkade the painter of light.

Mesmerized, I slowly approached the famous painting with the others. Like the rest of the known universe, I'd seen copies of the ubiquitous *Water Lilies* everywhere — in books, on posters, note cards, screen savers, even mouse pads. But they didn't even begin to do justice to the real thing.

I drank in the sapphire water, the rich grassy green lily pads, and the vibrant pink flowers — all exploding with light. And joy. Such joy. And those brush strokes! I moved closer. Brush strokes applied by Monet's own hand nearly a hundred years ago.

Tess came alongside me and squeezed my shoulder. "Beautiful, isn't it?" she whispered.

I nodded, unable to speak.

Now I understood how the children had been able to hide in the New York museum in *The Mixed-Up Files of Mrs. Basil*

E. Frankweiler. I'd have been happy to hide away in some forgotten nook at the Legion of Honor and come out again to explore the museum at length when everyone else was gone. I'd spend hours just in this very room.

"Chloe?" Tess's voice roused me from my daydream. "We need to catch up with Paige and Annette."

"Oh. I hadn't even realized they'd left."

"I know."

Reluctantly, I left Monet and followed Tess in search of the others. Becca, Jenna, and Kailyn were long gone from the museum, but we found Annette and Paige a couple rooms away standing in front of a huge oil painting of a shy-looking young girl at a well with a broken water pitcher at her feet.

"Look at her eyes," Annette said. "It's like she's starin' right into my soul."

Although I too was captivated by the mesmerizing eyes of the lovely girl in the painting, it was a smaller, less pretty picture just beside her that gave me pause. I'd never heard of the artist, Julien Dupre, but the young peasant woman in the field, holding on to a staff, caught my eye.

It was almost like looking into a mirror—if that mirror had reflected brown hair scraped back into a bun, rather than a ponytail. And if the girl in the painting had been wearing my glasses. And if she hadn't been dressed all in brown—a thick, heavy brown that weighed her down.

Then there was that whole sheep-tending thing.

Other than that, it was like looking into a mirror.

I longed to pluck the poor girl with the wistful expression out of her drab, realistic surroundings and set her smack dab in a rowboat in the middle of Monet's glorious water lilies. I closed my eyes, imagining it. She'd be wearing a long white cotton dress that ruffled in the breeze, her hair would be set free from its dutiful bun and flowing down her back, and her face would be turned to the sun, basking in the dappled light and warmth.

"Chloe?" Paige cleared her throat beside me. "If you want to make a quick stop in the gift shop before we leave, we'd better hurry, or we're going to be late to meet the others."

Half an hour later we entered the elegant lobby of the Ritz-Carlton in Nob Hill.

"Oh my," Annette whispered. "Are you sure we don't have to mortgage our homes to be here?"

"Only if you're checking in." The corners of Tess's mouth turned up. "Rooms can easily go for a thousand a night."

"No way," Annette squeaked. "That's my mortgage payment."

Becca rushed up to us, her face flushed and eyes snapping. "We're all set for our summer catamaran cruise around Alcatraz. You just need to go online when you get home and pay with your credit card." She handed us glossy brochures with a large sailing ship on the cover. "Did you know we actually get to sail *under* the Golden Gate Bridge? We'll be one of those dots on the water that we saw from the cliffs earlier."

My stomach clenched.

Tiny dots.

Big ocean.

Deep ocean.

"Um, shouldn't we go into the restaurant?"

Once we were seated, everyone began talking at once about their respective morning adventures.

All except me.

I couldn't stop thinking about the drab peasant girl all in brown. And the water lilies. And the artist's brush strokes. How incredible that something done over a hundred years ago could still touch people today.

Will I ever do anything that will touch people a hundred

years from now? I thought of the Monet quote magnet I'd picked up in the gift shop that said, "I would like to paint the way a bird sings."

I'd settle for either.

Tess nudged me.

"What?"

"Could you pass the cream please?" Paige asked. Apparently not for the first time.

"Oh, sure. Sorry."

Our waitress appeared with a three-tiered silver serving rack full of sweets and savories. Becca looked askance at the delicate finger sandwiches. "Those are supposed to fill us up? I might need a Big Mac on the way home."

"Just wait and see." Tess selected a couple sandwiches from the bottom tier.

We followed her lead.

I bit hesitantly into what our server had said was prosciutto with melon on light rye. Yum.

"Mmm, this cucumber, roquefort, and walnuts is delish," Annette said. "What do you think, Kailyn?" But her daughter was too busy inhaling a smoked salmon sandwich with pickled onion and caviar to answer.

I love smoked salmon. And I liked the caviar too, much to my surprise, having never had it before. But pickled onion? I removed it discreetly and set it off to one side. The real revelation of our lunch, however, was the lemon curd on a freshly baked scone. Heaven. Especially when topped with Devonshire cream.

"Now I know how Judith felt the first time she had tea at the Carey-Lewises home." Paige wiped her mouth with her linen napkin.

Judith Dunbar was the underprivileged but strong and steadfast English heroine in our April selection, *Coming Home.*

And the Carey-Lewises were the rich family of her rebellious school chum, Loveday, who took Judith in and unofficially adopted her when her mother and younger sister had to rejoin her government-employed father in the Far East.

I heaped a little more lemon curd on my scone. "The only thing missing is the gorgeous country estate in Cornwall."

"And the good-looking son of the manor." Paige expelled a wistful sigh. "Wouldn't you have loved to live in England at the time of *Coming Home?*"

"All except for the war part," Becca said dryly.

"But even that was kind of romantic."

Becca and Jenna—pacifists—sent Paige a look.

"I don't mean that war itself is romantic," she added hastily. "Not at all. But that time in history, the late thirties and forties, was sort of magical. Something we won't see again. If you look at movies from then, *Mrs. Miniver, Casablanca, Goodbye Mr. Chips*, it was a whole different world, full of honor, sacrifice, and nobility. And I think this book captured that world wonderfully. I *loved* it."

"Me too." I took a sip of my Earl Grey. "Rosamunde Pilcher tells such sweeping sagas and always has these rich, wonderful characters that you really get to know and love. Like Judith. I hated to come to the end of the book."

"I know," Kailyn said. "This was my favorite book since book club started. I loved all the description. Couldn't you just picture the glamorous dresses Diana and Athena wore?"

Becca tilted her head at Kailyn. "You know, you remind me a little of Athena."

"Really?" She preened. "Thanks."

"I'm not sure that was a compliment, honey," her mom said. "Athena was beautiful, but a teeny bit on the shallow side." Annette gave Becca an appraising look, and then drawled, "You remind me a lot of Loveday."

"I don't think so."

"I do." I slathered lemon curd on the other half of my scone.

The rest of the table nodded in agreement.

"No way," Becca said. "I'd never marry a guy I didn't love just so I could stay on my parents' estate. I wouldn't even care about an estate. And besides," she scowled at Annette, "Loveday was a spoiled brat."

Paige jumped in to the rescue. "No one's calling you a spoiled brat, Becca, but you must admit you do share a lot of other characteristics with Loveday. She was strong-willed and impetuous and definitely used to going after what she wanted."

"Well, I know what I want. And I'm not afraid to go after it. I don't think there's anything wrong with that."

"All depends on how you go about it," Tess said.

My turn to jump in. "Annette, you're definitely a Judith. You were in the military and served your country, just like she did. You too, Jenna."

"I've never been in the military."

"No. Sorry, I mean you remind me of Judith too. That whole strong and independent thing you've got going on."

Paige bobbed her head in agreement, and then turned to Tess. "And I think you're a three-way combination of the forthright nanny Mary Millyway, and Judith's friend Phyllis."

"That's only two," Tess said. "Who's the other one?"

"Well … I think you have a little bit of Biddy in you too."

"The flighty aunt who drank too much?"

"Only after her son died in the war. And just for a brief time. I think of her more as Judith's fun and encouraging aunt."

"She's nailed you, Tess." I sent my aunt a warm smile. "Okay, since we're playing this game, who am I, then?"

9

"So many books. Too many books … You're clearly an inveterate reader.

A girl after my own heart."

Coming Home

There was an awkward silence. Tess busied herself with her napkin and Paige asked Annette how similar her military service had been to Judith's.

Kailyn broke the silence. "Actually, you kind of remind me of Judith's mother, Molly."

"*What?* I'm nowhere near as old as that."

"I didn't mean old, I meant more the way that she was always kind of scared of … driving."

"I'm not afraid of driving. Other than in San Francisco."

"And certain parts of Sacramento," Becca said.

"That's just exercising discretion and showing common sense. Why would I consciously choose to drive through a bad neighborhood at night?"

My roommate shrugged her shoulders. "Oh I don't know.

Maybe to attend a once-in-a-lifetime concert from the band you've been dying to hear forever? A band who'd come to town to perform at a fundraiser for a new youth center?"

I could feel my face heating up. I really had wanted to go see Switchfoot, but they'd chosen to appear in a scary part of town known for its drug activity and gang violence, and I didn't feel like getting shot.

Try as I might, my good-girl, white-bread self just couldn't summon up the courage to attend, even when a small group from church invited me to go with them.

"You really missed out," Shannon from the singles group told me the next day at church. "It was so cool. The whole community turned out and the band played for almost three hours! At the end, everyone prayed, even the gangbangers."

"You're afraid of lots of things," Becca was saying. "Sharks, for instance."

"Anyone in their right mind would be afraid of sharks, Aqua Girl."

"Amen," Annette said. "I know I surely am. And don't no-body say nothin' about my menopausal mind either."

"Okay, so sharks were a bad example. But what about," Becca ticked off on her fingers. "Flying? And sushi? And *pedicures*?"

"*Cheap* pedicures. Didn't you hear about those women who got foot infections from salons where they didn't sterilize their instruments often enough?"

Becca rolled her eyes.

"Chloe, that was a few years ago," Kailyn said. "I read some-where that it's all regulated and inspected now. They can lose their license if everything isn't clean and on the up and up."

"Maybe so, but how often do they do those inspections? I'm not going to chance it. I'd rather pay a little more than get some gross bacterial fungus or something." I turned to Becca.

"And for your information, I'm not *afraid* of sushi. I just don't like raw fish."

"Then how come at the condo you told me you were worried about mercury poisoning?"

Way to break the sanctity of the roommate confidences. Sure, I was a little concerned about mercury—you would be too if you'd read some of the scary things I had—but mainly the thought of putting raw fish into my mouth just turned my stomach.

"Hey, I've read about mercury poisoning from eating too much raw tuna and other fish." Paige wagged her finger at Becca. "So don't be giving Chloe a hard time."

"Aw, but it's so much fun."

Jenna deftly changed the subject. "Didn't the Bay look inviting today? Really made me want to go swimming."

"In this cold weather? You're crazy. You could cramp up and drown."

"Like Natalie Wood. She had a lifelong fear of drowning, and that's how she died." Paige was always spouting old movie trivia.

"I read somewhere that what you fear the most—drowning, flying, whatever—is how you usually end up dying," Kailyn said. "I have a fear of birds."

"That's a crock. What, you think a bird's going to peck you to death or something?" Becca said.

"Happened in *The Birds*."

"Great Hitchcock."

"I'll say. But scary. After seeing it, I couldn't walk through the playground if I saw even a crow on the jungle gym," Tess said.

Becca sent Tess a surprised look. "I didn't think anything scared you."

"We all have our fears. Even you, fearless leader. C'mon, 'fess up. What are you afraid of?"

"Men in tights. That's just wrong."

Annette sighed. "I was just trying to broaden your cultural horizons."

"What can I say? Ballet and art museums don't float my boat. Guess I'm a Philistine." Becca grinned. "I prefer McArt. A quick drive-through is more my style."

"Want fries with that?"

"Yes, please. And ketchup."

"Becca, Becca." Tess shook her head. "What are we going to do with you? Art can't be wolfed down like fast food. You have to savor it, take your time with it, digest it, let it speak to your soul."

"It spoke to me all right," Becca said. "It told me to go outside, get some fresh air, and enjoy the art of nature."

Annette groaned.

Tess wasn't so easily put off. She told my roomie that she was hoping when we got to Paris, Becca would have an art awakening. "If you can't in Paris, there's no hope."

"Don't bet the farm on that." Becca cracked her knuckles loudly, completely oblivious to her chichi surroundings and the frowns from neighboring tables.

Or was she? My roommate liked to make statements, and they weren't always verbal.

"Anyway, adventures should be exciting and out-of-doors," Becca said.

"Says who, nature-girl?"

"Most of the world."

"But our group's not the most athletic bunch, except for you and Jenna." My eyes scanned the table. "And I don't know about you, but I was never any good at sports in school. I was always the last one to get picked for any team. And that saying 'you run like a girl'? That was invented for me."

Paige and Annette bobbed their heads like those touristy bobble-head dolls you find at only the best truck stops.

"It's never too late to change," Becca said. "That's why we're doing these adventures — pushing us out of our comfort zones."

"Like visiting an art museum?" Paige asked innocently.

When we got home that night from our adventure in the city, there was a message for me on the answering machine.

"Hi, Chloe. It's Julia. Uh, Mom and I are going shopping for my wedding dress next weekend, and we wanted to look at bridesmaid's dresses too. We'd love you to come, but if that would be too hard for you, I understand. Give me a call, okay?"

Why would it be too hard? Just because you're getting married to the man of your dreams and the man of my dreams dumped me.

I slapped the delete button. Then I logged on to my laptop to update my checking account after today's expenditures. Strange. My account balance looked unusually low. I scanned the transactions and quickly found the problem. There among the debits was a familiar amount. Becca's rent check must have bounced.

Hesitantly, I headed down the hall and knocked on my roommate's half-open door.

"Enter at your own risk."

Becca's room was always a disaster zone, so I usually steered clear of it. I stepped just inside the door which was the only clear spot in the entire room. It looked like a robbery scene or the donation sorting area at the Salvation Army, with clothes strewn everywhere. And in the midst of all the chaos,

Becca was perched cross-legged on her futon, the queen of her domain, flipping through a magazine.

"Um, this is a little awkward, Bec, but … your rent check bounced."

"It did? That's weird. I know I had enough in my account when I wrote you the check. Did you deposit it right away?"

"No. A couple days later, I think."

"That explains it."

"What?"

"Why it bounced."

"I'm not following."

"My paycheck was automatically deposited Tuesday morning," Becca explained patiently. "I gave you the rent check that night and then Thursday made a few ATM withdrawals. And I had plenty in my account then, so maybe the check hadn't cleared yet or something."

Was she serious?

"But if it hadn't cleared, why didn't you allow for that? Don't you balance your checkbook?"

"Nope. Math isn't my strong suit." She picked at the polish on her left big toe. "What can I say? I'm always robbing Peter to pay Paul."

But how about paying Chloe? I took a deep breath. "If you like, I could show you how to balance your checkbook and set up a budget so you don't run into this problem."

"Nah, that's okay. I'm not big into numbers." Becca bounced off the bed, yanked off her white tank, tunneled through one of the clothes stacks until she found a fresh tank top, black, and pulled it on. "Hey, want to go dancing? I'm meeting a couple friends from work at that new club that just opened."

"No, thanks. I need to get up early tomorrow for church."

"Oh yeah, I forgot. Well don't wait up, Chloe the Good."

She smirked, grabbed her keys from her crowded dresser, and left.

Yes, Chloe the Good had returned to church, but I made sure I went to the early service so I wouldn't run into Ryan the Wedding Killer. Also, it gave me a get-out-of-singles-Bible-study-free card this way.

Problem was, my family, including Justin, Julia's fiancé, all preferred the early, more traditional service and naturally expected me to sit with them — which I did for a couple Sundays. But I wasn't sure how much longer I could handle Justin and Julia (or as I thought of them, the double Js) and their cooing wedding talk and general all-around lovesick gooeyness.

Maybe it was time to check out another church.

Mom's eyes brimmed with tears as she gazed at her firstborn and favorite daughter in the dressing room of the bridal shop the following Saturday. "Oh, honey, you look so beautiful!"

Julia examined her white lacy self in the full-length mirror. "Really? Do you like this dress better than the second one I tried on?"

"Oh yes. It's much prettier and fits you like a glove — just needs to have the hem taken up a little. More you, don't you think so, Chloe?"

What I think is that I'm going to run screaming from this room full of tulle, satin, and lace any minute.

"Uh, yeah, Jules. I like that one better."

Julia fingered the soft satin at her waist. "You don't think it's too form-fitting?"

"On you, dear?" The bridal boutique manager sent Julia an admiring glance. "You've got the figure for it. I wish all our brides were as slim and trim as you. It would make things so much easier. Don't worry about a thing. You look absolutely beautiful. You're going to take his breath away."

Julia's shining eyes met Mom's shimmering ones in the mirror.

I turned away and started rummaging through the rack of bridesmaid dresses that looked like a giant box of Popsicles. "What color pink did you have in mind, Jules?"

"I was thinking of a happy cotton candy pink—all light and fluffy and swirly."

Of course you were. Fits me to a T. Light. Fluffy. And swirly.

Two hours and forty-seven minutes later, after trying on countless pink bridesmaid dresses—strapless and spaghetti-strapped, with sleeves and without, V-necked and scoop-necked—I "swirled" myself into my car, stuck in Rosemary singing "Don't Fence Me In," and punched in Tess's number.

"How ghastly was it?" she asked.

"On a scale of one to ten, I'd give it a seventy-five."

"As bad as all that?"

"Worse."

"Meet me at Dunkeld's in twenty. I'll stand you to a double latte."

"Make it fifteen and a triple, and you've got a deal."

Arriving before Tess, I headed to the travel section and started flipping through Paris guidebooks. I shoved my fear of flying down and began reading about the myriad art museums the City of Lights had to offer, besides the Louvre. And they were legion.

"Going somewhere?"

I whirled around and came toe-to-toe with Ryan's blue Chucks.

"As a matter of fact, I am. Not that it's any of your business."

His face flushed a dull red. "I was just trying to make pleasant conversation."

"But you and I don't do pleasant conversation."

"We used to."

"Before your roommate dumped me, you mean?"

"No. Before you and Chris started dating."

"That was a long time ago."

"Not that long. Less than a year."

"Seems like an eternity."

"We used to be friends, Chloe. I'd like to think we could be again."

"And I'd like there to be world peace in my lifetime, but I don't see that happening anytime soon."

"Chloe?" Tess popped her head around Ryan's broad back. "Are you ready for that latte?"

"More than ready."

"Hi, Tess."

"Ryan!" She hugged him. "I'm sorry. I didn't realize that was you. How's it going?"

"Not bad. How are those two sons of yours? They're juniors this year, right?"

"Oh, yes. They're sixteen. A wonderful age — especially when there are two under one roof."

"My mom felt the same way when my brother and I were in high school." He grinned. "Once we got jobs, though, it gave us a place to work off all that energy."

"I keep encouraging my boys to find jobs, but so far, no luck."

"Are they strong?"

"Relatively speaking. Why?"

"My boss is always looking for grunt labor on the weekends and especially in the summertime." He fished a card out of his pocket and handed it to her. "Have them give me a call if they're interested."

"Oh, they'll be interested. I'll make sure of that. Thanks, Ryan. I owe you."

"No problem." His eyes flickered to me. "Well, I'd better be going. Nice seeing you both again. Enjoy your lattes."

Tess watched him as he walked away. I could tell she was checking out his legs. "Too bad he's so young. Story of my life." She turned to me with a speculative look.

"Don't even go there. I'm so *not* interested." I steered her to the café. "I need caffeine and now."

"Hey guys, what's up?" Becca appeared at Tess's side. "Good timing. I'm just taking my break. Any chance one of you can loan me a couple bucks for a mocha?"

10

If you are lucky enough to have lived in Paris as a young man, then wherever you go for the rest of your life, it stays with you, for Paris is a moveable feast.

A Moveable Feast

The following Sunday afternoon, Becca was at work and I was taking advantage of the alone time in our apartment to simply bliss out and read, as a light spring rain softly pattered against the windows. Between work, the book club, and Becca, I rarely had any time to myself these days.

In my pre-Chris days, I can remember in the wintertime making a big mug of hot chocolate and walking across the creaky hardwood to the window seat in my cozy little apartment. Right outside the single-paned windows was an ancient oak that kept me company, and I would read away for hours, all warm and curled up in a thick quilt.

Although my new place didn't possess the charm or the solitude of the old one, it did have its advantages: two bathrooms, a modern kitchen—including a dishwasher. No more washing dishes by hand or schlepping to the laundromat with six loads of laundry on a Sunday afternoon.

Honestly, though? I kind of missed the laundromat. I could get all my clothes done in one fell swoop and read my latest paperback at the same time. But that was then and this is now, and it's time to forget what lies behind and press on toward what lies ahead—which includes Paris. Ooh-la-la.

California Chloe was becoming quite the daring world traveler. First, the Mexican Riviera and now France. What next? The Amazon?

Maybe not. Don't go overboard.

I knew our trip to Paris was still several months away, but I believe in being prepared. And to that end, I'd gone to the library and checked out a raft of books set in Paris, including *The Hunchback of Notre Dame*, *A Tale of Two Cities*, *Madeline*, and Hemingway's *A Moveable Feast*.

I'd read *A Tale of Two Cities* when I was in school, but that had been a long time ago, and I needed to refresh my memory beyond the great opening line: "It was the best of times, it was the worst of times."

Today, though, I stretched out on the couch with Hugo's *The Hunchback of Notre Dame* instead, hoping to get farther into the tragic tale of the lonely, hunchbacked Quasimodo and his unrequited love for the beautiful gypsy Esmeralda.

About Victor Hugo though? That guy really liked his description. I mean thirty or forty pages about the layout of medieval Paris in the fifteenth century?

So not happening.

Maybe I needed something a little lighter, both in weight and tone. I picked up *Madeline* and quickly lost myself in the enchanting story and wonderful drawings of Paris.

That night, to continue my Parisian education, I went over to Tess's to watch some movies set in the French capital with her and Paige. She'd invited the whole book club, but everyone else was busy with work stuff or something.

When I arrived, my cousins Timmy and Tommy were playing toss the baguette.

"Go long," Tommy shouted to his twin, just as I opened the back door and stepped into the kitchen to see a loaf of French bread come sailing through the air. Startled by the sound of the door opening, Timmy missed the baguette, and it bonked me on the forehead.

"Ow!"

"Sorry, cuz. My brother never was a very good catcher."

"Oh yeah?" Timmy lobbed an orange from a bowl on the kitchen island at his twin, who lunged for it and missed. Just. He sniggered. "What were you sayin' again, bro?"

"I was sayin'," Tommy grabbed a clump of grapes and began flinging them at his brother, one by one, "food fight!"

Timmy volleyed the grapes right back.

"Hey, cease fire! I'm injured here."

"Aw, don't be such a wuss, cuz. It was just a piece of bread."

"A piece of bread that's hard as a rock." I picked up the long, now-chipped baguette from the floor and tapped it on the counter, where it made a loud knock. A couple more chips of crust fell off.

Tess appeared in the kitchen doorway, her brow puckered. "What's going on here?"

"Nothin', Mom, we were just playin'."

"Yeah, we were just goofin' around."

She took in the splattered grapes on the floor and a stray one stuck to the wall. "Well quit goofing around and clean up this mess. Now."

I tossed the baguette into the trash can.

"What happened to my bread?"

The boys dropped to the ground and began scooping up all their grape ammo, their heads bent in studied concentration.

"I'm sorry," I said. "I kind of broke it."

"But I was going to serve that with Brie."

"Crackers would work too." A grape rolled in front of my flip-flops, and I kicked it sideways to Tommy.

Tess frowned, but the front doorbell rang. She left to answer it.

"Hey, thanks for getting our back," Tommy said.

"Yeah, cuz. You rock."

"You owe me. Big time. And don't think I won't collect," I said with a sweet smile before I headed to the family room to join Tess and Paige.

"Hi, Chloe. I brought a ton of movies for us to choose from." Paige began yanking DVDs and videotapes out of a brown grocery bag in a frenzy, all the while giving us a running commentary on each film.

Her hand shook a little as she folded up the now-empty paper bag.

"Are you okay?"

"I'm fine." Paige gave a short laugh. "Just got into it with my mother again."

"Do you want to talk about it?"

"Not really. I'd rather escape to Paris." She fastened a bright smile on her face. "So, what are you in the mood for? Doris Day or Gene Kelly?"

Paige had shared a little about her mom during some of our book club discussions, but not a lot. She wasn't the type to complain or to draw attention to herself and her problems. We did know that her mother was in her late-seventies and had a rash of physical ailments, including diabetes, cataracts, high blood pressure, and something else I couldn't remember. We also knew that she was forever calling Paige and needing her to come over "right now!" to do something for her. And when Paige didn't respond immediately, since she did, after all, have a job and a life, her mother would pitch a fit.

"The joys of being the only child in town," Paige had said once after one of her mother's meltdowns.

Guess there are some good things about having a sister nearby, even if that sister walks on water. Thankfully, my mom was quite healthy and still had a couple decades to go before she hit her seventies. Besides, my mother was the complete opposite of Paige's.

She wouldn't even begin to know how to be high-maintenance.

Mom and I may not have had much in common, and most of the time I felt that she didn't "get" me, but there's no denying that she was a good, nurturing mother to my sister and me growing up.

I focused back in on my aunt's flat-screen TV where Gene Kelly was singing and dancing his way through a Paris neighborhood.

"*C'est beau*," Tess said. "That man could dance his way into my living room anytime."

"Oh yeah." Paige expelled a blissful sigh.

He *was* pretty cute. Great smile. Incredibly talented. Knew how to move. But it was more than the famous dancer's fancy footwork that was drawing me in. His character was an artist. In Paris. Painting. How fabulous was that?

I couldn't even imagine. But then, I could hardly imagine that we were really going to Paris in nine months. It still didn't seem real.

Maybe it wasn't. Things don't always work out as planned, as my almost wedding proved. Better to keep a level head about it all. Besides, if the trip were cancelled for some reason, then that meant no flying.

Over the ocean.

In a plane.

For eleven hours.

I could live with that.

It was just after midnight when I returned home with visions of soufflé, escargot, and pâté de foie gras dancing in my head. After watching two movies, foodie Paige, who subscribes to *Gourmet* magazine and is always trying out new recipes, had grilled Tess relentlessly about French food and what we might expect to learn from our Parisian chef. "Do you think she'll teach us the secret to making a perfect soufflé? I've tried and tried, but I just can't seem to get the hang of it. Mine always fall flat."

Paige also thought it would be great if we could learn to make our own croissants and éclairs.

Sounded like it might be a lot of work. I'd just get my croissants from my favorite neighborhood breakfast spot, La Bou.

Back at the condo, I let myself in quietly, not wanting to wake Becca.

I needn't have worried.

"Hey, roomie, guess where I'm thinking of moving?" she sang out from the couch where she was sitting spread-eagled in boxer shorts and a T-shirt, peering intently at her laptop, a glossy coffee-table book open beside her on the cushion.

"New Zealand?"

Recently we'd rented the *Lord of the Rings* trilogy and spent an entire Saturday watching it from start to finish. Becca had fallen in love with the lush scenery all over again, and decided she just *had* to live there.

"No. Well, yeah. Someday. But now where I'd really like to live is … ta-da, China!" Becca gestured to the oversized book at her side. It had been a slow night at work, she said, so she was flipping through some books in the travel section and found "this really cool one on China." She held the travel book of glossy photos out to me, her dark eyes shining like tinsel on a Christmas tree. "Check it out. Wouldn't you love to live there?"

"Not especially."

"But there's so many great things to see! The Forbidden City, the Great Wall, Tibet, the Himalayas. *And* they're looking for English teachers. There are all these different organizations that will actually *pay* you to go there and teach English to high school and college students. How cool is that?"

I yawned and set the book back down beside her. "Very cool. But what's even cooler to me right now is the bed that's calling my name." I didn't have the energy tonight to discuss my roommate's latest and greatest idea. Especially since next week, or next month, Becca would have a different destination du jour.

Becca was always coming up with exotic new places to live—depending on which book she'd read, which movie she'd just watched, or which program she'd seen on the Travel Channel. I couldn't keep up. And no longer even bothered to try.

None of us did.

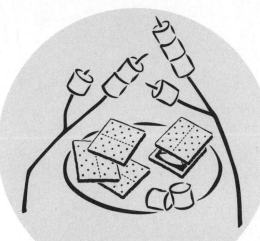

Part 4

MAY
A Walk in the Woods

11

Nearly everyone I talked to had some gruesome story involving a guileless acquaintance who had gone off hiking the trail with high hopes and new boots and come stumbling back two days later with a bobcat attached to his head or dripping blood from an armless sleeve and whispering in a hoarse voice, "Bear!" before sinking into a troubled unconsciousness.

A Walk in the Woods

I shifted impatiently from one foot to the other. "Aren't we done packing yet?" I looked at my watch again, hoping that might hurry the others along. "We were supposed to meet Paige and Jenna fifteen minutes ago."

"I know, I know. Hold your horses." Annette wedged a camp stove and a brand new box of enamel cookware from REI into the back of her ready-to-pop minivan. "Haven't you heard of the Boy Scout motto, *Be prepared*?"

"Yeah." Kailyn handed her mother two portable lawn chairs

to squeeze into the bulging van. "If we *have* to do this walk-in-the-woods adventure, I'm at least going to be comfortable."

"We're only going camping for the weekend—not for a whole month," Becca said. "And it's not like we're roughing it or anything. This campground has all the amenities of a small town—barbecue grills, picnic tables, a general store, showers, even restrooms."

Kailyn popped her gum. "Well of course it has restrooms. How else could you go to the bathroom?"

Smirking, Becca held up a small plastic shovel. "It's not just bears who go in the woods."

"Eww! TMI!"

After we'd begun reading my pick, *A Walk in the Woods* (too funny!), Becca had tried to convince me one night while we were watching a *CSI* rerun to choose a full-on back-to-nature rugged backpacking and hiking expedition along the Pacific Crest Trail for our adventure.

"Are you on crack or just insane?" I muted a Depends commercial. "A death march through the wilderness? Nothing doing. Kailyn could never handle that."

"Just Kailyn?"

"Annette too." Pause. "Although it's not really my thing either."

I've never seen what the big attraction is in staggering uphill with a heavy load on your back, tramping through a bug-and-rodent-infested forest and getting all sweaty and dirty. And then to top it all off, trying to sleep on a bed of tree roots, pine cones, and rocks. No thanks. "If God had wanted us to be one with Mother Nature, he wouldn't have invented the Hyatt."

"Guess that whole garden of Eden thing was just a fairy tale then?"

I threw my slipper at her.

Although I wasn't about to go backpacking, Tess and Becca had convinced me to at least give camping a try. So after searching the Internet and finding several state parks and campsites, I finally discovered one up north in the redwoods that sounded like it would work for our whole group.

The wheelchair-accessible trail sealed the deal.

At last Annette announced that she was finished packing the van. We all piled in, but it was a tight squeeze, so once we got to Paige's, Becca decided that she'd ride with her and Jenna instead.

When we finally drove into our campground near dusk, the good-looking ranger at the entrance whose name tag read Rick (yes, really) told us to make sure we kept all our food locked up in the car at night. "Bears have been seen in the area recently."

"Bears?"

"As in grizzlies?" Kailyn squeaked.

"Oh no. Not in this neck of the woods. These are just black bears looking for a little food. So make sure you put away all your chow whenever you leave the campsite and when you go to bed." The ranger wagged his finger at us. "No munchies in your tents, either. And be sure your cooler is airtight and locked in the car with all the windows rolled up tight."

"Can't we just crack the windows a smidge?" Annette turned on her Southern charm and sent him a winning smile. "Otherwise it gets so hot it might melt our chocolate. And you don't want to mess with a woman's chocolate."

"You could if you don't mind paying for new windows and seats. Bear can pop that window out with just one flick of his paw, he finds an opening. Couple in here a few weeks ago had over three thousand in damages to their vehicle when he yanked out the glass and shredded the upholstery to get to a candy bar in the backseat."

I scrabbled around in my purse until my fingers closed around my Almond Joy. I inhaled the candy bar in two bites.

Ranger Rick nodded his approval and then sniffed the air appreciatively. "Someone's wearing ... *Heavenly*, isn't it?"

"You have a good nose." Kailyn gave him a flirtatious smile. "*Heavenly* is my favorite Victoria's Secret fragrance."

"My girlfriend's too. But once you get to the campground, you'll probably want to take a shower and scrub it all off. Bears are just as attracted to the scent as men." Ranger Rick tipped his cap. "You ladies take care and have a nice weekend now."

Annette pulled forward several yards then slammed the car into park. "I vote we turn around and head back to that cute little B&B we passed a few miles back."

"For once, I'm in full agreement with you, Mom." Kailyn yanked out her cell. "Want me to tell the others?"

I twisted around in the backseat to see Becca, Paige, and Jenna pull in behind us and Ranger Rick make his hot way over to Paige's window to deliver his spiel.

"Nah, don't do that." Tess shoved Annette's purple umbrella that kept poking her in the neck between Kailyn's pink makeup case and about a dozen pillows. "We've come all this way, and packed all this stuff. All we have to do is take the necessary precautions, and we'll be fine. It's going to be fun. Trust me. I've gone camping with my boys plenty of times, and we haven't been mauled to death yet." She winked.

"Sounds like maybe you're overdue then." Annette met my eyes in the mirror. "What do *you* say, Chloe? This is your adventure, after all."

I say we turn this puppy around fast and head back to civilization. We can set up camp in the lobby of the nearest Hilton.

Except I was trying to be more adventurous these days. "Um ..."

A knock on my window made us all jump.

Becca and Jenna's grinning faces met ours. "Hey, you guys didn't get freaked out by Ranger Sexy's bear talk, did you?"

"What was your first clue?" Annette pried her hands from their death grip on the steering wheel and flexed her fingers to get the blood circulating again.

"Aw, they give those warnings all the time." Jenna waved off our concerns. "It's their job. No big deal. I've been camping a zillion times and never once have I seen a bear. Raccoons, yes. Chipmunks, yes. Even skunks a couple times. But no bears." She held up three fingers in the Girl Scout salute. "Honest."

"See?" Tess reassured Annette. "What'd I tell you?"

"I still think camping at that B&B down the road would be a safer choice."

"I'd even settle for a Motel 6," Kailyn said.

"Aw you guys, come on, don't be such wusses." Becca inclined her head toward Tess. "Besides, it's three against two."

Just then Kailyn's cell rang. "Hi, Paige. I hear ya. Okay, I will. Bye." She hung up, a huge smile splitting her face. "Make that three against three."

"Looks like we've got a tie," Jenna said. "Up to you, Chloe."

My eyes flicked between my aunt's loving but neutral expression, to Kailyn's and Annette's victorious expressions, and Becca's and Jenna's pouting ones.

No pressure here. The old play-it-safe, never-take-a-risk Chloe would have hightailed it out of there without a second's hesitation. But one word burned in my mind. "Safe." Chris had dubbed me safe. A nice euphemism for dull. Safe and sorry.

I took a deep breath. "Let's give it a shot."

Becca whooped and high-fived Jenna. "Yes!"

Annette and Kailyn chorused, *"What?"* and Tess gave me a proud smile.

"However," I added, "we have to do exactly what Ranger Rick said. Take all the precautions he suggested about food and perfume and everything. And the first time we get hint of a bear—Yogi or otherwise—or hear that any other campers have seen one or hear a rumor that someone may have seen a vaguely bear-shaped object on a distant ridge, we're outta here. Agreed?"

"Agreed," Becca and Jenna said in unison.

Kailyn muttered that I'd gone over to the dark side as Becca and Jenna clambered back into Paige's car and Tess navigated the way to our campsite. As we wound through the forest over a bumpy, winding dirt road, we marveled at the glorious cathedral of redwoods scraping the sky all around us.

"Did y'all know that some of these trees were standing when Jesus walked the earth?" Annette said.

And people say there is no God. I craned my neck to gaze up at the ancient redwoods and breathed a prayer of thankfulness. This kind of nature I could handle.

We passed by a small clearing planted with a rainbow striped VW van covered in Grateful Dead stickers. A long-haired guy in a bandana and holey jeans kicking back near a fire pit smiled and waved.

"Hey, wonder if that's Becca's brother," Kailyn said, staring hard at his Birkenstocks.

"Not unless there's something her mother didn't tell her." I returned hippie guy's wave. "Becca's an only child."

At Tess's direction, Annette pulled into the next campsite, where we began removing insane amounts of camping gear, clothing, and *stuff* from the van that looked like a woman in the last trimester of her fertility-treatment-induced pregnancy.

By the time the van had disgorged its final quintuplet—in

the form of Annette's hammock—it had grown alarmingly dark.

"Hold the flashlight steady so I can read these directions," Annette said to Kailyn as she pored over the set-up instructions for the shiny new six-man condo tent that she, Kailyn, and Paige would be sleeping in that night.

"I'm trying, but these mosquitoes keep biting." Kailyn slapped at another annoying parasite on her arm, jiggling the flashlight in the process.

"You need to go take a shower and get rid of that cologne," Tess reminded her. "Go on, now. We'll help your mom."

"Well, if you're sure." Kailyn grabbed her floral gym bag from the pile of luggage at her feet. "Which way to the shower again?"

Becca, who'd erected her individual pup tent in something like three minutes flat, the brat, offered to guide Kailyn to the facilities.

"Chloe, can you finish up here while I help Annette?" Tess asked.

"Sure. Piece of cake."

Feeling like Laura Ingalls, I pounded another metal thingamajig into one of the loops on my cousins' army green two-man tent that Tess and I were sharing. Unlike Annette's state-of-the-art, high-tech mondo-condo tent that weighed no more than a tube of lip gloss, Timmy and Tommy's decades-old Army surplus model was decidedly low-tech and high fragrance—eau de jock—and fashioned of a ludicrously dense canvas material that weighed about as much as the VW van next door.

While Annette and Kailyn's tent essentially erected itself in about fourteen seconds, our antique tent required a complex series of ropes, steel rods, connecting metal thingies, pulleys, and vast yards of duct tape.

After twenty-seven minutes of fighting with the pungent green tent, it sagged in the middle and the left pole looked dangerously unstable. But I figured it was good enough. By this time though, I was thinking it would have been a lot easier and infinitely more comfortable to sleep in Annette's minivan. I grabbed the final stake from the nylon mesh bag Tess had left me and moved to the back of the tent to secure the final corner.

All at once, something small, brown, furry, and probably foaming at the mouth with rabid drool streaked across my left tennis shoe and shot into the woods.

I screamed and dropped the iron stake on my foot. "Ouch!" I yelled, grabbing my foot and hopping around awkwardly on the other one. In the darkness, I tripped over the unstable left pole and crashed into the tent, flattening it beneath me.

Just call me uncoordinated.

They did. Always. Especially at school. And that was just the teachers.

12

One half of the world cannot understand the pleasures of the other.

Emma

Two hours later all the tents were up, and we were polishing off the last of the teriyaki chicken Paige had grilled for dinner.

"So, Annette, what's the deal?" Becca asked. "I thought you'd be really good at all this camping stuff since you were in the Air Force. Didn't you have to go through boot camp?"

"Basic training. And if you need marchin' lessons, I'm your girl. But beyond that not so much."

Jenna licked teriyaki sauce off her fingers. "But I thought part of basic training was physical conditioning and learning how to survive in the wild or a war zone."

"Not when I joined in the mid-seventies. At least for the women. We did have this one-day obstacle course and physical conditioning, but that was just runnin' around the track and doing a few sit-ups and female push-ups."

"*Female* push-ups? What the heck are female push-ups?"

"Hand me that towel and I'll show you."

Annette spread Kailyn's striped beach towel on the uneven ground and stretched out on her stomach. She placed her hands at shoulder-level, palms down, in standard push-up position, and bent her legs upward at the knees so that the soles of her feet pointed towards the sky. In that position, she raised her body off the ground, keeping her knees bent, and pushed up and down twice. "See? Like that."

"Those aren't even real push-ups!" Jenna said.

"What can I say? We were just followin' orders. When we ran laps, we had to hold our imaginations the whole way."

"Your imaginations?"

"Our boobs." Annette giggled. "Since male recruits often marched by the track where we were running and Uncle Sam didn't want them distracted by our runaway feminine charms, we were instructed to run with our fists pressed together beneath our bosoms, holding them in place. No jigglin' allowed."

"You have *got* to be kidding. Jiggle police?" Becca said. "How ridiculous is that?"

"You want to hear ridiculous?" Annette chomped on a Dorito and chased it down with a swig of diet cola. "One day our entire flight was lined up single file at attention while the beauty instructor went down the line one woman—"

"Beauty instructor?" Jenna yelped.

"Yep. One woman at a time and plucked our eyebrows with these special slice-and-dice tweezers. Ma'am, yes Ma'am!" Annette saluted. "Your tax dollars at work, ladies."

"Did you shoot your machine guns before or after the eyebrow plucking session?"

"Shoot? Women weren't allowed to shoot guns back then. It wouldn't have been machine guns anyway," she said. "While the male recruits were getting their M16 rifle training down at the shooting range to become proud American fighting men, we were reportin' to beauty class where we learned to walk, talk, wear our hair, and apply makeup." Annette waggled her sculpted eyebrows. "In the event we were ever taken prisoners of war, at least we would be fashionable POWs."

"What?" we roared in outraged estrogen unison.

"Oh, honey, I'm just getting started." Annette unzipped her hooded sweatshirt and fanned her face. "Is it hot out here, or am I flashin' again?"

"You're sitting too close to the campfire," Tess said. "Just back up a ways and tell us some more about your feminine boot camp. This is better than ghost stories."

"I'll say." Paige giggled. "Although I'm not sure which is scarier."

"Well, in the seventies, not only was the prevailing feelin' in Uncle Sam's Air Force that women didn't need to know how to shoot a gun — since of course they would never go into combat — what was *really* important was that our bars of soap were never marred by an errant bubble. During our daily inspection when our TI would go through our lockers, she inspected *every*thing. Even our soap. And if she found one tiny speck of lint on your bar of soap, or even a soap bubble, it was an automatic demerit."

"But that's impossible." I rubbed my eyes beneath my glasses. "No way can you use a bar of soap and not get a soap bubble on it."

"Exactly. Which is why after that inspection, every single bar of Dove, Ivory, and Zest in those dusty Texas barracks was wiped clean of any offendin' specks and put back into its plastic flip-top home inside each airman's locker — not to see the light of day again until those six weeks of basic were up. Basic training is a six-week mind game," Annette explained. "It's all about followin' orders, no matter how ridiculous or outrageous they may seem."

"I'd never have made it," Paige said.

"Me either." Kailyn looked at her mom with new respect.

"Never," I agreed.

"Oh you'd be surprised what you can do when you have to," Annette said. "Right, Tess?"

"You got that right."

Kailyn looked at Tess in surprise. "I didn't know you were in the military."

"I wasn't. But I went through my own basic training with twin seven-year-old boys after my husband died."

Tess didn't talk about that time much, but a look of shared sorrow flickered between us at the remembrance of my beloved Uncle Ted. One day at work he had just dropped dead of a heart attack at the age of thirty-nine.

"You learn pretty quick how to replace a broken toilet when you don't have money to hire a plumber," Tess said.

I squeezed her hand before directing my attention back to Annette. "What other kind of weird stuff did you do in basic training?"

"Oh, it wasn't all pointless and irrelevant activity. I learned the very valuable skills of foldin' my underwear into equal thirds, rollin' my pantyhose into a jelly roll measuring exactly three-fourths of an inch in diameter, and spacing my hanging uniforms exactly two fingers apart in my locker."

"That's absurd."

"How did you ever stand all that ludicrous Mickey Mouse stuff?" Becca asked.

"There were times I didn't." Annette gazed into the flames with a pensive expression. "Once I was lyin' on the floor beneath my cot, tugging the flat sheet through the chicken-wire frame that held my lumpy mattress to try to get a tautly made bed that would pass inspection. I started bawlin', and while the tears were running down my cheeks and into my ears, I thought, *What in the world am I doing here? I'm an intelligent, creative woman! How did I ever wind up here?"*

"And how did you?" Paige asked gently.

"Yeah. Why'd you join the Air Force in the first place?" I grabbed a handful of Doritos from the bag Becca was hoarding. "You don't seem the type."

"What type is that?"

"I don't know." I flushed. "Rugged. Athletic. Outdoorsy?"

"Those aren't the only kinds of women who join the Air Force, sweetie. In fact, when I joined in 1974, I heard from a lot of good ol' boys that there were only three kinds of women who went in the military." Annette ticked them off on her fingers. "Whores, lesbians, and women searching for a husband."

"No way." Jenna's high cheekbones darkened with anger.

"Yep. That was the mind-set at the time. Why else would a woman want to be in the military?"

"To serve her country and see the world?" Paige offered.

"Exactly. *And* to get the GI Bill to go to college afterward. My mama and daddy sure couldn't afford to send me," Annette said, "and I surely couldn't do it on my own. Besides, my daddy had his heart set on me marryin' the son of one of his good ol' boy pals—a boy who chewed tobacco and whose idea of a good time was to play pool and drink himself into oblivion at Virgil's Bar every Saturday night." She lifted her chin. "So I ran off and joined the Air Force instead. I thought my folks would burst a blood vessel, 'specially Daddy, but I'd just turned eighteen, and there wasn't nothin' they could do about it."

"Good for you." Becca gave Annette a vigorous thumbs-up.

Becca had also left her family the minute she became legal. Only it was her mother who had the drinking problem in the family, not her father. At least as far as she knew. Her parents divorced when she was in the first grade, and Becca had only seen her dad one other time after that, at her ninth birthday party.

Paige sent Annette a quizzical glance. "Tell me this. If you had it to do all over again, would you still join the Air Force?"

"In a heartbeat, honey. It taught me a lot, helped me grow up, and helped me get my college education. And the sweet cherry on top of my Air Force sundae was that by the time I was twenty-one, I'd visited thirteen countries. Not many people can say that."

That's for sure. I'd only been to one other country in my entire life: Mexico, on some high-school mission trips to help out at an orphanage, and, of course, on my honeymoon. On the second missions trip I forgot about not drinking the water and spent most of the trip bolting to the outhouse before I committed a hygienic indiscretion. My stomach threatened to turn at the memory, and I took a deep breath of fresh Mother Nature air.

"Hey, what's that funny smell? It's kind of sweet."

"Well, it sure isn't charcoal." Becca pressed her thumb and forefinger together as if she were holding something, raised the imaginary object to her lips, and inhaled deeply.

Jenna nodded in the direction of the hippie campsite behind us. "Talk about getting a natural high."

Duh. And I thought Kailyn was naive.

"I remember those days," Tess said.

"*You* smoked weed?" I stared at my favorite aunt and moral compass.

"I tried it a couple times when I was a teenager." She offered an apologetic shrug. "An eternity ago. But it never did anything for me."

"Me either."

The campfire lit up Kailyn's shocked face. "Mom! You got high?"

"Relax, baby girl. I tried smokin' pot once when I was stationed in Germany—it was the seventies, remember—but I didn't like it. And good thing, too. One of the guys in the supply squadron got busted with a couple joints and had to serve a few years in a German prison."

"Sounds like *Midnight Express*," Paige murmured.

"Except that was a Turkish prison. The German ones weren't as bad, but they were still nothin' I cared to see up close and personal. Giving up four years of my life to Uncle Sam was one thing—my choice. But spending four years in prison, and an overseas one at that? Not on your ever-lovin' life."

"Glad to hear it. Somehow I can't picture myself introducing you as my mother, the ex-con." Kailyn giggled. "Although, it's pretty hard to picture the pressed-and-proper woman who doesn't jaywalk, steal towels from the Holiday Inn, or drive over the speed limit, lighting up an illegal substance either."

We all laughed at the mental image of Sergeant Etiquette doing anything remotely illegal.

Paige speared two marshmallows on a shiny metal skewer and extended it over the flames. "I didn't realize we'd be playing *True Confessions* this weekend."

"Well, I'm all ears if you've got anything you'd like to confess," Annette said. "Like maybe who ate my last M&M?"

"No clue." Paige batted her innocent baby browns, removed her skewer from the flame, and slid the toasted marshmallows onto a waiting graham cracker with a square of Hershey's chocolate in the center.

The rest of us followed suit.

"Now that's what you call a little piece of heaven right there." Becca closed her eyes in rapture and licked the blackened marshmallow and melted chocolate from her upper lip.

"Thanks for bringing all the s'more stuff, Tess. I haven't had these in years."

"It's not a camping trip without s'mores. Ask my boys."

"Speaking of boys, how old are yours again?" Kailyn's man-radar blinked on full alert.

"Sixteen, so dial it on down a notch."

"Don't worry. I'm not into robbing cradles. That's more Chloe's territory."

"Kailyn!" Annette sent her daughter a reproving look.

"What? I was just joking. You know I was only teasing, don't you, Chloe?"

Every now and then Kailyn would come out with something totally snarky and sarcastic. I usually chalked it up to immaturity and insecurity. Even though she was the most gorgeous woman in our group, I sensed that at times Kailyn felt intimidated by some of our more well-read and intellectual members. So I let it slide.

Besides, the trees were wafting their evergreen perfume through the campsite and the stars were putting on a gorgeous silvery light show above our heads. Amidst all that natural beauty, I felt peaceful and magnanimous. "No prob. I know you didn't intentionally twist the Chris knife, Kailyn. That's all ancient history anyway."

I pulled out a couple of puffy air-and-sugar carb bombs and stuck them on the end of my skewer, holding it high above the flames and turning it slowly. I preferred a golden-toasted marshmallow to Becca's charred-to-a-crisp crudite.

As I removed my gooey stick from the hot flames though, I heard a twig snap. The hairs on my arm stood up. And all at once I got the uneasy feeling that we were being watched. Had hippie-boy heard our giggling over his weed-smoking proclivities? And was marijuana just the tip of his chemical-abuse iceberg?

Maybe he was high on methamphetamine and this very

moment was on his way over to take us all out with his honkin' Texas chainsaw.

Casually, ever-so-casually, I glanced toward the woods, where my eyes locked on another pair of eyes, bright and beady, and peering at me through the darkness. A soft hiss of air escaped through my clenched teeth. It couldn't be our hippie neighbor, unless he was skulking on his stomach, dragging his bloodied Black & Decker chainsaw behind him.

"Um, don't anyone freak out or anything," I said in as quiet and calm a tone as I could muster, "but, there's some kind of"—I swallowed hard—"*creature* in the woods staring right at us."

"Where?" Kailyn would have popped up like a jack-in-the-box if it hadn't been for Jenna's strong, restraining arm holding her down.

I cut my eyes to a cluster of trees just beyond the campground. "Right there. See?"

The glowing red eyes moved closer. I dropped my marshmallows into the fire.

"Relax," Becca said. "It's probably a chipmunk or possum."

"Aren't possums just giant rats with long tails?" Kailyn squeaked.

The bright, beady eyes cleared the undergrowth, and a dark blob waddled into the light.

"Aw, that's just a sweet little raccoon." Annette blew out a sigh of relief.

We all did.

"Isn't he cute? I love that little bandit mask they have."

"Sweet, nothing. Those little suckers are mea—" Becca broke off abruptly. "Kailyn, *what* are you doing?"

Our resident girly-girl had brushed off Jenna's hand and was walking toward the woodland creature with a couple graham crackers in her hand. "Shhh, you'll scare him away. I just want to give him a little something to eat." She made kissy noises. "Here little fella. Don't be afraid. I won't hurt you."

The raccoon advanced cautiously.

"Stop right there," Tess ordered.

"She's right. Put. The. Cracker. Down," Jenna said in her best *Young Frankenstein* voice.

"Oh, all right." Kailyn tossed the graham cracker to our raccoon guest, who deftly picked up the edible rectangle with his little black paws, held it, and politely nibbled at it with all the manners of a society matron at afternoon tea. "Isn't that sweet?" Kailyn cooed. "Didn't I tell you they were friendly?"

Rocky Raccoon took another two steps toward her and looked up expectantly.

"Aw, he wants some more." She started to reach for another cracker, but Tess stopped her cold.

"Don't do it," she warned. "Really. Not a good idea."

"Sorry, little fella. That's all." Kailyn waved him away. "Shoo."

The raccoon made an angry trilling noise and took a couple of additional steps toward her.

Kailyn began backing away cautiously. "Shoo," she said again weakly. She clutched the remaining graham crackers close to her chest.

The raccoon raised himself up on his hind legs.

"I think he's going to attack!" Kailyn's voice took on a hysterical tinge. She took another step back, and as the raccoon began to advance again, she flung the graham crackers past him toward the woods.

"Nooooo!" I screamed as visions of hungry, marauding bears filled my head.

Instantly, additional little furry bodies scurried from the darkness and pounced on the crackers Rocky Raccoon missed.

Only these furry creatures didn't have charming bandit masks. They were black with a broad white stripe down their backs.

"Nobody move," Tess ordered.

We froze as imaginings of not-so-heavenly and most definitely not Victoria's Secret perfume filled our trembling olfactory senses. But after the family of Pepé Le Pews finally finished up the last of the cracker crumbs, they wandered slowly back into the woodland darkness.

I let out my breath and dropped to the hard, cold ground. "Whew. I thought we were skunk spray for sure."

"I was already planning how I'd give us all a spaghetti sauce bath," Tess said.

"Spaghetti sauce?"

"Tomato juice is one of the best things to get rid of skunk smell. I had to drench our dog in it years ago when he surprised a skunk under our back deck—took forever to get him clean. But since we don't have any tomato juice, I figured spaghetti sauce would be the next best thing."

"Smokey the Bear and his buddies would have really come running for a little Italian dinner, don't you think?" Becca stood up and brushed off the back of her jeans. "That's an offer they couldn't refuse." She turned to Kailyn. "And on the subject of refusing, the first rule of thumb out here is *don't approach the animals*. And definitely don't feed them. Unless you want to wake up in the middle of the night with a hungry raccoon clawing at your sleeping bag. Those little suckers are mean."

Great. Now I could add raccoons as well as bears to my nightmare list. Thanks, Bec.

Jenna began collecting the dirty plates and shoving them into a trash bag. She assured us that as long as we put all the food and trash away and locked it up tight in the car, we'd be fine. Everyone pitched in on clean-up. Paige and I washed the cooking pans and silverware, Annette and Kailyn stored the leftovers in the largest cooler and then sat on it to ensure it snapped shut tightly, and Tess and Becca hoisted the cooler into the back of Annette's van.

After she locked her vehicle, Annette yawned. "I don't know about y'all," she said, "but I'm ready for bed." She picked up her industrial-sized flashlight. "Anyone want to hike to the bathroom with me first?"

"Count me in, Mom. I shouldn't have had that second soda."

"Actually, we should all use the restroom before we turn in," Tess advised. "Cuts down on having to get up in the middle of the night and make that trek alone."

That was all I needed to hear. This camper didn't plan on flying solo in the dark of night out here in the wild. Once we returned to our tents, Tess tossed me one of the air mattresses to stick under my sleeping bag.

"What? You think I'm a wuss or something?"

"Does a bear poop in the woods?"

"Don't even mention the B-word," I said as I climbed into Timmy's down-filled sleeping bag.

"You tell her, Chloe," Kailyn called out from the condo tent. "I vote for a moratorium on that word the rest of the weekend."

"Preach it, baby girl," Annette's voice wafted over to us. "Good night everyone."

"Good night, Ma; good night, Pa; good night, Mary Ellen; good night, John-boy," Paige sang out.

"Oh, put a sock in it," Becca grumbled from her pup tent next to ours. "And nobody'd better snore, either."

I sent up a heartfelt prayer before going to sleep. *Father, please protect us from bears and raccoons and any other wild creatures in the night, four-legged or otherwise. I know you made them all, but could you please make sure they stay in the forest where they belong? Amen.*

13

Pretty soon I wanted to smoke, and asked the widow to let me. But she wouldn't. That is just the way with some people. They get down on a thing when they don't know nothing about it. Here she was a-bothering about Moses, which was no kin to her ... yet finding a power of fault with me for doing a thing that had some good in it. And she took snuff, too; of course that was all right, because she done it herself.

The Adventures of Huckleberry Finn

"Chloe," Tess whispered. "Did you by any chance have beans today?"

"That's not me. It's your son's air mattress."

I was shifting in my cousin's sleeping bag. Every time I turned on my side, a little whooshing sound escaped from beneath my hip.

"A likely story," Becca said sleepily from just outside our tent wall.

Jenna snorted.

"Shhh. Some people are trying to get their beauty sleep."

Half an hour later, everyone was asleep. Except me.

Since counting sheep never worked, I played out the evening in my mind instead, smiling to myself at the image of a young Annette in basic training standing at attention and getting her eyebrows plucked. I rubbed my bushy brows. Time to do a little plucking of my own.

I stifled a giggle as I remembered Kailyn trying to make nice with Rocky Raccoon with the graham crackers. And then all at once, I bolted upright to a sitting position as I remembered that I'd dropped my marshmallows into the fire when the raccoon's moving eyes frightened me.

Had anyone picked them up and thrown them away? Or were they still on the ground calling out to Yogi Bear and Boo-Boo in all their sticky sweet smellingness?

Quit being so neurotic, city girl.

Sinking back into my sleeping bag, I laid flat on my back, staring up at the drab olive tent fabric and wishing for a moon roof so I could see the stars. Why couldn't I get to sleep? I never had any problems at home. I thought longingly of my silky soft, six-hundred-thread-count sheets I'd saved up to buy for my own Valentine's Day present, along with a box of See's chocolates.

Chocolate.

Maybe I shouldn't have had that last hot chocolate.

But I'd been pretty good at holding it when we were on long family trips in the car when I was a little girl, focusing in on something else so I'd be distracted from my bodily need, usually a book.

I picked up my copy of *Heidi*, switched on my flashlight, and tried to lose myself in the lush Alps with Heidi, Peter the goat boy, and the grumpy Grandfather who couldn't help but fall in love with his kind, sweet-natured granddaughter. The description of the warm goat's milk did me in.

"Tess," I whispered. "Are you awake?"

A light snore was my only response.

I shoved *Heidi* aside and scrambled out of my sleeping bag, flashlight clenched tightly in my hand and sending a bouncing ball up and down the tent walls. Shoving my feet into my tennis shoes at the foot of my makeshift bed, I grabbed my hoodie and stumbled through the tent flap toward Becca's pup tent.

"Hey, Bec." I leaned into the tiny tent and shook her shoulder. "Wake up."

She came at me, arms flailing, fists clenched, and snarling, knocking the flashlight out of my hand.

"Ouch!"

"Chloe?"

"I have to go to the bathroom," I whispered.

"So what's stopping you?"

"I don't want to go alone in the dark. I'll get lost. Or worse yet, run into another skunk or a raccoon or a mountain lion. Or even a—" But I couldn't bring myself to say the B-word.

Becca sighed and unzipped herself the rest of the way out of her sleeping bag. "Come on wussy woman. The sooner we go, the sooner we can get back to sleep." She clicked on her flashlight and splayed the beam over the ground, searching for the one she'd knocked out of my hands. "There it is—over there. See? Now hurry up."

My bladder made me only too glad to obey. I grabbed the fallen flashlight and switched it on. And as I did, a daddy long legs scurried down the shaft and across my hand. I dropped the flashlight again and swatted frantically at my hands.

"Now what?"

"Spider!" I squeaked.

"Oy vey." Becca picked up my flashlight, thrust it into my

hands, and yanked me forward to begin the dark, lonesome trek to the facilities. I tripped over a root and nearly went down, but righted myself just in time.

"Remind me again why camping is fun?" I whispered.

The next morning, I woke up freezing with a crick in my neck and needing to go to the bathroom again.

"Good morning, everyone," Tess sang out. "Are we all happy campers today?"

"Speak for yourself." I grabbed my towel and bag of toiletries and stalked off to the rustic bathroom, which turned out to be a little closer in the daytime. After using the facility, washing my hands and face, and giving my wilderness-filmed teeth a thorough brushing, I rolled my head from side to side until my neck cracked.

"Better now?" Paige, who'd also finished her morning ablutions, asked.

I swatted away a pesky fly. "I'd be even better if I were home in my climate-controlled condo with screens on the windows, indoor plumbing, and a soft, comfortable bed to sleep in."

"You and me both. Face it: we're just not the great outdoors types like Jenna, Becca, and Tess."

"You got that right. Although, Tess is actually more of a Renaissance woman. She can do anything—all this outdoor, athletic junk, but cultural stuff too. She loves music, fine dining, the theater, and art. She really knows a lot about art."

"I can't wait for her to show us around Paris." Paige bubbled with excitement. "Now *that's* a trip I'm looking forward to."

Me too. All except for that flying part. Thank you, God, for Xanax.

"Hey, you two." Annette and Kailyn met us on the path, each lugging a makeup case and toiletry kit, their towels flung over their shoulders. "Any hot water left?"

"Left?" I grunted. "There wasn't any to begin with."

Tess joined us, all bright-eyed and bushy-tailed. Annoyingly so. "How'd you all sleep last night in your fancy new tent?"

"Pretty good," Annette said, blotting beads of perspiration from her forehead with her towel.

"Not bad," Kailyn grudgingly admitted.

"Great," Paige said. "It was surprisingly comfortable — especially with the air mattress."

I rubbed my neck. "Wish I could say the same thing."

"We've got plenty of room. Why don't you sleep with us tonight?" Annette offered.

"Really?" I looked at Tess. "Would you mind if I abandoned you?"

"Not at all. Gives me more room to spread out."

Becca jogged up. "Hey, Jenna said to tell you she's starting breakfast, so you'd better hurry." She glanced at Kailyn's open tote bag. "You brought a *blow dryer* camping? Really roughing it there, aren't you?"

Kailyn shot a disdainful look at Becca's bed head hair. "You never know who you're going to meet in the woods. And a girl should always be prepared. Isn't that the Girl Scout motto?" She flounced toward the bathroom.

Fifteen minutes later we were finishing up our muffins and the scrambled eggs that Jenna had cooked on the camp stove when Annette and Kailyn returned to the campsite, skin glowing and not a hair out of place.

Tess whistled. "Got a hot date or something?"

"Yeah, with the coffee pot." Annette hustled over to the fire. "Any left?"

"We'll need to boil some more water." Paige held up a jar of brown crystals. "Sorry, but we've only got instant."

"That's really roughing it. Hang tight, Mom. I've got a

little surprise for you." Kailyn headed to the condo tent and emerged moments later, proudly extending a coffee grinder and a Krups coffeemaker to Annette. "Ta-da!"

"Um, not wanting to burst your bubble," Paige said, "but didn't you see *City Slickers*? Where the guy brought his coffee grinder on the cattle drive and spooked all the cattle when he turned it on? We probably don't want to be too loud out here in nature."

"Yeah. Respect the environment," Jenna said.

"*You* respect the environment. I'm having my coffee."

"Not unless there's an electrical outlet on one of these trees."

"Oh." Kailyn sat down hard on a redwood stump and kicked the dirt at her feet. "Stupid nature."

After all the food was secured in the coolers again and locked in the car, we headed out on our hike through the redwoods with Becca, Jenna, and Tess leading the way. Paige, Kailyn, Annette, and I brought up the rear on the wheelchair-accessible trail.

I gazed up at the ancient trees on either side of us, mesmerized by their sheer size and beauty. And age. What was it Annette had said? That some of them had been standing when Jesus walked the earth? I reached out my hand to touch the rough bark.

"Ow!" Kailyn yelped.

"What's wrong?" We stopped so abruptly I collided with Paige.

"I broke a nail!"

"Quick, call the Mounties," Becca said. "Or better yet, Ranger Rick at Fashion Emergency 911. Maybe he'll have nail glue in his first aid kit. If not, we might have to send you to basic training beauty school instead."

"That's one school you'd flunk out of," Kailyn snarked.

"Now girls—"

"Shh." I lifted my head. "What's that noise?" I whispered. "I hear a rustling."

"Again with the rustling?" Tess looked at me over her glasses.

"It's probably just my Rocky Raccoon pal from last night," Kailyn said as she examined her torn pinkie nail.

"I don't think so." The sound increased from a mere rustle to a full-on crashing through brush. "A raccoon wouldn't make that much noise."

"Maybe it's Bambi? Or his mother?"

"Is Bambi big and black?" Paige stared beyond me into the woods.

"Not the last time I looked," Tess said.

"Well, there's something big and black out there."

"Where?"

She pointed to a large black shadow weaving in and out of the trees as it galumphed through the forest alongside us.

Tracking us.

Sniffing us.

Playing with us.

Any minute now the dreaded B-word would come crashing through the underbrush and have a little Chloe or Kailyn for dinner. Except ... maybe it wasn't a bear at all. Maybe it was a wolf. A rabid wolf with yellow eyes and huge, snarling fangs dripping with blood from his last kill.

My practical side took over. *Imagination run away with you much? Stop being such a wuss. This isn't the seventies, baby. Step up to the plate.*

We could hear the creature panting heavily now. It was getting closer—its hot breath just yards away.

All at once it came crashing through the trees toward us. Instinctively, I stepped in front of Annette and Kailyn;

fists raised and ready to fight the beast off with my bare hands — although I wouldn't have minded a baseball bat or my heavy flashlight back in the tent.

The beast, however, turned out to be a gigantic slobbering Newfoundland with a wagging tail and a big, goofy dog grin on his face. I lowered my shaking arms, dropped to my knees, and buried my head in the friendly dog's fur in relief.

"Traveler, where are you? Here, boy." Our hippie campfire neighbor appeared out of the woods, laughing.

"Dude. I see you've met Traveler. Hope he's not bothering you."

"No," I said, blowing a stray dog hair out of my mouth. "We were just afraid he was a bear coming for his dinner."

"The only way Traveler could hurt you was to lick you to death."

I wiped some dog drool off my arm. "Yeah, I see that."

june
*H*eidi

14

I'll always say my prayers after this, as Grandmamma
told me to, and if God doesn't answer them at once I shall
know it's because He's planning something better for me.

Heidi

What was God planning for me? I thought I'd heard his voice
when I said yes to Chris's proposal, but maybe that was just
water in my ear. I had just finished taking a swim in my parents' pool.

After squealing yes to Chris's proposal in the shallow end,
we'd told my family and celebrated with a bottle of champagne.
Then Chris left to tell Ryan the good news.

"Honey, are you sure?" Dad asked as he walked me to my
car later. "You two haven't known each other that long."

"Neither did you and mom when you got married. And
look how that turned out."

He held up his hands in mock surrender. "You got me
there." He hugged me. "I just want you to be happy."

"I am. Don't worry. And don't worry about going bankrupt

either with both daughters getting married in the same year. Maybe your golf club can give you a two-for-one special," I teased.

Just not a double wedding. No way was I going to share my big day with my sister. Besides, I already knew she was planning a big fancy blow-out. And small and simple was more my style.

Of course, styles can change. For instance, it's never been my style to stand up to rampaging carnivorous beasts in the woods, so who'd have thought I'd step between my friends and that bear. Er, dog.

"I still can't believe how brave you were, Chloe," Kailyn said at book club a couple weeks later. "How you stood up to what you thought was a bear, ready to protect me and my mom. I take back everything I ever said about you being afraid of everything."

"Hear, hear." Jenna clapped.

Tess smiled. "I always knew you'd rise to the occasion."

Annette grabbed her umbrella from beneath the table we'd commandeered in one corner of the Dunkeld's café. She tapped it lightly on my left shoulder and then my right. "I hereby dub thee Chloe the Brave!"

Everyone stood and raised their lattes high. "To Chloe the Brave."

"Sit down. You're embarrassing me." Although I must admit, it was a good embarrassment. All my life I'd been known as Chloe the Timid, Chloe the Fearful, Chloe, the Non–Risk Taker. It was nice to know that I wasn't as much of a wuss as everyone — including me — had always thought. Maybe it was time to start taking some risks in other areas of my life too.

Like daring to wear white after Labor Day.

Getting a tattoo on my ankle. A small cross, I think.

Confronting Becca about not doing her fair share around the apartment.

Flying.

I drew the line at sushi though. Some mountains just aren't worth dying on.

As I raised a forkful of turtle cheesecake up to my mouth, I spied someone in the sci-fi section giving me a thoughtful look. Did the guy live in the bookstore or what? He nodded at me and turned away. Becca gave Ryan an appraising once-over. "It's too bad he was going to be the best man, 'cause he's seriously hot."

"I'll say. If only I were twenty years younger," Tess said.

"Hey, could we stop thinking about men for a minute and get back to the business at hand?" Kailyn rapped her French-manicured nails on the table.

"Who are you and what have you done with my daughter?"

"What?" Kailyn stuck out her lower lip. "I just want to discuss our latest book. That's why we're here. Right?"

"Right." Tess drained her latte. "Okay, everyone, listen up. Kailyn has the floor."

"Thanks. So—"

Just then, Paige rushed up, pulled a chair over from a neighboring table, and sat down, all out of breath. "Sorry I'm late. I had to pick up a prescription for my mom and the pharmacist took forever, then I had to drop it off at her house on the way here, and while I was there, she needed me to pull down a few things from the top of a bookshelf, including Mr. Spitz, her cat." She blew out her cheeks. "Did I miss anything?"

"Just Chloe's knighthood into the Order of the Brave."

"Ignore the woman behind the curtain." I pushed a bottle of water to Paige. "Actually, Kailyn was just opening the book club discussion. Kailyn?"

"Thanks, Chloe. Glad you made it, Paige. I was just about to ask everyone what they thought of *Heidi*."

"Loved it. How could you not?"

"Classic. Charming. Delightful."

"Old-fashioned but in a good way. Made me feel all warm and fuzzy."

"One of my favorite books from childhood."

"Mine too." Annette released a dreamy sigh. "Made me want to go sleep in a hayloft with a round window in the ceiling, so I could look up at the stars every night."

"And living in the Swiss Alps wouldn't be too shabby either."

Not shabby at all. While the others extolled the virtues of the book, I thought of what it would be like to live in a hut like Heidi's in such pristine, beautiful, and relatively solitary surroundings. I wouldn't mind living in a little hut high up in the gorgeous Alps either. As long as it came equipped with electricity and indoor plumbing. And plenty of Swiss cheese and chocolate.

I could see it now. By day I could set up an outdoor easel and attempt to capture the mountain's majesty, and by night I could curl up in front of the roaring fire and read to my heart's content.

How's that for a flight of fancy? Becca must be rubbing off on me.

"The whole thing was a little too much on the sugary side for me," Jenna said, making a face.

"Really? I thought it was sweet."

"Like I said."

"You're such a hard-hearted Hannah."

"Why? Just because I don't like my fiction syrupy?"

"No, you like it all dark, shadowy, and mysterious."

"What can I say? I like mysteries. Something that makes

me think and try and figure out who did it. More interesting. Too much sweetness and light gives me a toothache."

"Somebody call the dentist," Becca said.

"So who was your favorite character, aside from Heidi?"

"The grandfather, definitely."

"The blind grandmother."

"Clara."

"Toss-up between the old doctor and the gruff grandfather."

"I liked Peter the naughty goatherd." Becca broke into a "Lonely Goatherd" yodel.

"Julie Andrews?"

Jenna made a gagging sound.

"Watch it." Paige frowned at Jenna. "I love Julie. *The Sound of Music* and *The Princess Diaries*. And, of course, *Mary Poppins*."

"Keep that spoonful of sugar close."

"Movie rabbit trail again," Becca said.

Paige ducked her head. "Sorry. Can't help myself. Once a movie geek, always a movie geek."

Jenna shifted in her chair, an odd expression on her face.

If I didn't know better, I'd say it was uncertainty. But Jenna was never uncertain about anything. I focused on what she was saying. "Actually, since we've taken this little conversational detour, I have an announcement to make."

"Ooh! You're getting married!" Kailyn's face lit up.

"No, that would require a groom. And the fact that I'm not dating anyone at the moment would make it kind of difficult."

"What, then?"

"You're not quitting book club, are you?" Becca sent her a mock menacing look.

"No."

"You'd better not."

Jenna took a deep breath and released it slowly through her teeth. "I can't go to Paris with you guys."

"What?"

"You're kidding!"

"How come?"

She squared her shoulders. "One, it's a lot of money that I really can't afford to spend; and two, there's this major triathalon that same Saturday you leave that I've been wanting to do *forever*. I thought it was going to be the previous week, but I had the date wrong."

"So catch a later flight."

"It's an entire weekend event. And my boss just announced that he is taking the following week off. Since he just made me assistant manager, I have to hold down the fort while he's gone."

"Well, that sucks." Becca stuck out her lower lip.

"I'll say," Paige said. "It won't be the same without you."

"It's okay. To be honest, I wasn't sure how well I'd do as a vegetarian in Paris anyway. The French are pretty big carnivores."

"Couldn't you eat fish?" Kailyn asked.

"I don't eat anything with eyes."

"Salmon doesn't have eyes."

Jenna stared at her. "Of course it does."

"Not any that I've ever eaten."

Paige and I began to giggle, Becca let loose one of her trademark snorts, and soon the whole table was laughing.

Annette swiped at her eyes and then turned to her daughter. "Has any chicken you've ever eaten had eyes?"

"No. Eww!"

"Well it did before it got to the grocery store. Lamb too. And beef."

Becca mooed.

"Oh." Kailyn flushed. "Duh."

It's not that Kailyn was dumb, just clueless. And a little naive. And as her mother always said, she didn't have a lick of common sense.

Tess stuck a fork in the salmon to test it, pronounced it not quite done and re-covered it with tin foil before sliding it back in the broiler for a few more minutes.

After Kailyn's book club faux pas, Tess and I had gotten a craving for salmon but decided not to eat out since we were both trying to save all our spare pennies for Paris. Instead, we stopped at the grocery store where Tess selected two medium-sized pieces of fresh salmon from the fish guy in the back and I grabbed a salad in the bag, some microwavable rice, and ice cream.

Once home in my condo kitchen, Tess turned the oven on to broil and placed the salmon in the center of a large piece of aluminum foil I'd set on the granite countertop.

"Now watch closely. This is the tricky part." She seasoned the salmon with a little lemon-pepper and a couple small dabs of butter, loosely wrapped the foil around the fish, and crimped the ends. Then she stuck the foil package in the broiler. *"Voila!"*

"That's it?"

"That's it. Easy as pie. Now we just let it broil for ten or twelve minutes." Tess washed and dried her hands. "And now, my cooking-impaired niece, you can add salmon to your gastronomic repertoire, along with hot dogs and macaroni and cheese."

"Don't forget French toast. I make some mean French toast."

"Yes you do. *C'est bon.*"

"I hope our Paris cooking lessons are this easy." I pulled

the package of rice from the freezer, poked a hole in the plastic, and stuck it in the microwave for three minutes.

"*Je ne sais pas.* But I don't think they'll be too difficult." She took a drink of her iced tea. "My client who recommended our French chef couldn't stop raving about her. And this same client, who admitted that she's never been any good in the kitchen, said she came home with three delicious, fail-proof recipes that her husband absolutely loves." Tess's mouth curved upward. "She also said it made him much more attentive and romantic."

"Well there you go. We'll return from Paris these amazing French cooks and the guys will be beating down our doors."

"Or at least sniffing around them." She raised her glass. "Here's hoping."

Was I really ready for some new guy to come into my life though? I was doing pretty well on my own and with my paperback girlfriends. Who'd have thought?

The microwave dinged, and I pulled out the steaming rice in a bag as Tess grabbed two oven gloves and removed the salmon from the broiler. I shook some salad into two bowls and dropped a few cherry tomatoes on top. Then I dumped a serving of rice onto our plates next to the salmon Tess had artfully placed on two oversized leaves of lettuce, and picked up the plates.

"Kitchen or dining room?"

"Dining room. We need to start practicing civilized eating habits so we're prepared for France." Tess grabbed the Ranch dressing and our iced tea and followed me to my little-used dining room table.

We said grace, and I took a bite of fish.

"Mmm. *C'est* delicious. I can't wait to try this out on Becca. Makes a nice change from our usual Budget Gourmets and Lean Cuisines." I munched on my salad. "So … Paris. Tell me what you're most looking forward to. The food, the art, the Eiffel Tower?"

"*All* of it," Tess said. "The museums, the monuments, the sidewalk cafés, the Gothic cathedrals, the Seine with its bridges and bookstalls." Her eyes turned soft and dreamy. "Paris is like no other city in the world: fabulous food, amazing museums, the most beautiful architecture I've ever seen anywhere. And walking everywhere rather than driving, just the whole pace of life. There's so much variety in Paris. And wait until you see the art." She closed her eyes and expelled a blissful sigh. "Absolutely breathtaking. I'm counting the days until I can go to the Orsay and see my Renoir, *Woman Reading.* It's one of my favorite paintings, for obvious reasons."

"Are you sure you're not my mom?" I teased. "Mom's never been into art or reading. I mean, how can anyone *not* read?" I fixed Tess with a knowing smile. "C'mon, admit it. You got pregnant when you were sixteen, left town with your married sister, and when you came back again six months later, bam! Mom had a new baby girl. That's the only thing I can figure.

"Mom and I are so different. *You* and mom are so different. It's hard to believe you're even sisters."

"You mean like you and Julia?"

"*Exactement.*"

"Honestly?" Tess said. "I don't know too many sisters who are all that alike, unless they're twins. And even then ... Maybe it's that whole sibling rivalry thing, each of us vying for our parents' attention—I don't know. And yes, Karen and I are as different as—wait for it—night and day, but that doesn't mean I don't love her and wouldn't be there for her in a heartbeat if she ever needed me. And I know the same is true of her. You and Julia too."

"I'm not so sure about that."

"I am." Tess added dressing to her salad. "How is Julia? How are all the wedding plans coming along?"

"Perfect, of course. Could you imagine anything less?"

My sister had wedding planner books, binders, and checklists out the wazoo. One binder alone was filled with flower choices; another, menu options and still another, wedding cake possibilities. And as the maid of honor, wedding etiquette dictated that I help her with all this stuff.

Only I just didn't have the heart for it. It wasn't exactly my thing, either. So Julia and I were both relieved when her best friend, Katie, her senior bridesmaid, offered to step into the unofficial maid of honor capacity and help Mom and Julia with most of the wedding details.

Worked for me.

"Last I heard, Justin's friend Andrew is going to sing Stephen Curtis Chapman's "I Will Be Here" while they take communion, Julia has booked a harpist to play classical music both at the wedding and reception, they are riding in a horse-drawn carriage to the reception, *and* they plan to release white doves into the air when the ceremony is over."

"Sounds like quite the production."

"I'll say. Mom, Julia, and Katie are spending every waking moment going over all the myriad details. And it's still nearly five months away!" I set my fork down. "They've got lists for everything: the food, the music, the decorations, the order of the ceremony. They're driving everyone absolutely crazy. Everything has to be just so." I made a face. "If I ever get married — *big* if — I think I'll just elope to Tahoe."

"You and me both. I'd rather spend my money on a killer honeymoon." Tess started to apologize for saying the once-hated H-word, but I cut her off.

"I'm so over that now. Ancient history."

If only some of the sweet, Grandma-knows-best old ladies at church would leave it at that.

The first Sunday I returned to church after Chris had dumped me, several well-meaning friends of my Grandma Chloe's, whom Mom had inherited by proxy upon Grandma's death, descended upon me like a lavender cloud, dispensing sympathy and words of wisdom.

"Now don't you worry, sweetheart." Alice Cullifer patted my arm. "God's working on Chris. He just got cold feet. He'll be back."

Ethel Roushia, her blue-haired crony, nodded in agreement. "The Lord just needs to do a work in him. He's putting him through the fire so he can be refined. And he'll come back to you a better man. Meanwhile, you just hold on tight to Jesus."

"Men never know what's good for them," Lucy Hetland said. "That's why we women have to show them. Gently and quietly, of course, as it says in 1 Peter."

Others took a different approach.

"God stopped that wedding just in time."

"The Lord has something better for you."

"God has the perfect man that he created just for you. And he'll reveal him to you in his own perfect time. You mark my words."

"God's ways are not our ways."

"God's the best matchmaker."

Blah, blah, blah.

Over the next few weeks, the lavender ladies inundated me with flowery cards in the mail filled with Scripture, usually Proverbs 3:5.

To be fair, everyone was just trying to help the best way they could—but what exactly do you say to someone who's just been left at the altar?

And as the weeks passed with no new word on the Chris front, David Crooke, a former member of the singles group, now married, who fancied himself a spiritual giant, approached me after service with his Proverbs 31 wife in tow.

"Chloe, have you ever considered that maybe God's called you to be single? Like Paul?"

No, Dave. Have you ever considered that maybe God's called you to be bald and unemployed and sitting on a corner with a little cup and a sign that says Will work for food?

15

Accidents will occur in the best-regulated families.

David Copperfield

I was back in my worst nightmare. The fitting room of the bridal shop. The absolute last place on earth I wanted to be. But the store had called Julia and told her they needed her to come in so they could check the new hemline and also finalize the bridesmaid dress choices. Katie was voting for the strapless cotton-candy pink, while I was hoping for something a little less Pepto-Bismolish.

Mom was supposed to go with her favorite daughter, but she was in bed with the flu. So, with Katie out of town for the weekend, it was up to me.

When I arrived at the bridal store, I put on my best happy maid of honor face as I entered the little shop of horrors with my morning latte. The clerk ushered me to the back where the faint sounds of Pachelbel's *Canon* wafted over all the tulle and lace. I knocked on the dressing room door. "Jules? It's your maid of honor."

Pushing open the ivory door, I entered chaos.

The middle-aged seamstress was trying to zip up Julia's dress — *trying* being the operative word, since there was a stubborn one-inch gap between the two sides of the zipper that refused to close. And in that gap between her shoulder blades gaped an extra inch of creamy skin on Julia's slender body.

Who knew? The perfect, beautiful Julia had back fat.

I straightened my back and sucked in my stomach.

"Now don't you worry." The fitter was soothing my sister, whose head was bent to the side as she held her cascade of caramel hair away from the recalcitrant zipper. "Lots of brides gain weight before the wedding — it's all the stress. A few less carbs and some extra trips to the gym and you'll fit into your dress perfectly again."

Julia raised her head. Her wet eyes met my startled ones in the mirror. "No, I won't!" Tears rained down her face in a torrent. "I'll never be able to fit into this dress again."

She sniffed and whipped around to face me. "What is that *smell*?" Julia glanced at the triple-shot latte in my hand, and clapped her hand over her mouth, gagging. "I'm going to be —"

"Watch the dress!" The seamstress grabbed a wastebasket and shoved it in front of her just in time. Julia upended the contents of her stomach, her chest heaving.

Her suddenly voluptuous chest.

When did that happen? Did my sister get a boob job?

"Okay now, dear?"

Julia nodded miserably to the saleswoman, who gingerly pulled the trash can away, holding her breath.

I thought of saying "Cleanup on aisle seven" to add a little levity to the situation, but decided against it. Instead, I grabbed a tissue from my purse and handed it to my sister, careful to maintain my distance. "Sorry you're sick. You must have caught Mom's flu."

The sickly sweet smell filled the small, stuffy room, and I yanked another tissue from my purse and pressed it to my nose.

"I don't have the flu!"

I stared at her. She had just ralphed because of a *latte*. "Julia?"

She refused to meet my eyes. "I'm ... pregnant."

"*What?* Julia the Perfect?" My turn to clap my hand over my mouth.

Oh no. Did I say those words out loud? *Nice.* Not exactly what Jesus would do. My face suffused with heat and shame. The seamstress shot me a dirty look and slipped out with the trash can, grabbing my latte offender on the way, and murmuring something about giving us some privacy.

"I knew you'd be thrilled," Julia said through fresh sobs. "You've been waiting for me to blow it for ages. Well, I've blown it big time. So what are you waiting for? Why don't you call Aunt Tess and tell her so you two can gloat about it in your intellectually superior way?"

She drained her water bottle in a long gulp and then wiped her mouth with the back of her hand. "Or better yet, put an announcement in the bulletin at chur—" A fresh onslaught of tears streamed down her face, and she collapsed on the dressing room chair, her newly voluptuous chest spilling out of her too-tight dress.

Where was my mother when I needed her?

I shifted uncomfortably. Mom would have known what to do, what to say—how to soothe and comfort her firstborn daughter.

Or would she have been as stunned and dumbstruck as I was?

A part of me instinctively longed to rush to Julia's side, but another part held back. We hadn't been close since grade school when we still said our Now-I-lay-me-down-to-sleep prayers together. And as we grew up, our differences pushed us further and further apart. I sneaked a furtive glance at my beautiful sister, who didn't look so beautiful right now with her mascara-streaked face, puffy eyes, and shaking shoulders.

Julia was always the sweet and pretty angel of goodness and light with perfect hair, perfect teeth, and perfect manners who was homecoming queen in high school and had a bevy of boyfriends and giggling best friends, while I was the messy, uncoordinated, moody bookworm with runaway hair and braces who never went to homecoming or prom, and whose best friend—outside of Tess—was *Anne of Green Gables.*

But still.

Julia was my sister.

My only sister.

And she'd been there for me when Chris bailed. Or she'd tried to be. I just hadn't let her. She'd even returned Grandma Chloe's cherry wood secretary desk.

I took a deep breath. "I'm sorry, Jules. I'm a mean, jealous pig who is evil and must be destroyed." Awkwardly I hugged my sister's weeping body next to mine. "It's going to be all right. Really. You'll be a wonderful mother—you were made to be a mother, more than anyone else I know."

"But I've let *our* mother down." Julia sniffled. "And Daddy." She wiped her hand across her face. "And God." She cried harder and then lifted her tear-stained face to meet my gaze. "At least you waited."

"Easier said than done. And the only reason we could wait was because Chris and I were together just five months, not two years like you and Justin. Otherwise ..." I lifted my shoulders. "I can't imagine lasting two *years.*" I reached to stroke her tangled hair, but my hand dropped. How long had it been since I'd shown affection to my sister?

One step at a time.

"It's not the end of the world. Forgiveness is God's specialty, remember?" I handed her another tissue. "Here. Blow your nose. You've got snot all over your face."

"Ah, that's the Chloe I know and love." She relinquished a wan smile and blew her nose.

"This is quite the red-letter day. What does Justin say?"

"He doesn't know yet. I just found out, and I'm not sure how to tell him. Or Mom and Dad, for that matter."

"What?" I yanked Julia's sundress off the hook on the back of the door and handed it to her. "Mom and Dad can wait. You need to get to your fiancé immediately and share the good news."

Julia lifted hopeful eyes to mine. "You think it's good news?"

"Of course."

"But what about the wedding?" She fingered the folds of her too-tight dream wedding dress. "All our plans?"

"Pull a Scarlett O'Hara and think about that tomorrow. Right now you need to go tell the man of your dreams that he's going to be a daddy. But first, you might want to wash the mascara and boogers off your face."

Justin was over the moon.

He wanted to drive up to Lake Tahoe that very afternoon and get married. But both sets of parents — who'd initially been dismayed by the news, but after they got over their surprise, were supportive — convinced him to wait two weeks so they could pull together a lovely, intimate wedding in my parents' backyard.

Our whole family pitched in to help.

Dad corralled Timmy and Tommy to help him cut down and cart off a diseased mulberry tree that Mom had been after him to get rid of for ages, Tess and I pulled weeds, Mom planted extra flowers, Justin spread fresh bark in all of Mom's flower beds, and Julia deadheaded roses — the only manual labor her protective fiancé would allow her to do.

"But, honey, I'm pregnant, not incapacitated," Julia said when Justin balked at her mowing the lawn. "I'm perfectly capable of cutting the grass with Dad's power mower. I do it all the time."

"No need. I'll do it, sweetie. You just sit back and relax."

She did, with a sweet smile. Behind the sweetness, though, I thought I detected the tiniest trace of resentment. I was probably just imagining it.

Then Mom decided that with guests coming, both bathrooms needed sprucing up. She picked up a few gallons of paint — celery green for one, vanilla cream for the other — and we prepped the rooms for painting. We'd masked everything off, and Julia was about to pry the cover off the celery green paint when Justin skidded around the corner from the living room into the hallway and yelled, "Stop!"

Mom's hand fluttered to her chest. "Justin, you gave me a start."

"Sorry," he said distractedly as he approached, his focus solely on Julia. "Sweetie, let someone else do the painting — the fumes aren't good for you or the baby."

"Is that right?" My sister narrowed her eyes at him.

Ooh. Big mistake, Justin. Do not condescend to a pregnant woman.

"Hey mom, let's go get a glass of your wonderful lemonade." I steered her down the hall toward the kitchen. "I'm super thirsty, and I'll bet everyone else is too."

A few minutes later, Timmy, Tommy, Tess, and I were

congregated around the butcher block island scarfing down homemade oatmeal cookies and lemonade while Dad ran to the hardware store for some weed killer.

Mom was refilling my glass when Julia stormed into the kitchen and grabbed her purse. "Hey, Mom, are you ready to go to the store now and pick up those new bathroom rugs and shower curtains? Your grandchild and I need some fresh air."

I relieved my mother of the lemonade pitcher. And by the time she and Julia returned two hours later with several shopping bags between them, my sister had cooled off and both bathrooms were painted.

Two weeks later, Julia made a beautiful June bride.

Radiant and beaming in a simple white eyelet dress that floated about her when she walked, she caught my eye and winked as our little cousin Erica finally got to march across the grass, preening in her flower-girl finery and regally dropping clumps of rose petals in her imperious wake.

Amazing what a little unplanned pregnancy and all-too-human fall from the perfect sister pedestal can do between two sisters. Katie and I followed Erica the Flower-Girl in complementary linen column dresses — Katie's was soft pink, mine, a cool mint green — that we could wear again after the wedding. The swirly, cotton-candy pink confection remained at the bridal shop ready to ensnare the next maid of honor who walked through the door.

Thanks, Jules, I owe you, I thought as I walked across the freshly mown lawn.

When Justin first saw Julia come walking toward him on our father's arm, he gasped. And then he wept.

I love that in a man. Don't you?

Then I wept when Justin said his vows, his eyes never leaving my sister's face, holding her hands as he emphasized each word loudly and clearly after our pastor: "For better, for worse. For richer, for poorer. In sickness and in health." Justin gazed deeply into Julia's eyes, completely oblivious to everything and everyone else. He squeezed her hands tightly. "As long as we both shall live."

I blubbed. And so did every other woman present.

Then, as their first act together as husband and wife, Julia and Justin took communion as Justin's friend Andrew sang, "I Will Be Here."

More blubbery.

"Man, those two really did me in!" Tess wiped her eyes as she joined me in the shade of the big oak tree.

"Tell me about it. Too bad Justin doesn't have a brother."

"Or an unmarried uncle. Widower father. Whatever. That boy's got romance in his genes."

"Looks like he's not the only one." I nodded to where Tommy was flirting with Clemmie, my folks' cute sixteen-year-old next-door neighbor.

"That's not romance; that's hormones," his mother said with a sigh.

"Don't you worry about your boys, Tess," Dad said as he came up behind us. "I'm keeping an eye on them. Besides, they're so busy at those summer construction jobs and so tired when they get home, they don't have time to get into trouble."

"From your lips to God's ears." Tess glanced at Tommy, who'd just been joined by his twin. "I think I'll just go tell Clemmie how nice she looks." Her lips curved upward as she headed across the grass to her sons and the object of their mutual affection.

Dad looped his arm around my shoulders. "How are you doing, sweetheart?"

"I'm fine." I reached up and squeezed his hand. "I'm really happy for Justin and Julia. They have what I want, *someday*. But not right now."

As I spoke the words, I realized they were true. I wasn't just telling my father what he wanted to hear. I sent the bride and groom a thoughtful look. "I realize now I didn't have that with Chris. That whole steady, unconditional love and acceptance. And I don't want to settle for anything less."

"You'd better not. *Both* my daughters deserve the best." He planted a kiss on my forehead and offered me his arm. "Shall we go find your mother? I have a feeling there's a million and one things she needs us for."

"Lead the way."

Half an hour later I was standing in front of the cake table, trying to explain to the flower girl from Hades why she couldn't have a piece of wedding cake "with lots and lots of frosting *right now!*"

"Erica, we need to wait for the bride and groom to come cut the first piece of cake before anyone else can have any." I bent down to her height and nodded to the nearby food table. "But look. There's still lots of food at the buffet. Would you like to have some more cheese and crackers? Or some delicious grapes? Yum. I love grapes, don't you?"

"Don't want grapes!" She stomped her pink Mary Jane–shod foot. "Wanna piece of cake. Now!"

"I'm sorry, you can't have any now. You have to wait."

Like everybody else.

"Don't wanna wait! Don't wanna wait!" Erica began to wail.

"Sounds like someone needs a nap," an all-too-familiar voice said.

I straightened up quickly, realizing that from my bent-over position, I was probably revealing my white lacy bra and way too much cleavage.

"Ryan. Hi. What are you doing here?"

"I was invited. Justin and I are in a men's Bible study group."

"Ah. Right. Sorry. Didn't mean to be rude."

"That's okay," he said wryly. "I'm kind of used to it by now."

"About that. I — Erica, no!"

The frosting-obsessed flower girl, taking full advantage of my Ryan distraction, had scooted behind me and plunged her chubby little hand into the bottom layer of my sister's beautiful, three-tiered lemon chiffon wedding cake.

"Stop right there," I ordered my cousin from the netherworld.

Erica glared at me, her eyes filling with angry, rebellious tears, and screeched, "Mommy!"

"It's all right. You don't need to yell," I said in a calm, soothing tone. "Now you're going to gently pull your hand out so you don't break Cousin Julia's wedding cake. Okay?"

She nodded.

Aunt Gabby came rushing up. "Sweetheart! Are you okay? What happened?"

Erica played her mother like a violin and turned on the waterworks in earnest. "Cousin Chloe yelled at me."

"I'm just trying to prevent her from ruining Julia's wedding cake," I said. "Now stop crying, Erica, and let's pull your hand out nice and slow like a good girl. There you go. That's right. Almost done."

Her fist cleared the cake.

"Good girl." I grabbed a napkin and slid it beneath her still-clenched fist to prevent any more crumbs and frosting from falling on the white linen tablecloth. "Now go with your mommy, and she'll get you all cleaned up."

Erica shoved her hand in her mouth and gobbled greedily at her fistful of cake. Then she flung herself at her mother's legs and held on for dear life.

"Ooh! Careful, honey. You're getting Mommy's muumuu all sticky."

Erica wailed as Aunt Gabby led her off to the bathroom.

Ryan whistled softly as he looked at the damaged cake. "Looks like a meteor blasted through there."

"Asteroid Erica." I stared in dismay at the three-inch hole smack dab in the center of the bottom layer of the cake. "What am I going to do? I don't want anyone to see this. Especially Julia. She may not have gotten the original wedding of her dreams that she'd planned on, but I don't want this one to turn into a nightmare."

"Can't you just turn it around to the back where no one can see it?"

"Then the bride and groom cake topper will be mooning everyone."

"So take the topper off and turn it around."

"I can't. The florist secured all the flowers on the top tier to the topper. It would destroy the whole arrangement."

"Ladies and gentleman," my dad's voice boomed out over the backyard. "The bride and groom are now going to cut the cake, so please, make your way over to the cake table. Thank you."

I looked hard at my sister's beautiful lemon-chiffon cake, thinking fast. "Cover me," I hissed to Ryan.

As he camouflaged my actions from the crowd, I plucked some daisies out of my bouquet and shoved them into the hole and around all sides of it, creating a sunburst effect. Then I repeated the same design on the middle layer so it looked like it was planned.

Finally, I turned my denuded bouquet around so the empty spots weren't facing front and turned around to smile at the approaching horde.

"I owe you an apology, Ryan."

We were sitting on a stone bench in my mother's freshly weeded and spruced-up cottage garden, eating wedding cake by the delphiniums. "You were right. Chris and I weren't a good match. We *were* too different."

A knowing grin split his face. "I thought that was you behind the Picasso that morning at Dunkeld's."

"What can I say? I've never been very good at hide-and-seek. Or at admitting when I'm wrong." I stuck out my hand. "Friends again?"

Ryan set down his cake and shook my hand. "Friends." Did he linger, with my hand in his? He released it with a little smile and stretched out his legs.

"How do you feel about becoming an aunt?"

"Good." I wiped my sweaty palm on my napkin. "Except for the whole infant part."

"What?"

"I'm just not into the baby thing." I lifted my shoulders. "I know I'm supposed to be transported to heights of maternal gooeyness whenever I see a little bundle of joy, but I'm just not. Remember when Drew and Trista had their baby and brought it to singles to show everyone?"

"Vaguely."

"Well, every girl within a hundred-yard radius went into overdrive and started gushing about how cute it was."

"I think 'it' is a boy."

"Whatever. They all look alike to me. Anyway, all the women were smiling and cooing and taking turns holding the baby. Except me. I just don't get the big fascination. All they do is eat, sleep, cry, and poop."

I slid a hesitant glance at Ryan. "So do you think I'm awful?"

"No. Why?"

"Because I'm not into babies."

"So? I'm not into cats."

"Yeah, but a lot of guys aren't. Cats are a girl pet. That's why so many old ladies have them. But babies are definitely a woman thing." I sighed. "I think I must be missing the whole baby bonding gene or something. I'm just not feelin' it.

"And I've tried. Believe me, I've tried. I even worked in the church nursery for a while." I squeezed my eyes tight against the memory. "Talk about a disaster. Every time I picked up a baby, it would cry; I couldn't figure out how to do the bottle right; and I gagged when they spit up on me. And don't even mention diaper duty. I saw colors that I've never before seen in nature. The smell nearly knocked me out."

Well, haven't I become the Chatty Cathy all of a sudden? What's up with that?

"I'm not big on diapers myself." Ryan laced his fingers behind his head and leaned back on the bench. "And as far as the whole bonding thing goes, I bet that will change when you have your own baby."

"Ya think?"

"That's what I've heard."

"I hope so. Meanwhile, I sure hope Julia doesn't get her feelings hurt when I'm not all goopy over little Julia or Justin during the initial baby phase. But once my niece or nephew starts walking and talking" — I stabbed the air with my plastic fork — "I'm all over it. I think they're adorable when they waddle around with those cute, chubby thighs, sucking their thumbs and clutching onto their blankie. And I can't wait to be cool, fun Aunt Chloe and take her — or him — everywhere. The park. The zoo. The library."

"The ocean?"

"Don't push it."

Part 6

JULY
The Adventures of Huckleberry Finn

&

AUGUST
Dove

16

Dove nosed into her slip at the Long Beach marina, her sails furled like a bird resting its wings after a storm.

Dove

We didn't get off to a very auspicious beginning on our Huckleberry Finn rafting trip down the American River. First, Jenna's six-man raft had to be inflated, but she'd forgotten her motorized pump at home, so one by one we took turns blowing the raft up with a foot pump. Not quite the same as pumping up a bicycle tire. Just when I thought my leg would fall off, a family of four showed up and loaned us their automatic pump.

Then, as we launched the six-man raft—Annette had begged off with a migraine—Kailyn squealed as we stepped into the water. "You promised I wouldn't get wet!"

"Chill," Becca said. "It's just your feet."

"The feet wearing my Michael Kors flip-flops."

Designer-impaired Becca and I both gave her blank looks.

"They cost nearly a hundred bucks!"

"Are you serious? That's insane. Mine only cost seven bucks." I lifted my right foot out of the water to show off my cute black rubber flip-flops. "Target."

"They're not quite the same."

"Who wears expensive shoes rafting anyway?"

"People who were told they wouldn't get wet." Kailyn scowled at Becca.

"It doesn't take a rocket scientist to know that you don't wear leather on the river."

"Maybe if someone had bothered to tell someone else that we'd be stepping *into water*, the rocket scientist wouldn't have worn her favorite pair of Michael Kors."

It was Jenna's turn to give Kailyn an incredulous stare. "How else did you think we'd launch a raft?"

"I have no idea. I've never done this before." Kailyn held her metallic leather flip-flops high in her left hand as she gave a feeble push to the rubber raft with her right.

"Girls, let's not squabble, okay?" Tess said. "This is a day of fun and relaxation. Kailyn, you might want to put your shoes in one of those extra plastic bags I brought. And let's shove off and get this party started."

A few minutes later we finally got the raft launched and everyone hopped in, with Becca and Jenna manning the oars for a relaxing three-hour drift down the Lower American River. That's the only way they'd gotten me to come — the promise of no whitewater rapids and the assurance of a gentle, peaceful ride down the lazy river. Becca also pledged that we wouldn't see any sharks. This time though, just to be sure, I Googled in advance to verify.

She was right. Sharks live in salt water.

I adjusted my prescription sunglasses and trailed my hand languidly over the side of the raft. Tess, who had rafted with her sons countless times, attached a small cooler full of bottled water and soda to the back of the raft to float along behind us.

We'd all slathered on the sun block and were enjoying the quiet reverie of a lazy drift down the river when Kailyn of the perfect body and gorgeous long blonde hair decided she was hot and took off her T-shirt. Big mistake.

"Woo-hoo! Yeah, baby!" shouted some teenage boys coming up behind us on another raft. "Lookin' good, white bikini!"

One scrawny guy who probably hadn't even started shaving yet clutched his hand to his chest and shouted, "Will you marry me?"

The rest of us were wearing bathing suits too — with shorts. But when you're in a raft with Heidi Klum, who's going to notice? All at once, I was pelted between the shoulder blades with a hard stream of water.

I whirled around to see another raft of laughing, sunburned guys — frat boys, by the looks of the Greek logos on their ball caps — all aiming an arsenal of weapons at us: water pistols, water bazookas, even buckets.

So much for our quiet, peaceful drift down the river.

Kailyn shrieked as a bucket of water drenched her from head to toe.

"Now that's what I'm talkin' about!" The beefy guy holding the now-empty bucket high-fived his buddies.

"Okay, this is war." Tess whipped out a heavy-duty water pistol that I hadn't even seen her bring on the raft, leaned over and proceeded to squirt bucket boy right in the face.

"Score!" Becca yelled.

Tess cut her a grin and tossed her a squirt gun. But before Becca could even take aim, a seriously sunburned frat boy knocked it out of her hand with the force of his water bazooka.

Jenna rode to the rescue. She strong-armed the cooler into the raft and grabbed a bottled water from inside which she opened and proceeded to upend over sunburned frat boy's head.

"Yowser! That's freezing!" he yelled.

"And there's more where that came from." She flexed her biceps. "So why don't you go play somewhere else?"

"Bring it on babe, bring it on." He laughed, along with his buddies who then proceeded to launch into a renewed water attack that left Paige and Kailyn—sitting on the side of the raft closest to them—drenched and shivering.

I thrust a towel at Kailyn. "Here. Wrap this around you and change places with me."

Kailyn did, gratefully, and the guys groaned. "Aw, we'll be good. Promise."

Beefy bucket guy's beer breath hit me in the face as he and a couple of his brawny buddies reached over to pull our raft closer, tipping it a little in the process, which made my heart jump to my throat and elicited a squeal from Kailyn.

That did it. Time to bring out the big guns.

Adopting my most beatific Mother Teresa expression, I looked beefy boy square in the eye and said, "Do you know Jesus as your personal Lord and savior, my friend? If you died tonight, do you know where you'd spend eternity? Would you like to ask him into your heart right now?" Then I began to sing, "Shall We Gather at the River?"

Tess and Paige joined in reverently. And then Kailyn, who was wearing her T-shirt once again.

"Just our luck." The guys groaned. "A bunch of church chicks." They paddled away in disgust, on the prowl for fresh, unsuspecting rafters to sneak attack.

"Well that's the most original brush-off I've ever heard."

Becca's pearly whites gleamed. "I'll have to remember that one."

The rest of our afternoon on the river passed uneventfully, and we ended our day with a picnic at a park where we got into a lively discussion on the merits of Huck Finn and whether or not Mark Twain was a racist or a visionary casting a light on the racism of his day.

We couldn't come to a consensus, but all agreed we were happy to close the book on the hateful N-word that had been so freely bandied about in its pages.

When I checked my messages that night, there was one from Julia and one from Ryan.

I read Julia's text. NAMES: EMMA, MADISON, SOPHIA? JAMES, JOSHUA, LUCAS?

I texted back: SOPHIE & LUKE?

Ryan wanted to know how our day on the river had gone and to remind me it was my turn to bring goodies to Sunday school. "I really like the doughnuts with the chocolate sprinkles," he said.

Three weeks later, Becca stood at the front edge of the boat, her torso extended off the railing, arms outstretched and charcoal hair ruffling in the wind as the large catamaran sailed over San Francisco Bay. "Hey, look! I'm King of the World!"

"You don't look like Leonardo DiCaprio," Jenna said dryly, rolling her eyes.

Becca, in her element, ignored her. "Isn't this cool?"

"That's one way of putting it." I gripped the railing.

"Aw c'mon, Chloe! Don't be a baby." Jenna zipped up her windbreaker. "Just relax and enjoy yourself. The wind is really calm and the water's smooth as silk today."

"You said that about rafting too."

"The river was mellow, it was those guys on the other rafts who weren't."

When we'd first boarded the *Adventure Cat* at Pier 39 for our hour-and-a-half cruise around Alcatraz and under the Golden Gate Bridge, I'd been a little nervous.

"Couldn't we do some of our adventures on dry land?"

"At least on this water adventure we won't have to deal with the drunken, testosterone-fueled frat pack," Paige said.

"No, just sharks and riptides and who knows what other kinds of underwater dangers."

"Oh, chill," Becca said.

Jenna stepped out of the relative safety of the glass-enclosed cabin. "Let's go out front. I want to feel the breeze and smell the salt air."

"I'm fine in here for now," Kailyn said from her seat on the bench, her right hand on the opening to the life preserver storage.

"Me too."

"Chloe, you have to face your fears head on." Becca pulled at my hand. "Come on."

Well … it wasn't like we'd actually be *in* the water. And it was a pretty big boat, and they did make this trip a couple times a day, so it must be safe. Tentatively, I followed Becca onto the open deck as the thirty-foot-wide catamaran cleared the dock area and entered the Bay.

"I can't believe how stable this is," Tess said.

"So much smoother than a regular sailboat." Becca's eyes lit up. "Now that's a white-knuckle adventure."

I sat down between Tess and Paige on the fiberglass deck of the catamaran and gingerly stretched my feet out in front of me onto the thick, woven trampoline-style net that made up the front end of the boat. There were pontoons on either side — that, apparently, is what makes it a catamaran rather than a boat. But still. The only thing between us and the shark-infested water was a net.

Just fabric. What shark can't bite through fabric?

Are they serious?

Jenna and Becca didn't seem concerned. They plopped down on the netting, which wasn't springy like a regular trampoline, and it held them securely. They stretched out on their backs with their hands laced behind their heads, staring up at the perfect August sky. Then they flopped over on their stomachs. "How cool is that?" Jenna said. "You can see the ocean right beneath us."

"This is so much better than a glass-bottomed boat." Becca looked through the net into the brownish green ocean below. "I wonder if we'll see any of my little nurse sharks."

Paige and I both yanked our feet off the netting.

"Very funny. Reminds me of something my sons would do," Tess said. "And they're sixteen."

"What can I say? I like to stay young."

"Understatement of the year," Paige grumbled.

"Oh look!" Annette pointed to a dark spot in the water up ahead. "There's a seal or something. See him? Oh, he just went under. There he is again. There's his little black head. Isn't he cute?"

"Just so we don't see a big, ugly gray head and a dorsal fin."

I decided I'd be more comfortable standing. Good thing there were lots of things to hold on to. We left the bustling tourists and playful sea lions of Pier 39 behind us as the boat nosed into the open water. In front of us, the sparkling San Francisco Bay spread out like a gorgeous IMAX panorama with an amazing view of the Golden Gate Bridge and surrounding hills.

Wow.

"It's beautiful." I stood on the side deck clasping the railing a few feet from Becca and Jenna who'd bounded to their feet to stand at the front of the boat yearning into the wind.

The gentle rocking of the boat was soothing. And I realized I didn't need to cling to the metal bar quite so tightly. I relaxed my grip and decided this was going to be a good adventure after all.

Tess came and stood beside me. Silent. In shared appreciation.

A yell from the skipper startled me. The engines stopped. "What's wrong?" I grabbed Tess's arm in panic. "Are we sinking?" That's when I heard the click and swooshing of the sail being raised into position.

"No." She pointed to the first mate hoisting the sail. "We're just getting started."

And with a fhwoomp, the wind filled the sails and we were moving—more like flying—over the water. Seagulls soared overhead and a quartet of ducks skimmed the water's surface, ducking beneath and resurfacing moments later.

"What do you think?" Tess asked a few minutes later.

"It's great! I hadn't realized how peaceful it would be." I lifted my head into the Bay wind, reveling in the scent of the sea. "And freeing." Coasting over the water was so much better than actually being in the water.

Becca and Jenna maintained their position at the front of the catamaran, feet planted firmly on deck, their bodies arching into the wind, looking for all the world like twin modern-day figureheads.

Strong, athletic, and fierce.

And not in a catwalk, supermodel way either.

I wonder what it would be like to be that strong and fearless.

But then again, I am on a sailboat skimming across the ocean. Who'd have ever thought?

Paige and Annette joined us. "Is Kailyn still hunkered down in the cabin?" Tess asked.

"Hunk being the operative word."

"What?"

Annette thumbed over her shoulder. "Leave it to my baby girl to hone in on a man on our girls' adventure out. On the open sea, no less."

I glanced back toward the glassed-in cabin where I saw Kailyn engaged in animated conversation with a guy.

"Only Kailyn," Tess said. "But who knows? Maybe he'll be able to convince her to come out on deck. He doesn't look like the indoor type."

"It doesn't matter what type he is," I said. "Once a guy meets Kailyn, he sticks to her like glue. Indoors or out."

Meow.

"What are you guys talking about?" Becca popped up beside us with Jenna in tow. "Or should I say who?"

My face warmed, and I sheathed my claws, deciding it would be better if I focused on our surroundings instead.

Alcatraz Island loomed on our left, the prison buildings high on the hill and a large sign still posted warning that people caught helping prisoners to escape were subject to prosecution and imprisonment. I stared at the once impenetrable fortress, now a popular tourist attraction. "It must have been horrible to be a prisoner there. So isolated. I'd have gone crazy." I looked back at the San Francisco skyline. "Especially seeing the city all the time. So close and yet so far."

"Haven't you ever taken the Blue and Gold ferry to Alcatraz?" Becca asked.

"Nope."

"We'll have to do that next time. And get our picture taken in one of the cells."

"I did that with a date once," Jenna said.

"That sounds romantic." Annette pushed her wind-whipped strawberry-blonde hair behind her ears.

"He took me to a computer show for our second date."

"What was he, a CSI nerd?"

"Engineer."

"Ah."

"And I thought my dates were bad." Paige chuckled.

"Hey, you girls had a chance with some really nice guys." Annette wagged her finger at us. "So don't complain. Y'all are just too picky."

"Easy for you to say when you got the cream of the crop." Tess linked her arm with Annette's. "Does your Randall have any brothers, by chance?"

"Only one and he's married. Sorry."

As we sailed past Alcatraz, the contrast struck me—the freedom of sailing versus the prison on the rock. This is how young Robin Graham must have felt as he sailed *Dove* over the open sea.

I'd never felt so free. And I was surprised to discover I wasn't the least bit afraid either. No wonder so many poets wrote odes to the sea and so many men fell in love with her and left women behind for her.

The *Cat* turned, and we were sailing directly toward the Golden Gate Bridge. Ahead of us a little ways on the left—is that called starboard?—I spotted three sailboats, each with different-colored sails, one white, one sunburst yellow, and one turquoise blue, zig-zagging through the water. As I tracked their progress, sails billowing, all at once the turquoise sail caught the wind and it puffed out into a giant blue ball.

"Look!" I pointed. "That sailboat's pregnant!"

"And how. Looks like she'll be going into labor any second," Paige said.

"That's what you call sailing." Tess broke into the song

of the same name—a perfect accompaniment to the mood of the day.

Kailyn finally surfaced from her glass sanctuary and introduced us to her latest lap dog, Doug. He *was* cute. I noticed him checking out Becca as she scampered around the deck like a happy puppy in her shorts and red hoodie. Not Kailyn's lap dog after all.

Definitely a dog though.

All at once, a wave lifted the catamaran up slightly and then dropped her back down on the water, splashing water on deck and splattering us with a little sea spray.

"Eek!" Kailyn jumped back. At least this time she'd left her fancy flip-flops home.

The boat lifted again as another wave rolled beneath it.

She blanched. "Are we going to tip over?"

"Not a chance," Jenna said. "That's just the *Cat* reacting in the wake of that other boat that went by. Happens all the time. No biggie."

"Still, I think I'll go back inside." Kailyn flicked a droplet of water from her blonde mane. "Coming, Doug?"

"Nah. Think I'll just chill here and catch some wind and rays."

Kailyn's eyes flicked to Becca, who was oblivious to Doug's apparent interest, caught up as she was in her whole sailing adventure.

"Chloe, want to join me?"

"No thanks. I'm fine out here. Actually, I'm really liking it."

Becca and Tess whipped up two enthusiastic and athletic thumbs up. "What'd I tell you?" My roommate bounded over and said loudly into my ear, "It is nothing to die; it is horrible not to live."

"Who said that?"

"Jean Valjean in *Les Misérables.*"

"Oh. I thought maybe it was Robinson Crusoe."

The *Cat* glided across the water like a warm knife through butter.

"This is really somethin'," Annette said. "I think everyone should do this at least once in their life."

"Oh yes." I drank in the beautiful towers of the Golden Gate silhouetted in the distance, the freedom of the open sea, the wind and salt air in my face, and the gentle rocking of the water.

This wasn't something I could read about. This was something that had to be experienced.

"Wow. Who knew this would be such a rush?" Annette said. "Thanks for suggestin' it for the Paperback Girls, Becca." She giggled. "Although, maybe we should rechristen our group the Getaway Girls."

"That's not a bad idea."

As we approached the bridge, there was a dark stripe in the water—the shadow of the bridge stretching across our path. And as we entered the bridge's shadow, we could feel the temperature drop several degrees—something normal and expected when you walk under the shade of a tree, but here at sea, it was different somehow. The hills were now only to our sides as the bay opened into the ocean. Looking forward, it was just water and sky across the whole horizon. But looking up, we could see the belly of the Golden Gate.

"I've never seen it from this angle," I murmured.

"Not many people have," Tess said. "Relatively speaking. One of the most famous structures in the world, yet most people only see it from above, not from down here."

"It's so high." Jenna gave the metal structure a thoughtful glance. "No wonder the jumpers never make it."

"Leave it to Agatha Christie to go there." I gazed back across the open ocean. "And talking of making it, would you ever go sailing around the world alone like Robin Graham did?"

Before Jenna could reply, Annette jumped in with her slight Southern drawl. "Honey, I wouldn't go in the Jacuzzi alone."

"I would." Jenna offered her brilliant grin. "Sail around the world, I mean."

"So would I," Becca agreed.

"There's adventurous, and then there's stupid." Tess looked at our two wild-and-crazy daredevils over her glasses with a smile.

Becca lifted her chin. "I don't think it's stupid to do something where it's just you against the elements, with no one else telling you what to do, having to live by your own wits and strength."

"Isn't that what Captain Ahab did?" I asked. "We all know how that ended up."

"I can tell someone never finished *Moby Dick*," Tess said. "Captain Ahab wasn't alone. He was the captain of the ship, and in his obsession to get Moby Dick, he not only killed himself but his entire crew too—all except for Ishmael."

"Glad no one here has that kind of obsession."

"My only obsession at this moment is food," Annette said. "I don't know about anyone else, but I'm starved."

Part 7

september
ℳarjorie Morningstar

17

A book is so soon made, costs so little, and can go so far!

The Hunchback of Notre Dame

As I sprawled on the couch reading *Marjorie Morningstar,* Tess's favorite coming-of-age tale, on a sunny September afternoon after a grueling week at work, I tried to read it through my aunt's eyes, to see if that would make it more relatable.

Marjorie Morgenstern dreams of becoming an actress, much to the dismay of her conventional Jewish parents, who would rather see her settle down with a nice Jewish boy, raise kids, and never work outside the home. Yet time and time again Marjorie steps outside of the family conventions.

No wonder Tess loved it.

After she'd graduated from high school, she spent the summer backpacking around Europe — over her family's objections. And unlike my mother, who'd married shortly after her eighteenth birthday and happily settled into her home-and-hearth calling, Tess traveled and established herself in her career before meeting Uncle Ted and marrying him at the age of thirty.

They didn't have kids right away because they wanted to enjoy time alone together first—just the two of them. After three years of marriage, Tommy and Timmy were born.

Seven years later, Uncle Ted was gone.

My phone rang, Tommy's cell number flashing on the display. I snapped it open. "Hey, Tommy."

"Hey cuz, wanna come over and play Scene It tonight?"

"Guys against girls again?"

"What else?" Timmy said through his brother's speakerphone.

"I see. You *want* to get skunked again." The last time Tess and I had played with her sons, we'd beaten them mercilessly.

"Yeah, well we'll see who's wearing a white stripe down their back when the night's over," Tommy—or was it Timmy?—said.

"That's right," his twin agreed, "so be sure and wear a black shirt, cuz." They sniggered and hung up, neglecting to mention their secret weapon.

Ryan.

I was surprised to see him when I arrived at Tess's that night, but he was the one who got the boys their summer job, after all. He and my cousins had worked together all summer long at various construction sites, so I guess when I thought about it, it wasn't that much of a surprise.

Tess had a surprise in store for her sons, however: her own secret weapon.

Paige.

And we weren't the ones wearing the white stripe down our backs that night.

"Women rule!" I shouted after we won our second game in a row.

"Nice ringer Tess brought in," Ryan said as I walked him to his car at the end of the evening.

"Hey, all's fair in love and war."

"War's over. Remember?" He threw me a teasing smile. "We called a truce."

"Not when it comes to games. Have you forgotten my competitive streak?"

"I haven't forgotten anything."

"Hey, y'all, check it out." Annette brandished her copy of *French Women Don't Get Fat* as she strode into Paige's living room the following week. "French women don't go to the gym! They just walk. *Everywhere.*"

"That's because if you drive in Paris, you take your life in your hands," Tess said dryly. "Especially around the Arc de Triomphe on the Champs-Elysées."

"Ooh, the Champs-Elysées." Paige released a rapturous sigh. "Don't you just love the sound of that? So musical."

"Yeah, I'll bet it's really musical with all those cars honking at you." Jenna slid over to make room for Annette on the sofa.

"Works for me." Annette patted her voluptuous hips as she squeezed in between Jenna and Tess. "I'll take cars honkin' at me any day rather than go to the gym. No offense, trainer girl."

"None taken."

"I'm with you, Annette. I'd rather walk around a gorgeous city than on a treadmill any day," I said. "Have you gotten to the part yet where she says we should never eat standing up or on the go?"

"Hey! No fair talking about the book this early. We're not discussing it until January, remember?" Kailyn said.

"What I want to know is how do French women get any-thing done?" Becca asked from her cross-legged position on the floor. "I'm always eating on the run. Who's got time to sit down to a meal?"

"The French make the time because food is a way of life to them," Tess said. "It *is* life. Eating isn't just fuel to them. Dining is a ritual—an event unto itself. A pleasure to be savored."

"I'd like to know how they can eat all that fattening French food and sauces and still stay so slim." Kailyn crossed her capri-clad legs.

"Well, if you open the book, it will tell you. That's what we do in our book club. We read." Becca spelled it out slowly. "R-e-a-d."

"Really?" Kailyn made her eyes all big and round. "Gee, I thought this was a knitting club. Guess I'd better put these long needles away." She sent Becca a piercing stare from Paige's floral wingback. "Or maybe I can find some other use for them."

"Hors d'oeuvre, anyone?" Paige waved a platter of fragrant, fresh-from-the-oven appetizers under our noses.

I snatched up one of the bite-sized goodies and popped it in my mouth, reveling in the savory goodness. "Yum. What is this?"

"Escargot in brioche."

I swallowed hard.

Becca spit hers out into her napkin.

Paige offered the tray to Jenna.

"No thanks. I don't eat animals, remember?"

"Escargot's not an animal."

"No, it's a slug." Becca shuddered and drained her ever-present water bottle.

Tess extended her napkin. "I'll take Jenna's and Becca's both."

Paige beamed.

"Me too." Kailyn wolfed down two of the salty starters

in rapid succession and licked her lips. "Now that's what I'm talkin' about."

"Since when did you become all daring?" Becca asked.

"You'd be surprised."

"That's for sure. There's more to my baby girl than meets the superficial eye." Annette ruffled Kailyn's blonde hair.

I popped another escargot into my mouth. I had to admit it was pretty delicious — as long as I thought of it by its French name.

Paige and Tess had decided we needed another movie night to prepare for our upcoming Paris trip — one that all the Paperback Girls could attend. And once again, Paige was assigned the task of selecting the films.

She chose an Audrey Hepburn double-feature. "We're going to start with Audrey and Fred Astaire in *Funny Face*," Paige said as she settled onto the floor next to Becca.

"Just so he doesn't do any ballet." Becca bit into her crunchy French bread.

"Hey!" Paige brushed baguette crumbs from her shirt. "Didn't your mother ever teach you not to talk with your mouth full?"

"Sorry," Becca mumbled behind the hand she'd clapped to her mouth.

"*Quelle horreur!*" Kailyn exclaimed.

"Ah, I see someone's been practicing their French."

"*Mais oui. Maman, aussi.*"

Paige started the movie and Kailyn, much to my surprise, lapped up all the fifties fashions. I cringed, however, at a musical number that swathed everyone and everything in an all-too-familiar pink.

And then we were in Paris.

"Wow." Kailyn propped her chin in her hands. "What a beautiful city."

"I can't wait to go back," Annette said.

"I can't wait to go for the first time." I gawked at the screen, devouring all the amazing sights. "And I don't care how touristy it is, I'm getting my picture taken at the Eiffel Tower."

Becca agreed and said she was also planning to send postcards to everyone she'd ever met.

"I was toying with the idea of sending a postcard to my ex," Paige said. "He's always wanted to go to Paris. But that would be mean, wouldn't it?"

"Uh, *no*," Jenna said. "Mean is leaving you for the bimbo kindergarten teacher. I say send away."

"Yeah, and you should casually mention that you're in the most romantic city in the world with a great boyfriend while you're at it," Becca added.

"Which would be a lie."

"You never know. You could meet some hot French guy and fall head over heels."

"How come old movies always have to end with a woman in a wedding dress?" Jenna asked as the credits rolled.

"Because it's romantic," Paige said. "Besides, it didn't end with an actual wedding—she was just modeling the wedding dress for the fashion show."

"Right. But it did end with the two of them floating off into the sunset together."

"And what's so wrong with that?"

"It's not realistic. And it just sets up all these happily-ever-after fairy-tale fantasies for young girls."

"What's wrong with believing in happily ever after?"

Jenna sent Paige a look. "You of all people need to ask?"

Paige lifted her chin. "That doesn't mean I'm ready to give up on love. I still believe in it. Marriage too."

"Hear, hear," Annette said.

Tess added a hearty amen.

"Come on, Becca. Chloe?" Jenna sent us a beseeching look. "Help me out here."

"I agree with Jenna," Becca said. "I haven't seen many marriages last—beginning with my parents' who split when I was six. No offense, Annette, but I pretty much think all that happily ever after stuff is a crock."

"But how do you really feel?" Tess said. "Don't sugarcoat it."

"I feel that most women have been raised on destructive fairy tales that promote the myth that some prince is going to come along and *rescue* them from their lonely, miserable-with-out-a-man, cinder-scrubbing life. Then he'll spirit them away to a magical marital kingdom in the suburbs where they'll frolic happily ever after in the land of Pledge wipes, Jacuzzi tubs, and granite countertops."

"Ah, but Pledge wipes are my friend," Annette said with a wink.

"And happy marriages aren't a myth," Paige said. "There's plenty of them around."

"Paige is right." I inclined my head to Annette. "What about Annette and Randall? And my parents? And Tess and my Uncle Ted?"

"What about someone in our age group?"

"My sister and Justin."

"Yeah, like that's really going to last," Becca said. "Getting hitched because you're knocked up is always a good way to start a marriage."

A heavy silence filled the air as the Paperback Girls exchanged uncomfortable looks.

"Julia and Justin didn't get married because she was 'knocked up,'" I said in a level tone, although I could feel my eyes shooting off sparks. "They got married because they love each other. Deeply. Fully. Unconditionally. And because God brought them together." I looked hard at my roommate. "And what God has joined together, let no man—or woman—put asunder."

"Okay, okay. Don't get your panties in a knot."

"Time for a commercial." Tess stood up. "Paige, didn't you say you'd made some delicious dessert? May I help you serve it?"

"Yes, please."

"I'll help too." Kailyn jumped up and followed Tess and Paige.

Annette decided she needed to use the little girls' room and Jenna trailed after her, murmuring that she was next in line.

Way to clear a room.

I grabbed a copy of Paige's latest *Gourmet* magazine and yanked it open, furiously flipping through the pages without really seeing them.

Becca drummed her Birks on the floor in an awkward staccato beat as I turned another page. She cleared her throat. "I didn't mean to make you mad, Chloe. But I thought you didn't like your sister. You're always trashing her—calling her Julia the Good, Julia the Perfect, Julia the golden child."

"You're right." Heat crept up my neck. "I am. Was. But I'm allowed to—I'm her sister. Chalk it up to sibling rivalry. Jealousy. Whatever."

And that makes it okay?

"Not that that makes it all right, but I'm working on that." I took a deep breath. "Even though I was dumped at the altar, that hasn't turned me against marriage. I still really believe in it and I'm sick of everyone giving it a bad rap."

"Sorry," Becca mumbled.

"I'm sorry too. I shouldn't have jumped down your throat like that. Guess I'm a little defensive."

"Ya think?"

"Is it safe to come back into the war zone?" Tess called from the kitchen.

"All clear."

The girls returned to their seats. "Mmm, this pear tart is yummy, Paige." Jenna forked up another bite. "What's this stuff on top?"

"Crème fraîche."

"Is that French for whipped cream?" Becca asked before inhaling the rest of her tart.

"That's la crème fouettée. Crème fraîche is actually slightly fermented cream that's been thickened with lactic bacteria culture."

"Bacteria?" Kailyn scrunched up her nose in distaste.

"What do you think's in yogurt, baby girl?" Annette said. "Ever hear of acidopholus?" She turned to Paige. "So, how'd you make it? And is it the same as what we'll get in Paris?"

"Pretty much. In France, their cream is unpasteurized, so it already contains the necessary bacteria to thicken it naturally into crème fraîche. Here, since all our cream is pasteurized, you have to add buttermilk to whipping cream in a glass bowl, cover it, and let it stand at room temperature from eight to twenty-four hours, until it achieves the necessary thickness."

"Way too much work," Becca said. "I'd just use whipped cream in a can."

"But it's nowhere near the same thing."

Jenna sent Paige an affectionate look. "You're such a foodie."

"What can I say?" Paige looked ruefully at her midsection. "And I know it shows. That's why I'm really loving *French Women Don't Get Fat*. I can't wait to try some of the recipes."

"Me too," Annette said. "Like that miracle leek soup she said helped her lose weight."

Kailyn frowned. "Remember: no talking about the book until we're all finished reading it."

When *Charade*, our second movie of the night, ended, Jenna said she liked it a lot better than *Funny Face*.

"Well of course you did," Tess said. "People kept getting killed, and we never knew who the real bad guy was until the end."

"That's what kept it interesting."

"Cary Grant kept it interesting for me," Annette said. "Mmm-hmm. That was one sexy leading man."

Paige expelled a dreamy sigh. "Think we'll find Cary Grant or Fred Astaire in Paris?"

"If we did, it wouldn't be pretty, since they're both seriously dead," Becca said.

"Funny." Paige made a face at her. "I meant meeting a man like that in Paris."

"Yeah, and having him sweep me off my feet, or dance me off my feet," Kailyn said.

"More likely you'll meet Inspector Clouseau and he'll stumble over your feet."

Paige said that next time we'd watch *Amélie*.

"Is that the French film from a few years ago?" Jenna asked. "I've heard it's really good. And quirky."

"Subtitles?" Annette scrunched up her face. "I hate having to read a movie. If I wanted to read, I'd open a book."

"It's better to help people than garden gnomes," Becca intoned.

"What?"

"There she goes again," I said. "The queen of the non sequitur."

"It's from *Amélie*."

Jenna grinned. "Now I really want to see it."

Part 8

OCTOBER

*M*urder on the Orient Express

&

NOVEMBER/DECEMBER

*L*es Misérables

18

Laughs are like wild mushrooms: they don't deliver themselves to you — you have to go in search of them, whether by pursuing the unexpected, or by being totally crazy ... to keep the adventure of living adventurous.

French Women Don't Get Fat

A few weeks later after church, I stopped by Julia and Justin's with Chinese take-out for lunch and *Goodnight Moon* for my soon-to-be niece or nephew.

Julia was feeling a little hormonal, so after we finished the Kung Pao, I urged Justin to go spend some guy time with his buddies. "Ryan said at church that he hasn't seen you in a while. He told me to let you know that he's going to play hoops with some of the college group if you want to join them."

"Really?" Justin's eyes lit up. He delivered a hopeful look to Julia. "Would you mind, honey?"

"Not if you bring me back some Chunky Monkey. And mangoes. I've really got a craving for mangoes."

"Will do, babe." Justin gave her a quick peck, and then

bussed her stomach. "Bye-bye little one. Be good for your mom while I'm gone. Don't kick her too hard."

Julia called after Justin's retreating back. "And pistachios too. We're all out of pistachios."

After the door closed behind him, Julia shifted on the couch and exhaled noisily. "I owe you. Justin's been driving me crazy lately, hovering over me like a mother hen. I told him earlier to go see his friends so I could have a little space, but he didn't want to leave me alone."

"Aw, that's sweet."

"Not 24/7 it isn't. I'm pregnant not terminal. I don't need round-the-clock care." Her eyes lit on the plastic take-out bag. "Hey, toss me another one of those fortune cookies."

"Someone's got an appetite."

"Well, I am eating for two, you know." Julia crunched into her cookie and fixed me with a knowing look. "So, what's the deal with you and Ryan?"

"What do you mean?"

"I mean you guys have been hanging out and his name seems to be cropping up a lot in conversation these days. So are you dating?"

"Ryan and me?" I laughed. "Serious?"

"Serious."

"He's just a friend."

"You sure about that?"

"Positive."

"Just checking." She shifted uncomfortably on the couch again. "Has he heard from you-know-who lately?"

"It's okay. You can say his name. And yes, Ryan said he heard from Chris a month or so ago. He moved to Alaska."

"Alaska? Why?"

"He got a job as a kayaking guide."

"Sounds right up his alley."

"Yep. Apparently he met this 'cool chick' who was vacationing in San Diego from Alaska. She's a kayak guide up there and told him there were always jobs available for athletic guys like him."

"Ah." Julia offered me a fortune cookie and a smile. "Well, that just proves that you two wouldn't have worked. Jock Chris and Chloe the book geek? Not in a million years."

Guess I'm not the only one in the family who assigns names. Chloe-the-book-geek? Not bad. Pretty accurate actually.

"You're right, Jules. Next time I'm going for a guy who reads."

"Agatha Christie kept me guessing until the very end," Paige said at our October book club meeting. "Each time I thought I knew who the murderer was, she'd drop another clue that made me change my mind."

"I know!" Annette said. "Usually I can solve mysteries halfway through the book, but here I was stumped."

"That's why she's considered the master of mystery," Jenna said, preening a little that her book club selection had gone over so well.

Since *Murder on the Orient Express* had taken place on the world-famous luxury train from Istanbul to Paris, Jenna had wanted to re-create that train-trip adventure by having us all ride the Skunk Train, a historic steam engine up north that chugs through the redwoods. Unfortunately, since Fort Bragg was more than a four-hour drive from Sacramento, it would have required an overnight stay in a hotel, which our Paris-saving budgets couldn't afford.

Jenna had settled on the murder mystery theater instead. On Halloween night, no less. We'd all gone in costume and had a blast. Becca had even been tapped to play one of the interactive roles during the mystery.

Of course.

"*Bonjour Mademoiselle, je voudrais la glace au chocolat, s'il vous plait. Merci.*"

"*Excusez-moi, Madame. Je suis malade. Où est la toilette, s'il vous plait?*"

I felt a tap on my shoulder and turned around from my bedroom desk where I was intent on the task before me.

Becca's mouth moved, but I couldn't hear what she said. I pushed my earphones down around my neck.

"What did you just say?" she repeated.

"'Hello, I'd like chocolate ice cream, please. Thank you.' And, 'Excuse me, I am ill. Where is the restroom, please?'"

"Uh-oh. Did you get ill from the ice cream?" She scrunched her face. "Remind me not to have any while we're in Paris."

"Actually, you're going to want some. There's this amazing ice cream place not too far from Notre Dame with more unusual flavor combinations than Ben and Jerry's." I licked my lips in anticipation. "And you'd better start practicing your French, too, smarty. We'll be there in less than three weeks."

"Only twenty days." Becca plopped down on my bed. "How cool is that?"

"It would be even cooler if you spoke the language a little."

"But I do. Check it out: *Bonjour, Mademoiselle. Parlez-vous anglais?*"

"You need to be able to say more than that."

"Why? They all speak English, don't they?"

"No. Why should they? They live in France."

"Yeah, but English is the universal language."

"Maybe—although I think Spanish may have recently passed it. But either way, don't you think it would be a good idea, since we're going to their country, to learn just a little of their language?"

Careful. Climbing up on your soapbox there.

I leaned back in my chair. "French is such a beautiful language. Like classical music with a hint of jazz."

"Well, aren't you waxing poetic?"

"*Ce n'est rien.* It is nothing."

"You're right. It does sound a little like classical music."

Becca's cell blared—not a classical music ringtone—and she raced to answer it. She returned a few minutes later, a pleased smirk on her face.

"Who was that?"

"Brian."

"Brian who?"

She stretched out on my bed and clasped her hands beneath her head. "Brian Rhodes. He's this customer I met at the store today. We're going out tomorrow night. He's cute *and* smart. He needed my help in finding a philosophy book for his master's class."

"I thought you had a date with Nick tomorrow night." It was difficult to keep up with my roommate's love life. Every month, sometimes every week it seemed, there was a new romance du jour. But Becca always kept things fun and casual. She wasn't interested in serious.

She made a face. "I'm so over Nick."

"I thought you liked him. He seemed really sweet."

"He was. And I did. At first. But after the third date he started getting clingy. I hate clingy."

"I know. Any idea why?"

"Why? Because I don't like guys that follow me around like a puppy dog."

"And that's because … ?"

"Because it's creepy. Stop trying to analyze me, Dr. Phil."

She changed the subject. "I keep forgetting to ask, how'd Sophie's doctor's visit go? Everything okay?"

"Fine, thank goodness!"

It had been a little scary when Julia's baby — Sophie Rose — was born a little early the week before Christmas. She showed signs of an infection, so couldn't go home right away, much to my sister's and Justin's concern and dismay. Actually, we were all concerned. Lots of prayers went up for that little baby. Thankfully, though, the doctors released her with a clean bill of health a few days later, to everyone's collective relief.

Sophie was the best present under our family Christmas tree. My mom had sewn her a soft red velvet dress with hand-embroidered white rosebuds for her first Christmas two days ago and Julia had put her in those white legging thingies that unsnap easily for quick diaper access. My contribution had been a pair of white satin booties trimmed in red.

"Sophie looks great. She's gaining weight, her color's really good, and she got this really big smile on her face when I was reading her *'Twas the Night Before Christmas*. My mom said it was gas, but I know better."

"Is this the same woman who said all babies look alike and they're boring until they can start walking and talking?" Becca teased.

"What can I say? Sophie is an exceptional baby. Very smart. Gorgeous too."

"Spoken like a proud auntie." Becca bounded off the bed. "Well, I'd better go. I'm meeting Jenna at the gym, and on the way I'm going to give Nick the boot."

"Hey," I said before she disappeared. "Promise me one thing."

"What's that?"

"Don't do it in a text message, okay? At least talk to him on the phone."

"No prob. You know me. I've never been one to take the coward's way out."

I practiced my French for another fifteen minutes and then decided to reward myself with a well-deserved snack. I padded down the hall toward the kitchen in my fuzzy red slippers and favorite flannel pants and sweatshirt to get some tea and chocolate chip cookies. Shivering, I punched up the heat on the hall thermostat to dispel the coldness of the wet, drizzly December day.

In the kitchen, the empty cookie package and a smattering of crumbs on the countertop mocked me.

Typical.

Becca was always finishing off food and leaving me to clean up behind her. I decided to have tea and crackers instead. Filling the teakettle with fresh water, I returned it to the stove, turned on the burner, and opened the cupboard to get a mug. But like Old Mother Hubbard, I found the cupboard was bare. I'd asked Becca to run the dishwasher earlier, but of course she'd forgotten.

Again.

Opening the jammed-to-the-hilt dishwasher, I pulled the least dirty mug out, gave it a quick swipe with the soap wand, and rinsed it out. Then I filled the plastic well with detergent, closed the dishwasher door, and hit start.

While I waited for the water to boil, I went in search of my copy of *Les Misérables*. I'd fallen asleep on the couch reading it last night and remembered setting it on the coffee table before I went to bed. But it wasn't there now.

I checked the cushions to see if maybe it had fallen down between them. No luck.

Dropping to my knees, I peeked underneath the couch. Nothing, except one of Becca's missing Birkenstocks, which I pulled out and placed next to the chair she always sprawled in where she'd be sure to see it.

Resuming my search for my wayward book, I checked the dining room.

Nada.

The kettle whistled, and I returned to the kitchen, where I poured a cup of cinnamon tea and grabbed some peanut butter crackers and a napkin. Maybe I'd taken it to my bedroom after all. I checked my nightstand and alongside my bed.

Nothing.

I sipped my tea and munched a cracker, thinking. There was only one other place it could be.

Becca had lost her copy a couple weeks ago and hadn't wanted to shell out money to buy another one, so I'd told her we could share. Only, could she please wait until I was finished before she started? I was down to the last few chapters.

I guess she couldn't wait. Well, neither could I.

I approached Becca's room with fear and trembling. You never knew what you'd find in there. How can I put this gently?

She's a slob.

I've never been a neatnik like my mom and Julia, but compared to Becca, I'm the queen of clean. Yet she paid rent — usually on time — and it was her room, so as long as she kept the door closed when people came over, I figured the state of the room was her business.

Today, though, she'd left her door open. Hoping to find the book on her nightstand just inside the door so I wouldn't have to invade the Becca sanctuary, I stuck my hand inside her room while still standing in the hall and fumbled for the light switch.

The shower scene music from *Psycho* filled my head. Mountains of clothes, and piles of books and papers, sports gear, damp towels, and stray empty water bottles carpeted the disaster-zone floor, obscuring the actual carpet beneath.

Averting my eyes from the havoc Hurricane Becca had wreaked, I glanced at the small wooden bookcase next to her bed that did double duty as a nightstand. One of my Fiesta-ware plates with hard, caked-on spaghetti sauce from dinner three—no, wait, four—nights ago perched precariously on a stack of paperbacks.

Gingerly I lifted the plate, and as I did, the whole stack of books tumbled to the floor out of my reach.

Now I'd have to go in.

Carefully, I stepped over another stack of paperbacks, and as I did, my foot crunched down on an empty soda can trapped beneath a magazine. At least I hoped it was empty.

I picked up the can of Diet Dr Pepper and the fallen stack of books. Unfortunately, *Les Misérables* wasn't in the stack. Sighing, I returned the paperbacks to the clean spot on the top of Becca's dusty bookshelf. I stole a quick glance at the other shelves, but Victor Hugo was nowhere to be found. Not even a Quasimodo.

"Sanctuary!"

No way was I going to venture any farther into the recesses of Becca's room. I already felt like a trespasser. Besides, there was no telling what I'd find. I'd just have to ask her when she got home to please return my book. I switched off the light and headed back down the hall with the empty can on top of the dirty plate.

As I passed by her bathroom, I spotted a familiar book cover on the floor. The very dirty floor.

Becca returned home at midnight to find me sitting on the couch in my robe and pj's sipping another cup of cinnamon tea. "What are you still doing up?" she asked. "Don't you have church in the morning?"

"I was waiting for you." I took a deep breath and tucked my feet underneath me. "We need to talk."

"That sounds ominous. Those are the same words I used on Nick earlier." Becca plopped down in the chair facing me, the corners of her mouth turned up. "Don't tell me you're going to break up with me?"

"No ... but we do need to make some changes around here." I held up my bloated paperback with Cosette's orphaned face on the cover, crumpled and peeling back from the spine. "I found this on your bathroom floor."

"I'm sorry. I dropped it in the tub when I was reading last night, and I was trying to let it dry out." She smiled wryly. "Guess it didn't work. But don't worry—I'll buy you another one at work tomorrow."

"Thanks. I appreciate it."

Becca yawned and stood up. "So we're good now?"

"Not exactly."

She sat back down.

I took another deep breath. I hated confrontation more than just about anything—including camping. But there was no help for it. "Bec, you can't leave dirty plates in the bedroom with dried food on them. We'll get bugs. Or even worse"—I shuddered—"mice."

"What were you doing in my room?"

"Looking for my book, the book that I'd asked you to wait to borrow until I'd finished reading it."

She had the grace to blush.

"I poked my head through the open door to see if it might be on your nightstand, and I saw a stack of paperbacks. But a plate was covering them—a dirty plate with dried-on food. And when I moved it to see if my book might be beneath it, the whole stack of books fell. The only reason I went into your room," I continued, "only two steps, by the way, was to pick up the fallen books and put them back where I'd found them." I smiled to show her I wasn't the enemy and this wasn't a war. "How do you even get to your bed?" I teased. "Do you take a running leap or what?"

"I manage." She looked at me curiously. "But since when did you become Mrs. Clean? You told me you hate cleaning."

"Just because I hate it doesn't mean I don't do it. Besides, there's a difference between messy and dirty. I don't mind stacks of books or piles of paper ... have you looked at my desk lately?" I cut a wry look her way. "But it does bother me to see dirty dishes lying around and grody bathrooms." I got to my feet and motioned for her to follow. "I want to show you something." I strode down the hall, smiling to myself at my little surprise and flung open the hall bathroom door with a flourish.

"Ta-da!"

"What?" She turned confused eyes to mine.

"What do you mean *what*? Look at the bathroom. It's sparkling."

"O-kaaay?"

"Are you telling me you don't see any difference?"

"Am I supposed to?"

"You're kidding. I spent nearly two hours cleaning that bathroom."

"Serious? Why?"

"Because there was hair all over the floor, the trash can was overflowing, the tub had a thick ring of soap scum around it, there was toothpaste spattered all over the sink, and don't even get me started on the toilet." I rubbed my eyes beneath my glasses. "Have you ever heard of cleanser? Or Lysol? A pumice stone, maybe?"

"Like the one I use on my heels?"

"No. Like the one you use to get rid of the nasty ring inside the toilet."

"I don't have time to deal with all that stuff." She puffed out a how-boring-can-you-get sigh. "Besides, it's *my* bathroom. You've got your own to play Suzie Homemaker in."

"It's not just your bathroom. It's the guest bathroom too — the one people use when they stop by. And you may not care if it's dirty, but I do. It's embarrassing."

"Maybe to your überclean mother and sister but not the rest of the world."

I puffed air out my cheeks in a frustrated sigh. "Clearly we have very different ideas of how to live."

"And what's so bad about that? I'm serious," Becca said in earnest. "Differences are what make the world go round."

"I thought that was love."

"Whatever." She flashed her pearly whites. "Besides, ya know you love me. You have to. Isn't that one of the commandments? Love thy roommate?"

"It's love thy neighbor."

"My room's right next to yours. You can't get any more neighborly than that."

I jerked my head to the now-pristine bathroom. "And this is right next to my room, and it really bothers me when you don't keep it clean. Or at least moderately clean." I offered a small smile. "That love-thy-neighbor thing works both ways, you know."

"Okay," she said slowly, "but can we work out some kind of cleaning compromise?" She fidgeted and scuffed her foot. "Honestly? I wouldn't even know where to begin. Maybe that's because my mom never showed me how to do this kind of thing."

Way to tug at the heartstrings.

"Deal, seeing as I learned at the knee of the Queen of Clean. And if you'd ever like some help in your room too — say, before book club comes over next week? — just let me know. I'm all over it."

Part 9

january
French Women Don't Get Fat

19

One can no more prevent the mind from returning to an idea than the sea from returning to a shore.

Les Misérables

Becca took me up on my offer, and for three nights in a row, we did a cleaning blitz when I got off work. The condo hadn't been that clean since right before the wedding that wasn't.

The following week, all the Paperback Girls except Jenna came over so Tess could give us our final Paris prep session.

"I just love your place. Especially the granite countertops and stamped concrete floor," Kailyn said. "And how fun to live downtown." She released a wistful sigh. "I can't wait until I can afford to move out and have my own place."

"You and me both," Annette said.

"Hey!"

"It's not that I don't love you, honey. It's just that your daddy and I are lookin' forward to being empty-nesters so we can dance around the house in our underwear." Annette waggled her eyebrows. "Or even naked if we want."

"Eww!" Kailyn said. "TMI."

"Yeah, Annette." I put my hand over my eyes. "I could have gone my whole life without that visual."

"And have some pity on those of us who don't have dancing partners," Paige said.

Annette turned from the bookshelves where she was checking out our hardback collection to face us. "You could have. Every one of those guys I introduced you to way back when we finished *Emma* were nice, eligible men, but you didn't give them a chance."

"Yes I did," Tess said. "I went out with James a couple times, and you're right, he was very nice."

"You did?" I stared at her. "How come you never told me?"

Annette beamed at my aunt. "Tell *all*."

"Yeah," Paige said. "We want all the juicy details."

"There's really nothing to tell." Tess shrugged her shoulders. "We went out to dinner twice. He's smart and interesting, a nice guy. Good-looking too, but he spent most of the time talking about his dead wife. He's still grieving for her—which I understand." Tess's eyes flickered. "He just wasn't ready to be dating yet."

"But that was months ago," Annette said. "He probably is now. You should call him."

Kailyn agreed. "Smart, nice, interesting, and hot to boot? I'd be all over that."

"He has my number," Tess said. "End of subject. And now if you'll excuse me ..."

"Well it's nice to know that at least someone followed through on my fix-up adventure," Annette said as Tess headed down the hall to the bathroom.

"Actually, Will did call me after our infamous karaoke/

sushi night," I admitted, "but I didn't go out with him. It was still too soon after Chris."

"Yeah," Becca kicked off her Birks and flopped down in her favorite chair. "And I went out with that ballet dude once, but he was way too uptight for me."

"At least he wasn't clingy," I snarked.

Annette threw up her hands. "I give up. You girls are impossible."

"Not me," Paige said. "I'd have gone out with my blind date again, only he never called. Story of my life."

Tess rejoined us and said she liked what we'd done with the bathroom. "Very fresh. What kind of candle is in there? It smelled wonderful."

"Crème brûlée." It took great self-control to refrain from looking triumphantly at Becca. "In honor of Paris."

"Only six more days!" Paige clapped her hands. "Let's get this Paris party started."

Using both hands, I slid the heavy quilt wall hanging to one side so we could watch the travel DVD Tess had brought.

"Ooh!" Annette's eyes glittered in big-screen envy. "My husband would kill for that TV."

"We're taking Super Bowl party rental reservations now," Becca said. "Five hundred bucks, and it's his for the day."

"For that much, y'all better supply the buffalo wings and ranch dressing too."

I popped in the travel DVD, and we oohed and aahed our way through the wonders of Paris, making notes of the sights that were must-sees. The only thing that gave us pause was when the travel host tried steak tartare.

Kailyn shuddered. "No way would I ever eat raw meat."

"You eat sushi all the time."

"That's different. It's not beef. I don't want to get mad cow disease."

"You can get that even when beef is cooked."

"Well, simonella or whatever. You know what I mean. Eating raw beef is just gross."

"For once, you and I are in agreement," Becca said. "And it's salmonella, by the way."

Tess cleared her throat. "Since our date with Paris is just a few days away, I wanted to offer some last-minute tips that will make things easier once we arrive. First off, contrary to the impression that everyone has about the French, they're not rude. They just do things differently than we do—they're a little more formal than we are," she said. "And since we're visiting their country, it seems only appropriate to make an effort to learn a little about their culture and how to act when we're there."

Annette nodded. "Such as always saying *'Bonjour, Madame,'* or *'Bonjour, Monsieur'* anytime you walk into a shop or restaurant. I learned that the hard way when I went there on leave years ago. To the French, it's very rude to walk into a shop and not greet them with a polite *'Bonjour.'*"

"Exactly. And while we're at it," Tess sent an apologetic look to Annette. "It's not 'bone-joor.' The accent goes on the first syllable, but very lightly." She illustrated with a musical lift. "*Boh*-zhur. Also," she continued, "if you at least make an effort to speak their language, you'll find the French quite helpful and accommodating." She handed us all laminated, credit-card-sized lists printed with what she considered the Top Ten phrases to help us get by in Paris:

Hello or good day: *Bonjour*

Please: *S'il vous plaît*

Thank you: *Merci*

Do you speak English?: *Parlez-vous anglais?*

I don't understand: *Je ne comprends pas*

I don't speak French: *Je ne parle pas français*

I'm sorry: *Désolé(e)*

Excuse me (to get one's attention): *Excusez-moi*

Excuse me (to pass): *Pardon*

Good-bye: *Au revoir*

Kailyn scanned her list and frowned. "What about 'how much'?"

"That's my shopaholic daughter."

"Actually, that's a very good question, since I'm assuming you'll all want to buy souvenirs," Tess said. "What you would say is, *'Combien, s'il vous plaît?'* Which translates to 'How much, please?'"

"How do you spell that first word?" Paige asked, her pen poised over her pocket-sized travel journal.

"C-o-m-b-i-e-n."

I scribbled in my travel journal too.

"What about 'I ate too much pâté and I need to find a potty *right now?*'" Becca asked.

Kailyn giggled.

Tess didn't even bat an eye. *"Où sont les toilettes?* Where are the toilets?" She continued with her helpful hints. "Make sure you always have small change on you since many restrooms cost to use." The corners of her mouth curved upward. "And don't be surprised to find unisex bathrooms or men's and women's rooms that share a common lobby."

Kailyn's eyes widened. "Serious? Are we supposed to say *'Bonjour'* in the bathroom?"

It wasn't the bathrooms that concerned me.

I picked at my cuticles. "Tell me again that flying's not a big deal. That people do it all the time. And we're not going to crash into the ocean and be shark food."

"Flying's not a big deal," Paige said. "People do it all the time."

"And we're not going to crash in the ocean," Annette added.

"You just need to do what my girlfriend Cameron does whenever she flies," Kailyn said.

"What's that?"

"Take a Valium."

"Better living through chemistry." Becca grinned.

"Chloe?" Tess sent me a gentle look filled with love. "Who's in charge of your life? Remember, 'not a single sparrow can fall to the ground without your father knowing it. And the very hairs on your head are all numbered.'"

I did know that. But what if my number was up?

The next morning, since it was once again my week to bring treats to Sunday school, I dropped by the grocery store on the way to church to pick up some bagels and cream cheese along with a few muffins and doughnuts.

Including one with chocolate sprinkles.

When I entered the empty Sunday school room, my arms full of goodies, Ryan was there, measuring out coffee into the coffee urn.

"*Bonjour*, Ryan. *Comment allez-vous?*"

"Don't rub it in, brat."

I gave him an innocent look as I set down my purse. "What do you mean?"

"What do I mean?" He mimicked me. "While some people are cruising around Paris having the time of their lives, the rest of us will be slaving in the salt mines."

I gave him the Gallic shrug I'd seen in so many French films. "*Désolée. C'est la vie.*"

He put the lid on the coffee pot and hit the on button. "I don't suppose there's room on this Paperback Girls trip for a paperback boy, is there?"

"Sorry. Girls only."

"I could go along as your luggage carrier." He threw me a hopeful look.

"No need. I'm only taking one small rollaway suitcase." I began arranging the pastries on a platter. "But thanks for the generous offer."

"Official food taster? You never know what you're going to get in those fancy French restaurants. Snails, fish heads, liver, tongue, even eyeballs. My taste buds and cast-iron stomach would be willing to run the *Fear Factor* gauntlet for your sensitive little stomach."

"No thanks. And my stomach's not sensitive. Have you forgotten who was the last person standing at the salsa bar challenge, Mr. Whoa-there's-a-lot-of-jalapeños-in-this?"

"You got me there. But I have only one word for you." He fixed me with a steady gaze. "Sushi."

"Sushi's the last thing I'll be eating in Paris. I'm thinking more coq au vin, cassoulet, and crème brûlée. And chocolate éclairs, of course."

Ryan shook his head sadly. "Oh well. Maybe someday before I'm old and gray I'll get the chance to visit the most beautiful city in the world."

"So what's stopping you? Haven't you ever heard of carpe diem? Seize the day, my friend. Seize the day."

"Chloe?" He cupped his ears and drew his eyebrows together in a puzzled line. "The woman before me looks like my friend, but she doesn't sound like her. Those words would never pass her practical lips."

I lobbed a packet of cream cheese at him and missed.

He dropped his hands from his ears. "It *is* Chloe. You still throw like a girl."

"You wouldn't want me to change everything, would you?"

"Not at all. Then you wouldn't be the Chloe we all know and love." Ryan's eyes flickered, and for a second I thought I saw a glimpse of—I don't know—something. But he bent down and scooped up the packet of cream cheese from the floor, holding it with both hands like a basketball and arced it into the trash can.

"Score! Two points, thank you very much." He wiped his hands on his pants. "I hope you have a great time. Take lots of pictures and climb to the top of the Eiffel Tower for me, okay?"

"Deal." We shook on it.

The Sunday school class began drifting in and Ryan released my hand, but not before leaning over and whispering, "And watch out for those French guys. Don't be taken in by their smooth ways and romantic accents."

Who knew so many people in my life wanted to go to Paris?

That afternoon when I stopped by my parents' house to give Mom the extra key to my apartment so she could water my plants in our absence, she yielded a wistful look. "I've always wanted to go to Paris," she said. "Ever since I saw Leslie Caron dance with Gene Kelly in that white skirt on the banks of the river." She released a dreamy sigh. "And then when *Phantom of the Opera* came out, oh my! That opera house was so beautiful. I wonder if it's really like that in real life. Are you and Tess planning to go there?"

"I'm not sure. Maybe." I slid her a tentative glance. "I never knew you wanted to go to Paris." I was beginning to get the feeling that there were a lot of things about my mother I didn't know. I hesitated, knowing it was way too last-minute. "Would you like to come with us?"

"Oh goodness, no, honey. This is a group trip with your book club and I'm not a part of that. You know I'm not much of a reader. Besides, I can't leave Julia. She's still a little uncertain with Sophie." She beamed her proud grandma smile. "Isn't she the most beautiful baby you've ever seen? She's getting so big!"

Tess had advised us to travel light for our weeklong trip and to take only one carry-on piece of luggage and a backpack or oversized purse, so we wouldn't have to spend so much time at baggage claim and customs. So to prepare, Becca and I decided we should do a practice run first to see what would fit in our limited luggage.

Becca threw all her clothes into her suitcase and zipped up the bulging bag in less than ten minutes. *"Voilà!"*

I continued to fold each shirt, skirt, and pair of pants neatly into thirds lengthwise, and then rolled each item into a tight jelly roll and carefully tucked it into my suitcase, while my roommate watched, bemused. "Ah, the ever orderly Chloe."

"In an old house in Paris that was covered with vines, lived twelve little girls in two straight lines," I recited.

She looked at me blankly.

"Gotcha!" I smirked. "You don't recognize *Madeline?*"

"Is that anything like *Eloise?*"

I straightened the folders on my desk, having already handed off my pending projects to my coworker Todd, set up my email to out-of-office automatic reply, and logged off my computer.

Then I headed down to the break room to retrieve my lunch tote from the fridge.

As I approached the break area, I could hear the familiar drone of the gossip girls.

"Can you believe Janelle?" Betty Jo was saying. "Where does she get off telling me what to do?"

"She thinks she's so—" Michelle broke off as I entered.

Carol offered a plastic smile over her strawberry yogurt.

"Bonjour," I said to the snarky trio as I walked over to the fridge and removed my plaid lunch tote. "Please, don't let me interrupt. I'm just off to Paris for a week with a friend." I gave a little wave. *"Au revoir."*

The buzz began before I'd even left the room.

20

All around us are people, of all classes, of all nationalities, of all ages.

Murder on the Orient Express

I clenched the armrest, squeezed my eyes shut tight, and tried to focus on Rosemary Clooney in my ear buds in an effort to drown out the high-pitched whine and roar of the engines as the plane hurtled down the runway.

And then we were off. Up, up, and away. My doctor-prescribed Valium kicked in, and I was able to look out the window at the patchwork fields below without losing my cookies.

I thought back to a year ago at this time when Becca first suggested we step out of our comfort zones and start to live out some of the adventures in the books we read. Who'd have imagined we'd have come so far? Except Becca. Although she had her faults—which I saw up close and personal living with her, and they sometimes drove me crazy—I had to give her credit. Thanks to her, we were on our way to Paris. I hit my

French music playlist, leaned back, and lost myself in "La Vie en Rose."

"No wonder French women don't get fat," Annette said as our motley crew huffed and puffed our way through the long, dark Paris Metro tunnels. "It's all these miles of walking they have to do."

"I'll say," Kailyn grumbled as she adjusted her shoulder bags. "I'll take my Civic any day."

"*C'est fou ça!*" Tess said. "I told you not to pack more than you could carry."

With a travel agent as an aunt, I'd learned to pack light early in life. Backpacker Becca too.

Annette and Kailyn? Not so much.

Kailyn was laden with a massive rolling pink suitcase, a hanging clothes bag over each shoulder, a heavy-duty makeup case, and, of course, her latest designer purse. For just a week.

Annette was a mirror image of her daughter, minus one shoulder bag.

We took pity on the overloaded duo and relieved them of their hanging bags — distributing them among the rest of us. Guess I should have taken Ryan up on his luggage bearer offer after all.

As we rounded a bend in the underground tunnel, civilization appeared in the form of a multitude of carts, stands, and shops offering myriad tantalizing treasures calculated to inspire lust in every die-hard shopaholic's heart.

Kailyn moved as if in a trance to a cart full of leather handbags. "Ooh, check out all the fab purses! I have to get one."

"We didn't come to Paris to shop," Paige reminded her. "We came to cook."

"Maybe you did, but I'm not going to be in the fashion capital of the world and not stop to buy something."

"Right now you are," Becca said. "You'll have plenty of time to shop later. Keep moving so we can get to the hotel and dump all this stuff and start exploring."

Kailyn wrenched herself away from the purse stand with a heavy sigh and yanked her mega suitcase behind her.

"*Mon dieu!*" a trim, well-dressed, thirty-something woman said as the heavy case banged into her ankle. She let loose a stream of what I can only imagine were invectives in French.

"Oh, *pardonnez-moi.*" Kailyn's face flushed crimson. "I'm so sorry."

The woman fixed her with an icy stare before click-clacking away in her black high-heeled boots onto the Metro.

"Way to get off on the wrong stiletto," Becca said.

Tess led the way into the Metro car, the rest of us piling in behind her, tossing out *pardon*s left and right as we lugged our mountain of baggage through the packed car. Annette managed to snag the last remaining empty seat—but the rest of us had to stand in the crowded car, holding on to metal poles for balance.

From my standing vantage point I noticed that the annoyed madame whom Kailyn clipped with her suitcase wasn't the only well-dressed French woman on the Metro. Everywhere I looked, the women were well put together. Not one sweatsuit or California casual in the bunch. And since French women are known for being fashion icons, I studied them discreetly to see what it was they had that we didn't.

The answer was scarves.

Nearly every woman, from the black-blazered, twenty-something professionals to the elegant grandmamas with their translucent crepe-paper skin, seemed to be wearing a scarf knotted casually at the throat. I determined then and there to go home with at least three.

Shoes were the other thing that set the Parisian women apart.

As I stole a covert glance at their French feet, a sea of black and brown footwear in every height — from narrow, flat-soled walking shoes to spiky stilettos — filled my vision. And not one French woman was wearing the wide, comfortable white tennis shoes that are de rigueur for every soccer mom, jogger, and middle-aged woman in the U.S. The few glimpses I caught of white tennis shoes clearly belonged to American tourists.

Annette noticed too. She tucked her glaring white Pumas that seemed to be emitting an otherworldly glow discreetly behind her big rolling suitcase. Then she leaned over and whispered to Kailyn. "Tomorrow, we're going shoe shopping."

Grateful that I'd worn my favorite low-heeled black leather boots, I uttered a prayer of thanks that I'd been able to talk Becca into wearing her black clogs rather than her bright red Birks on the plane.

When we disembarked and struggled to street level again, Annette wheeled her largest suitcase off to the side, away from the roiling crowds spilling out from the Trocadéro stop, and sat down on it. "Can y'all give me a minute to catch my breath?"

The rest of us set our luggage down, and I massaged the palms of my hands to relieve the suitcase handle burn.

"Are we almost there?"

"Pretty close," Tess said. "Just a few blocks and we'll be at the hotel."

"A few *blocks*?"

A gust of wind sliced through us.

"I'm cold," Kailyn whined. "And thirsty. And it looks like it's going to rain any minute, and I don't know which suitcase my umbrella is in."

Becca leaned over and whispered in my ear, "Do you know

if the French believe in capital punishment? Because I think I'm about to kill somebody."

"Okay, girls, chop chop." Tess picked up her luggage. "Let's get moving."

Becca and I followed close behind Tess, while Paige, Annette, and Kailyn brought up the rear. We walked past a few buildings, turned the corner, and then stopped dead in the middle of the sidewalk.

Even Kailyn became uncharacteristically silent as six American girls stood utterly still in quiet reverie at their first sight of the Eiffel Tower looming above the city, dark against the glow of a pale gray sky.

It looked almost close enough to touch.

"There it is!" Paige's mouth hung open. "We're actually here. In *Paris*! Can you believe it?" Becca gaped, at a loss for words. First time since I'd known her.

I felt the same way. I'd seen the Eiffel Tower a million times in a million pictures. So why did I feel as if I was going to burst into tears any second? It's just a building. Not even a building. A structure. Of iron, no less. I'd never seen anything like it.

"Magical, isn't it?" Tess said.

"I always thought the Golden Gate Bridge was the most gorgeous man-made structure I'd ever seen," I whispered. "Until now."

"This is why we didn't take a taxi. I figured a few sore arms and backs would be worth it."

"Oh yes," I breathed, unable to tear my eyes away, even as a continuous stream of people walked up and down the sidewalk around me.

"Just wait until you see her at night all lit up like a Christmas tree." Tess kissed her fingers.

She was even more magnificent up close and personal.

We trundled our bags over a stone bridge traversing the Seine as we approached the beautiful iron madame. That's what she was to me—an elegant, ageless woman with a lacy web of crisscrossing lines on her face and a backbone of iron.

Becca whistled. "Look how huge it is."

"Amazing."

"I didn't know it was brown, though." Kailyn scrunched her eyes at Paige. "Did you?"

"Uh-uh. I always thought it was black. That's what it looked like in every movie I've ever seen."

"Well, you do watch a lot of black-and-white movies," Tess remarked dryly.

"I thought it was black too." I stared upward at the brownish-bronze tower, still entranced by the iconic sight.

"Well, black or brown, I can see why so many couples come here for their honeymoon and why so many guys propose here too." Kailyn sighed. *C'est très romantique!"*

Annette's face lit up. "I might try and get your daddy to bring me here for our thirtieth wedding anniversary."

"Only if I can come too."

"Now *that* would be really romantic."

"Romantic-shmomantic." Becca stuck out her tongue. "This is a girls' adventure, remember? And I vote we start our Paris adventure by going all the way up to the top of the tower."

"We will, but later." Tess pushed her rumpled hair off her forehead and eyed our bedraggled appearance. "We look like a group of refugees. Let's get to the hotel ASAP."

We picked up our bags again and followed Tess. A few minutes later, though, she stopped, frowned, and pulled out her pop-up Paris map.

"Oh no," Kailyn wailed. "Don't. Don't tell me we're lost."

"We can't be lost, baby girl," Annette soothed. "The Eiffel Tower is right behind us."

Tess looked at her map, then back in the direction of the Tower. She turned her map a couple times. "Aha. Not lost, just taking a long cut. Sometimes you take a short cut, sometimes you take a long cut. Back at the edge of the park there were three streets that came together. We simply took the wrong spoke."

If looks could kill, my favorite aunt would have been dead five times over.

"So how many more blocks to the hotel?" I shivered as another gust of wind cut through me.

"Looks like about four."

"I knew we should have taken a taxi," Kailyn said.

"This is all part of the adventure. You'll laugh about it when we get home."

"Is that before or after we starve to death?" Becca sent Tess a dark look.

"Personally, I can think of worse things than to be lost in Paris." I gazed at the elegant creamy buildings all around us. I'd thought watching the travelogues and all the movies set here would have prepared me for Paris. I was wrong. Nothing compares to the real thing. It was so much more than I ever imagined. "Just look at all this gorgeous architecture."

"*You* look at it," Kailyn grumped. "I'd rather take a nap."

"No sleeping allowed," Tess advised. "At least until we've had some lunch and done a little sightseeing. What we're doing now—walking around outside—is the best thing for jet lag."

"Tell that to my bunions." Annette rubbed her foot.

"If Jenna were here, she'd say no pain, no gain." Paige picked up her bags. "So in honor of our absent member, I vote we get moving."

After checking into our small, *charmant* hotel with a green awning and a reserved, albeit polite concierge (who revealed his name was Arnaud after prodding from a flirtatious Kailyn), we agreed to meet back in the lobby in ten minutes to begin sightseeing. Becca and Paige disappeared through the dining room to the back of the hotel where they were sharing a room on the ground floor. And Arnaud the chivalrous helped Kailyn and Annette load their mountain of bags into the narrow elevator that would take them to their fourth floor room.

Tess and I started to follow.

"Alors, I am sorry," Arnaud said, "but I am afraid the *ascenseur*—elevator—is *petit*. If you wait, I will send it back down for you."

"Petite is right." I sucked in my stomach when Tess and I squeezed into the narrow, claustrophobic space a couple minutes later. Thankfully, when we exited the *ascenseur*, our room faced us. Tess turned the key in the lock and opened the door.

An explosion of red toile met our eyes. Toile wallpaper, toile curtains, toile lampshades, even a toile bedspread.

On the lone bed. A double.

"Uh, didn't we ask for twin beds?"

She frowned. "Yes." She dropped her purse on the pastoral bedspread and picked up the phone. "I wonder what happened. Let me call down to the front desk."

While Tess talked to the concierge in rapid-fire French, I took the opportunity to use the bathroom/water closet. This, like the elevator was also petit. But sparkling clean, I was thrilled to see, with a full bathtub and shower.

A casement window in the shower wall opened onto the street, beckoning me. As I approached, I realized I could see into the apartment building directly opposite—where a man, whose back was to me, was getting dressed.

I shut the window and backed away quickly, then took advantage of the facilities.

Looking around for the handle to flush, I couldn't find one in the usual places. I glanced at the floor to see if maybe there was a button on the ground to press with my foot. Nothing.

I noticed a framed pen and ink sketch of a nude hanging above the toilet. Only in Paris. Beneath the tasteful sketch of the naked woman (that didn't really show anything other than her back and some discreet curves), two white plastic spheres were affixed to the wall—one large, one small.

Cautiously, I pressed the larger of the two spheres.

Whoosh.

I washed my hands and dried them on my jeans, not wanting to dirty the towel for the next guests since I knew we'd soon be vacating the room once Tess had straightened out the single-bed mix-up.

I returned to the room of toile. *A girl could get lost in all that toile.* "Hey, what's the deal with these two different circles above the toilet?"

"One's for large loads, the other, for small. Water conservation, you know."

Well all righty then.

I picked up my purse and suitcase and opened the door. "So, what's our new room number?"

"603."

I looked from Tess to the number on the door. "But this is 603."

"*Oui, oui.*" She walked over to the window. "Although I made our reservations ages ago, a couple days before we left, it occurred to me that we might like a room with a view instead, so I emailed them with the upgrade and, *voilà!*" Tess pulled open the toile drapes with a flourish.

Over the rooftops at a kitty-corner angle, I could see the entire top half of the Eiffel Tower.

I gasped.

"The only room with a view was a double. Not the choice I'd intended, but just look at that sight! Isn't that worth a little coziness?"

"Well …" I plopped down on the far side of the bed with its busy pastoral scenes in red and white. With my head on the toile pillow, I looked out the window again.

The glorious Tower filled my eyes.

"If you don't like this, the concierge said there was one with two twins left on the second floor that looks out at the alleyway."

"I think I can manage if you can."

"*Bon.*" Tess released a pleased smile and pushed open the bathroom door. "And now my turn."

I quickly unpacked and peeled off the green turtleneck I'd been wearing since yesterday morning, exchanging it for a fresh black pullover. I brushed my hair and pulled it back into a black hair tie just as Tess opened the bathroom door.

"Good idea." Tess glanced at my top and exchanged her red sweater for a white button-down blouse and brick red leather blazer. "You ready to go explore the most beautiful city in the world?"

"Duh. Or should I say ooh-la-la?"

"Mmm. This has got to be what heaven will smell like." Paige sniffed appreciatively as we entered the creperie.

It had been a little tricky deciding what to do for lunch — getting six women to agree on something is like getting Dr. Laura to agree with Howard Stern. Paige, Kailyn, and Annette — now sporting brown leather loafers — wanted to dine at a sidewalk café, while Becca and I longed to just grab something from the small pâtisserie around the corner so we could begin exploring the city.

Tess cast the deciding vote. "First rule of thumb: Never grab and eat. Although McDonald's has made it to Paris—unfortunately—the French abhor the whole concept of fast food. When they eat, it's usually a two- or three-hour affair."

"Three *hours?*" Becca wailed. "That's valuable sightseeing time wasted!"

"Good food and good conversation is never a waste. However, for our first day, I know we're all eager to explore my favorite city in the world, so we'll compromise." Tess looked at her watch. "There's a little creperie nearby that serves amazing crepes, and we can probably be in and out in under an hour."

Hesitant to try anything too exotic for my first meal in France—there'd be plenty of time for that later—I ordered a basic and incredibly delicious crepe with ham and gruyere cheese.

"Mmm, that was divine," Paige said, after swallowing the last bite of her smoked salmon with crème fraîche and lemon crepe.

"Told you you'd like it." Tess finished off her chicken crepe and murmured something in French to the passing waiter.

"What'd you say?" I downed the rest of my Evian. "I couldn't quite make it out."

"You'll see. It's a surprise."

Moments later, the waiter returned with three more crepes, which he set down in front of Tess. "*Bon appetite*, Madame."

Becca cut her eyes at Tess. "For a little person, you sure eat a lot."

"This is dessert, and it's for all of us." Tess cut each crepe in half and transferred the portions onto our plates. "You haven't lived until you've tried Nutella."

"Nutella?" I eyed my half warily.

"Chocolate hazelnut spread."

"Well, why didn't you say so?" Annette speared a piece with her fork. "I haven't met a chocolate yet that I didn't like." She popped the bite into her mouth and moaned.

Pretty soon our whole table was moaning in chocoholic rapture.

"Keep it down," Tess hissed. "You sound like Meg Ryan in *When Harry Met Sally.*"

I giggled. Then Kailyn and her mother. And then Paige. In seconds we had all dissolved into fits of laughter.

Must have been the jet lag.

"I can't understand what they're saying." Becca stabbed at the buttons on her armrest that controlled her headset as the tour bus pulled away from the Eiffel Tower.

"Me either." Annette crossed her eyes. "It's all Greek to me."

"Mine's Japanese." I held up my headphones, stuck out my lower lip, and adopted my best baby voice. "Waaah. Fix it, Aunt Tess. It's broken."

"Whoa," Becca said. "For a minute there, I thought maybe Kailyn had a twin."

I stuck my tongue out at my roommate as Tess moved from seat to seat on the upper level of the double-decker, open-air bus, setting the audio guide to English. At last we were on our way, checking out the most romantic city in the world.

Well, not that romantic when you're with a bunch of women. But who cares?

I was in Paris!

21

When a man understands the art of seeing, he can trace the spirit of an age and the features of a king even in the knocker on a door.

The Hunchback of Notre Dame

I hunched into my black pea coat and wrapped my arms around my middle to ward off the damp January air.

"We could sit down below if you're too cold," Tess suggested.

"No way. I don't want to miss a thing. What's a little cold when you're in the most beautiful city in the world?" The wind whipped my hair around my face as I gazed all around.

The elegant architecture with all its ornate detail and carvings was a far cry from all the bland California stucco I was accustomed to. Most of the stately stone buildings we passed were white and creamy. Like vanilla ice cream. Or whipped butter.

Annette huddled closer to Kailyn. "I read somewhere that

most European cities are considered masculine, but what sets Paris apart is that she's a woman."

We passed by yet another graceful and elegant whipped butter building.

"Oh no," I said. "Paris isn't a woman — Paris is a lady."

"Couldn't have put it better myself." Tess inclined her head to a gold-domed building. "Would anyone care to pay their respects to someone who was the farthest thing from a lady? Want to visit Napoleon's Tomb?"

"Why would we want to see where some old dead guy is buried?"

"Oh, I don't know," Annette answered. "Maybe because Napoleon was one of the greatest military leaders in history?"

"And one of the most egotistical," Becca said. "I'll pass."

"Me too. Sorry, Tess. Not really my thing."

"Mine either," Paige confessed.

"That's okay. We middle-aged menopausal types will come back later and check it out. Okay, Annette?"

"You got it."

"Hey!" Kailyn pointed off to the right as the bus turned the corner. "That looks like *The Thinker* between those shrubs over there."

"You're right." Annette waggled her eyebrows, Groucho Marx — like. "I'd recognize that butt anywhere."

"If you were listening to your audio guide instead of yakking, you'd know that's the Musée Rodin," Tess said. "And I don't know about you, but that's a must-see for me. Maybe tomorrow, along with the Louvre, or the Musée d'Orsay."

"Sounds good." I glanced around the group. "That's a definite for everyone, right?"

"As long as I get time to shop," Kailyn said.

Becca rolled her eyes and then turned to Tess. "Are you seriously planning to do two museums in one day?"

"*Mais oui.*"

"Not sure if I can hang with that or not."

"Sure you can." I patted her arm. "It's part of the adventure. We've only got seven days to see some of the most amazing art in the world, and some of those days will be tied up with cooking. So we'll need to double up on museums."

"Okay, but I reserve the right to bail if I get bored."

"Bored? In Paris?" Tess clasped her hand to her heart. "*C'est impossible.*"

"Ooh, speaking of art, check out that bridge with stone pillars and the gold-winged horses at the top." Paige pointed.

"That's the Pont Alexandre III. Most people consider it the most beautiful bridge in Paris."

"They got that right." Annette released a low whistle.

Everything was beautiful in Paris. I could hardly take it all in.

None of us could. We were like hungry kids with our faces pressed to the window of a candy store.

"Look at that building!"

"And that one."

"This one's really cool."

Just then the little tour guide voice in my ear said we were turning onto the Champs-Elysées. Becca and I swiveled our heads around to catch sight of the celebrated Arc de Triomphe at the far end of the world-renowned boulevard. "Ah. 'There is no limit to Paris,'" she said.

"Huh?"

"Victor Hugo, *Les Misérables.*"

"Of course. What was I thinking? But wait, we're going away from the Arc."

"We'll catch it all on the way back, don't worry," Tess assured me.

A tour bus crept by, then another, passing within inches of

my elbow propped on the rail. I yanked my arm inside. As we entered the Place de la Concorde, the traffic grew congested and chaotic with tour buses, taxis, and cars weaving crazily around each other.

"I'm sure glad I'm not driving," Annette said.

Kailyn flashed her perfect white teeth. "Aren't we all?" She leaned forward in her seat. "Hey, check out the killer fountain! That's the one we saw in *The Devil Wears Prada*. Remember? Love it!"

We all lapped up the sight of the graceful green-and-gold fountain arcing water.

Tess pointed out the Egyptian obelisk nearby and told us that during the French Revolution that's where the guillotine was set up — the guillotine where Marie Antoinette, Louis XVI, and so many others were beheaded in what was known as the Reign of Terror.

Kailyn loosened the scarf around her neck.

"She should never have said 'Let them eat cake.'"

Paige tossed a stick of gum at Becca.

A taxi honked its horn and whizzed by as our bus continued its route. Annette yawned and covered her mouth. "Sorry. I think the jet lag's startin' to catch up to me. Do you want to go back to the hotel and catch a nap before dinner?"

"No!" we all chorused.

"Guess I'm outvoted," Annette said dryly. "I can always get a nap later."

"That's the spirit, Mom. I knew you could hang."

"I'm not so sure *I* can." Paige slouched in her seat and released a yawn.

"Stop it right now." I shook my finger at her and adopted a threatening tone. "You're going to create a yawn domino effect."

"Here's a little something that might wake you up," Tess

said as the bus drove through an archway in the middle of a building. Beyond the archway was a ring of buildings surrounding a huge courtyard. "Musée de Louvre."

"That's the Louvre?" Becca gaped. "It's huge."

Paige sat up straight. "To hold over 300,000 pieces of art, it has to be."

"When I came here over thirty years ago, my favorite pieces—aside from *Winged Victory*—were all the Impressionists," Annette said. "But they're not here anymore."

"How come?" Becca asked.

"Because in the eighties, the Musée d'Orsay was opened, and the entire Impressionist collection moved there," Tess explained. "Don't worry, Annette. You'll see your Impressionists again. And I think you'll like their new setting even more."

"What's up with the glass pyramid thingie?" Kailyn pointed. "It doesn't look like it belongs with all the old buildings."

Tess gave a wry smile. "There are many Parisians who'd agree with you. It was quite the controversy when it was built a couple decades ago."

"Actually, I like the pyramid," I said. "Since it's glass, it doesn't block the stone buildings, and actually draws the eye in even more."

For once, a merger between the old and the new worked.

"Oh my!"

"What?" Tess shot me a look of concern. "Are you okay?"

"Notre Dame," I breathed. "We have to get out here." I shot from my seat as the bus made one of its frequent stops so the tourists could hop on and off. No way could I remain sitting. Not when the world's most famous cathedral that I'd read about in Victor Hugo's *Hunchback* was right there in front of me.

I grabbed my backpack and sprinted for the stairs.

"Hang on. Wait for us."

"Oomph." Becca ran into me on the sidewalk in front of the bus where I was standing, staring. "What are you waiting for? Come on."

"Just a sec. I want to drink it all in. We're here." I closed my eyes. "We're really here."

"Well, almost, anyway." Annette nudged me. "Let's get closer."

"It's so huge," Kailyn said as we crossed the street to the courtyard.

"Much bigger than it looks in the movies." Paige's mouth hung open. "Look. Those people are dwarfed by the doorways."

"And the archway doors are only the bottom third of the building," Tess informed us.

"There's something in front of that round stained glass window." Kailyn pointed. "What is that?"

"Statues of the Virgin Mary," Tess said. "Notre Dame means 'Our Lady.' "

"And then there are the bell towers," Becca's voice said behind me.

Paige began laughing.

"What's so funny?" I asked as we all turned around.

My roommate had wadded her scarf into a ball and shoved it underneath her jacket, high up on one shoulder. "Sanctuary!" Becca said, a little too loudly as she started limping, or rather, waddling, across the courtyard toward the cathedral steps.

Tess sighed. "You can dress her up, but you can't take her out."

As we walked through the massive doors into Notre Dame, a small group of people in front of us stopped to make the sign of the cross.

They might be pilgrims, visitors coming to visit this holy place. Annette and Kailyn made the sign of the cross too. More pilgrims.

We moved to the middle part of the dark, massive church—the nave, as Tess called it. It was strangely empty. All the windows were magnificent stained glass, but the arched panels couldn't match the round "rose" windows. The light filtering in through the stained glass onto the slab floor created a dappled, otherwordly feeling.

Even Becca was visibly moved.

"Let's just sit here for a few minutes," Annette whispered.

"Okay, but not too long," Tess cautioned. "It will make it difficult to get our jet-lagged selves back up again."

After lingering a little longer in the sanctuary, we met up outside the cathedral. Tess led us around to a charming tree-lined park with several benches and a great view of the back side of the cathedral.

"Perfect." Annette plopped down on a bench.

"Perfectly cold." Kailyn shivered. "I'm ready for a coffee, but I need to rest first."

"Ditto." I slouched between Paige and Annette.

Even though we were cold, it was wonderful to sit and people watch. And what a backdrop. In contrast to the tall rectangular front of Notre Dame, the back was all curves and angles—the tall steeple, the round roof, and all of the arches.

"Great view of the flying buttresses," Tess said.

"Where?" Kailyn scanned the sky. "I've always wanted to see a flying buttress."

"Pardon?" Paige asked.

"I heard about them in a Disney movie and hoped we'd get to see one."

"There they are." Tess pointed. "Buttresses are supports that hold up the walls."

"Oh." Kailyn blushed. "I always thought they were like bats or something."

"Don't feel bad," Annette said. "I thought we were going to see some nice Parisian butts flyin' through the air."

Back on the bus again after our *petit cafés*, Paris was a blur. As much as I wanted to pay attention, jet lag was winning the battle.

For all of us.

We walked back to our hotel after the bus dropped us off at the Eiffel Tower in the early evening and agreed to freshen up and change for dinner. Once we got to the hotel lobby, though, Annette and Kailyn could barely keep their eyes open.

Annette yawned. "I may just skip dinner and go straight to bed."

"You can't miss dinner out your first night in Paris!" Foodie Paige licked her lips. "This is what I've been waiting for."

"Well, if we leave right now," Annette said, "I can probably keep my eyes open for another half hour. Tops."

"Me too." Kailyn stifled a yawn.

I checked my watch, which I'd set to Paris time when our airplane landed. It was a few minutes after five. Behind me, I could hear Arnaud informing Becca that most restaurants didn't start serving dinner until seven.

"Two more hours? I'll be fast asleep by then. Sorry, girls." Annette punched the elevator button. "I'm way too exhausted to eat, anyway." She sent us a tired smile. "See, that French diet's already startin' to work."

The door opened, and Annette and Kailyn stumbled wearily into the narrow space.

I was strongly tempted to follow their lead, but my grumbling stomach and the rest of the group wouldn't let me.

Two hours later, Paige and I were splitting an order of

to-die-for escargot at a small—as in only four tables—restaurant called Chez Michèle two doors down from the hotel. I could tell Becca was about to break into her "I don't know how you can eat snails" tirade, so I kicked her under the table.

Almost gently.

Our chef, Michèle, who also acted as our server, and probably the dishwasher too, didn't speak any English, but Tess conversed with her freely in French.

And Paige and I practiced our few phrases.

"*J'adore escargot,*" I said.

"*Merci, et* blah, blah, blah ..." Michèle responded in a rapid torrent of French.

I shot a helpless look at Tess.

"She said thank you and asked what you would like for dinner," Tess translated.

Since Chez Michèle was a one-woman restaurant, she offered only two choices of *plat du jour*—the special of the day. Today's specials were *poulet* with vegetables and rice and *gigot d'agneau.*

Tess and Becca went for the chicken while Paige and I opted for the lamb.

I closed my eyes in rapture at the first bite. This was not my mother's Easter lamb with mint jelly.

Paige bit into her l'agneau and visibly swooned. "Oh my. How did she do that?" She sent an admiring look at our chef. "It just melts in my mouth. The rosemary really adds to it." She raised another bite to her mouth. "Poor Jenna, missing this. We need to send her postcards."

"Yeah, like that will cheer her up." Becca, who was pretty much inhaling her chicken, took a sip of wine. "Having a wonderful time. Wish you were here. Sorry you're stuck at home with all your sprouts and tofu while we're eating like Marie Antoinette." She dug greedily into her chicken again. "Of course when we all come home fat as pigs, Ms. Aerobics Queen will have the last laugh."

"We won't go home fat," Tess said. "We'll walk off everything we eat."

"Let's start tonight by walking up to the top of the Eiffel Tower!"

"First of all, you can't walk all the way to the top—only to stage two," Tess explained. "And secondly, the only walking I'm doing after this is back to the hotel, into the elevator, and then to my room, where I'm going to collapse on the bed." She opened her purse. "Besides, we need to wait for Kailyn and Annette to go up the tower."

"We can go back with them again tomorrow night. *Please?*" Becca wheedled. "I really wanted to end my first night in Paris on top of the Eiffel Tower."

"I'd never make it." Tess's eyes drooped. "I'm ready to fall asleep right now."

"Me too," Paige agreed. "Sorry, Becca."

Becca's face fell.

"I'll go with you," I heard myself offer.

Was that really *my* mouth those words came out of? What was I thinking—walking around at night in a strange city alone with Becca the wild and irresponsible, whose grasp on the French language is even more tenuous than mine?

"Serious?" Becca jumped out of her seat, her eyes snapping with excitement. "Well then, let's blow this popsicle stand."

"Tess, Paige, you're sure you don't mind?" I pulled out my wallet. "We'll definitely go again tomorrow night with the whole group."

"I'll hold you to that." Tess collected our Euros and paid our chef/waitress/dishwasher. "*Merci beaucoup, Madame. C'était très magnifique!*"

"*Merci, Madame.*" Paige kissed her foodie fingers. "*Très bien.*"

Chef Michèle smiled and said a bunch more words in French.

"*Merci,*" I began in my halting French. "*L'agneau c'est incroyable.*"

Becca patted her stomach. "*Merci. C'est* really good. Ooh-la-la." She tugged on my hand. "Come on, La Tour Eiffel is waiting for us."

"*Un moment,*" Tess said, looking at her watch as she led us out the door.

We stood in front of the restaurant, exchanging uncertain looks.

"Okay, now look up."

We gasped in unison.

The Eiffel Tower was lit up like a Christmas tree against the night sky. And not only lit up, but putting on a glorious light show for us, sparkling like diamonds.

Or thousands of shooting stars.

Inarticulate sounds came out of my throat. Not words, exactly. There were no words. In that moment, I fell. Hard.

"It's like the Fourth of July," Becca said.

"Better," I breathed, staring at what was no longer a famous monument made of metal and iron, but *my* tower. My beautiful tower.

"How long does this last?" Paige asked.

"For ten minutes. Every night, every hour until midnight. Twenty-thousand lights."

"Sweet!" Becca urged me forward. "Hurry so we can see it up close and personal."

"*Bonne nuit,*" Tess called after us.

Twenty minutes later we were atop my tower looking out over the lights of Paris.

Me.

On top of the Eiffel Tower.

Looking at the lights of Paris.

Does it get any better than this?

Tess had warned us that the lines to get to the top were often mind-numbingly long, but there were very few tourists waiting in line when we arrived at the base of the tower at nine-thirty.

They were probably sleeping off their jet lag in a nice warm bed.

When Becca wanted to climb to the second level though, I put my foot down. "Don't push it. I'd probably fall asleep on the third step." And then, as I stepped off the elevator onto the metal platform of the tower and looked out over this amazing city, for some strange reason, I felt like bursting into song.

What was up with that? I never sing in public. And especially not to the understated, less-is-more French public. I glanced around. Aside from Becca, there were only about seven or eight people with us on the pinnacle. And none of them were paying any attention to the crazy American girl who was about to make a fool out of herself.

C'est la vie.

Something in me needed to sing. Was compelling me to sing. But what? It wasn't just singing to be singing. Something was drawing me. Tugging at me. I thought about all the Paris songs I knew.

"Frère Jacques?" Too grade-school.

"La Vie en Rose?" Too touristy.

"I Love Paris?" Too peppy.

Then it came to me. The old Joni Mitchell song about being a free man in Paris. Tess had introduced me to Joni, one of her favorites, when I started college. "Every college student needs to listen to Joni Mitchell," she said.

I began to hum, not remembering all the words. Then I started to sing.

Soft and low. From the top of the Eiffel Tower into the wind.

Talk about being unfettered and alive.

22

When at last she found her voice, it was a hushed voice, the voice she used for church. "Just think, Jamie, Michelangelo himself touched this. Over four hundred years ago."

From the Mixed-Up Files of Mrs. Basil E. Frankweiler

Nothing, not even San Francisco's Legion of Honor had prepared me for this.

Eager to start our museum exploration, I'd talked the girls into a quick half-hour breakfast of croissants and café crème at a sidewalk café on Rue Cler. Then we caught the Metro to the first of our two museums of the day, the Musée d'Orsay, the beautiful former train station now home to the world's finest collection of Impressionist art.

And there I was, standing before the man. The myth. The legend.

Van Gogh.

I stared at the thick, frenzied brush strokes of his self-portrait in oil. Kaleidoscopic swirls of a pale turquoise-greenish background almost blended in with the same-colored jacket he wore, save for a dark outline around his back and shoulders. But it was the haunted, almost emaciated face that drew me in. The tense set of his mouth, the red, unkempt hair and beard, the anxious, tortured eyes, and the single ear.

"Dude. Check it out." Becca materialized beside me. "Think that was after he cut off his ear?"

"Maybe. Or maybe it's just the angle of the pose, and his other ear can't be seen."

She peered closer. "Nah. I think he'd already cut it off and just didn't want everyone to see."

As we moved on to the next Van Gogh, I was surprised to see a middle-aged woman sitting on a little stool with an easel set up before her — painting.

Copying Van Gogh!

I raised stunned eyes to Tess, who whispered, "Painters-in-training are allowed to practice their art, copying from originals. It's done all the time." She nodded to the far side of the room where a man at another easel was copying what looked like a Monet.

We continued to wander, dazed, through room after room of Impressionists — Renoir, Cézanne, Degas, Monet, Morisot. And then, out of the corner of my eye, I saw her. The woman with the green umbrella.

My breath caught.

I'd first been introduced to Monet's *La femme a l'ombrelle* in my junior high art class when my teacher was showing us examples from different artists. Monet's woman in white on a windswept hill with a blue scarf flapping in the breeze and a green umbrella resting on her shoulder had spoken to me like none of the other paintings the teacher had shown us.

She was so beautiful. So free.

So with my charcoal and colored pencils, I'd tried to capture her on paper. And failed miserably.

And now here she was. The real thing. In person.

Slowly, I made my way over to her. She was larger than life. So much larger than life.

My eyes welled up.

I'm not sure how long I stood there. I was vaguely conscious of the rest of the group moving on and other people coming and going, but still I stood there.

Staring.

Weeping.

Silently.

My fingers itched to pick up a paint brush again. I hadn't painted in over a decade—not since my sophomore year in high school when Billy Preston had jeered at my pathetic attempt at a self-portrait. I was the least talented student in my art class, and I knew it.

Everyone knew it.

And still my fingers itched.

A hand touched my shoulder. "Chloe?" Tess said. "We thought we'd have lunch here before heading on to the Louvre."

In the café on the fifth floor of the Orsay, we found a table behind the huge, gorgeous clock overlooking the river Seine.

Becca and I both ordered the *tartine paysanne*—a ham, cheese, and mushroom pizza-like sandwich on a toasted baguette.

"Mmm, this is to die for," Becca said.

I nodded, my mouth full.

"This is the prettiest museum I've ever been in," Kailyn said. "It's so open. The building itself is kind of like art. And I can't believe how many paintings I knew."

"Me, either—like that famous Renoir outdoor café scene

I've seen everywhere, all my life—except for the real thing up close and personal." Paige sighed. "I love Renoir's women. They're so lush and curvy. And *real*. Not like all the size zero models today."

"I knew there was a reason I should have lived back then," Annette said.

I didn't answer. I was still thinking of my Monet.

"I hear ya on the real women," Becca said. "That's why I liked the Toulouse-Lautrecs. The people in his paintings always look like they were having a good time."

"They were," Tess said dryly. "Sometimes too good a time. The absinthe really flowed freely back then."

Becca finished off her Evian. "But it was the sculptures that really rocked. Did you see that one cool polar bear? Huge!"

My roommate had a thing for animals, especially the more exotic ones.

"One statue ticked me off though," Becca continued. "A woman on her knees reaching out and begging a guy not to leave with another woman. I hate when women do that."

"Congratulations, *mon amie!*" A triumphant smile split Tess's face. "You have now had what we call an art awakening."

"Say what?"

"Art seeks to evoke some response from the viewer—good, bad, disturbed, excited," Tess explained. "The sculpture that so angered you is called *The Age of Maturity* by Camille Claudel. And the man she was begging not to leave was none other than Rodin."

"*The Thinker* Rodin?" Kailyn asked.

Tess nodded.

"But who's Camille Claudel? Never heard of her."

"Me either," Annette said.

"I'm not surprised." Paige tore off a piece of baguette.

"She's been pretty much relegated to obscurity. Camille Claudel was an incredibly talented sculptor who struggled against the male-dominated artistic establishment of her time. She became Rodin's muse and mistress — one of them, at least — but was an amazing artist in her own right. Unfortunately, she supposedly went mad, some say due in part to Rodin's rejection, and her family had her institutionalized. She spent the last thirty years of her life confined to an insane asylum where she died, never having sculpted again."

"You're kidding." I set down my toasted sandwich, my appetite gone. "How awful."

"Makes me glad I didn't live back then," Kailyn said. "Women really got the shaft."

"I'll say." Becca scowled.

Tess was staring at Paige. "I'm impressed with your art history knowledge. You've been hiding that from us."

"Actually ..." Paige blushed. "I only know about Camille Claudel because I rented the movie from Netflix."

"Still. You know more than I did." Annette finished her coffee. "That sounds like a movie we'll have to rent when we get home. Maybe on another Paperback Girls — I mean Getaway Girls" — she grinned — "movie night?"

"Count me out. Too depressing." Becca stood up. "Are we ready to go?"

"Not quite. We haven't even been to the gift shop yet," Kailyn said.

Becca recoiled in mock horror. "Oh no. What was I thinking?"

As we approached the gift shop en masse — minus Becca, who said she'd wait for us outside — I spotted a great white T-shirt with all the artists' signatures scribbled on it in black, including my favorites: Monet, Degas, Van Gogh, Renoir. I found a medium and held it up against myself. "I know this is incredibly touristy, but I'm getting it."

"Love it!" Annette said. "Do you mind if I get one too?"

"As long as you don't wear it on the same day."

"Deal."

Only problem, the sizes run small in France. I had to get a large instead of my normal medium.

"Bonjour. Excusez-moi, s'il vous plaît," Annette said to the slim young woman behind the counter. "Do you have anything *grande?"* She pointed ruefully to her hips. *"Je* Americans are *non petit."*

The dark-haired mademoiselle in a black pencil skirt and crisp white blouse gave a slight smile and shook her head. *"Non, madame. Désolée."*

"C'est la vie." Annette giggled. "I'll just have to lose weight when I get home." She bought two T-shirts, one for her and one for Kailyn.

Paige decided to buy the same shirt too.

And a Water Lilies watch.

And a Renoir tote bag.

And a Degas mug.

And an Impressionists calendar.

And tons of postcards.

"We're going to have to start calling you Kailyn," I said, staring at her loot. "I didn't know you were such a shopaholic."

"I'm not." She blushed. "I usually hate shopping. But who knows if I'll ever get back to Paris again in my life, so I'm going to take full advantage of it. You only live once, right?"

Annette gave her a thumbs up. "This is my first time back in thirty years, and I wouldn't be here now if it weren't for book club, so I say go all out!"

In addition to my artsy T-shirt, I picked up a small, easy-

to-pack, unframed print of my woman with her green umbrella. Then I caught up with Tess in the postcard section,
where she was trying to decide between a Monet and a Renoir
to send to my parents.

"Tell you what. You send the Renoir, and I'll send the
Monet."

"Deal." She headed to the cash register, three postcards
in hand.

"Is that all you're getting?"

"Yep."

"No prints for your house?"

"Nope. Once you've seen the real thing, nothing else will
satisfy."

"Really?" I looked down at the Monet I planned to hang
in my bedroom. Would it satisfy me now that I'd seen the real
thing?

I hesitated.

But then I thought of what Paige had said. And who knew
if I'd ever come back to Paris again? This print might be my
only remembrance of my lady on the hill. I took it to the cash
register. And while the clerk was ringing up my purchase, I
added in an address book with a Renoir dancing city couple on
the cover for Julia and Justin.

Becca whistled softly as we entered the Louvre less than
an hour later. "Toto, we're not in Kansas anymore."

"You can say that again."

"Toto, we're not in Kansas anymore."

I punched her on the arm.

"Be sure you hold on to your map of the exhibits so you
won't get lost," Tess warned. "It can be quite a maze in here
with all these different corridors."

"Where's my trusty GPS unit when I need it?"

On the Metro ride over, we'd agreed to get the Big Three

out of the way first: *Venus de Milo, Winged Victory*, and the *Mona Lisa*.

Venus de Milo was just as gorgeous as I'd thought she would be in all her white marble purity, but it was *The Winged Victory of Samothrace* all alone at the top of a long, sweeping stone staircase that took our collective breath away.

Even McArt girl Becca.

We stood rooted to the bottom of the stairs by the imposing vision. At last we began our ascent. Intellectually, I knew that the ancient sculpture at the top of the stairs was a stone statue—Nike, the Greek goddess of victory—but as we drew close, she looked so real, as if the draped robes around her body were rippling in a strong breeze.

I circled her slowly. Reverently. Transported back in time. Until Kailyn's voice brought me back to the present.

"What I want to know is how come all these famous women statues have parts of their bodies cut off? That's kind of creepy."

"In Venus's case, it was because Hercules was a little too rough when he was skipping stones," Becca said.

"*Anhhnh.*" Tess made a buzzer sound. "Wrong answer. Someone's watched too many Disney animated features. I read somewhere—and I think this was for Venus, although I'm not positive—that when the statue was found, it was dragged roughly across the ground to be transported and in the process, broken."

"Whatever. It's still creepy."

"What do you suppose Jenna would think of these statues?" Paige asked. "I don't think she'd like them." The corners of her mouth tilted up. "She'd think it was some kind of conspiracy to keep women silent and housebound, or in this case, museum-bound."

"And she'd have a point there."

"Serious?" I turned to my roommate.

"I'm just sayin'."

Tess linked her arm through mine. "Well why don't we go visit a woman who's managed to keep both her head and her arms?"

By the time we made it to the front of the interminable line to see the *Mona Lisa*, I was disappointed. I'd been expecting to be moved the same way I had been by *Winged Victory*, Van Gogh, and my Monet umbrella woman when I first laid eyes on one of the most famous paintings in the world.

Mona Lisa just didn't do it for me.

"She's so little," Kailyn said in a disillusioned whisper.

"Yes, but notice her eyes." Tess nodded at the painting. "Wherever you go, it's like they're following you."

Not me. Guess Mona just wasn't interested. Maybe if I'd taken my hair out of its ponytail that morning.

As we stepped away from the claustrophobic Mona crowd, we synchronized our watches and agreed to split into pairs and meet back at the Metro exit in an hour, well before the six o'clock closing, to beat the departing hordes. I set off with Becca in tow in search of the Rembrandts. But we got so turned around in the labyrinthine corridors that we never did find them. Lots of Greek sculpture and Egyptian antiquities but no Rembrandts.

Lots of aching feet too, even though we were wearing flats.

Becca finally mutinied. "And that's it for me too. I'm museumed out. Come on, I need an espresso."

"But we might not get a chance to come back here again."

"And that would be a problem, why?" Becca cut her eyes at me. "Look. My feet hurt, my eyes are glazed over from looking at so much art, and if I don't get some caffeine in me soon, I'll never make it through the rest of the night."

Kailyn and Annette had the same idea. We ran into them in a café under the pyramid, drinking café au lait and sharing a pastry.

"Great minds think alike," Annette said as we joined them. "I told Kailyn I needed a break. I was feelin' a little overwhelmed."

"Tell me about it." Becca plopped down in a chair.

"Don't get me wrong," Annette added. "The Louvre is really impressive—amazing, actually—but if I had to choose, I think I prefer the Musée d'Orsay. More intimate. I could be a bit biased though, since the Impressionists are my favorite."

"Mine too," I said. The waiter appeared, and Becca ordered espresso and a *pain au chocolat*, a croissant with a huge chunk of chocolate inside, while I opted for a hot chocolate and a *millefeuille*, which turned out to be the most delicious Napoleon I'd ever had.

We chatted for a few minutes about our cooking class beginning the next morning, and then Kailyn looked at her watch. "Time to go meet the others." She exchanged an eager smile with her mother. "And then you and I have a date to go shopping! Chloe, Becca, want to come?"

"It's what I've been dreaming of," Becca said. "Not."

I passed too in favor of a power nap on my red toile.

After a leisurely and amazing three-hour dinner that night—that had Becca twitching with impatience—we decided as a group to end our second day in Paris with a ride down the Seine on a Bateau Mouche. And as we sat in our seats waiting for the boat to launch, my tower did her twinkling Christmas tree magic once again.

"Ooh."

"Ah."

"Ooh." A chorus of delight and wonder in a dozen languages swept through the boat and a barrage of cameras clicked and whirred as Japanese, German, American, and every other kind of tourist began snapping away and the Bateau Mouche began its slow glide down the river.

I hit the French mix on my iPod and Edith Piaf sang "La Vie en Rose" in my ear as we glided by the still sparkling Eiffel Tower. I felt like I was in a movie. Or watching a movie of someone else's life.

This couldn't be *my* life. Safe, sedate, nonadventurous Chloe, drifting down the Seine in the City of Lights, passing glorious buildings and famous monuments bathed in amber lights against the night sky.

What could be better than this?

Drifting down the Seine in the arms of a man who loves me?

Maybe.

I looked around at the faces of my friends. They were all lit up and shiny and filled with wonder.

Maybe not.

As we approached Notre Dame, "Do You Hear the People Sing?" from *Les Misérables* filled my ears. I shivered. And not from the cold. My heart swelled and felt as if it would burst from my chest any moment. I motioned for Tess to come closer and stuck one of the ear buds in her ear. Her eyes widened, and a dazzling smile split her face at the same time as her eyes filled with tears.

"What are you listening to?" Paige, sitting on my other side, asked.

I gave her the other ear bud and watched her face do the same thing as Tess's. Paige gasped. And Becca, who was sitting in front of us, turned around and shot us a curious look. "What *are* you guys doing?"

On our return loop, just as we passed under the Pont d'Iéna bridge to the Trocadéro, the eleven o'clock Eiffel light show started. Once again, my iron lady was clad in a shimmering gown of sequins.

The entire boat gasped again, and cameras clicked all around me.

Jesus could have come and taken me home right then, and it would have been fine by me.

That night when we got back to the hotel, I sat in the lobby and tried to journal all that I'd seen and experienced so I'd never forget it. I wanted a record of all the special moments so that in years to come when I wanted to relive my Parisian adventure, the words would remind me.

But how can you capture with mere words something so beautiful? Something that needs to be *seen*?

I'm no writer. I can't use words to paint a picture.

I clicked my mechanical pencil, wondering if I should attempt to sketch the details of my amazing day. Closing my eyes, I once again saw my exquisite Monet umbrella woman standing on the hill, her scarf waving in the breeze.

My pencil wavered over the paper. Dare I try to draw her?

Not in this universe.

He was Monet, and I was just Chloe.

I set my pencil down and closed the journal.

23

The French do live by one principle that Americans sometimes forget, despite having coined it most eloquently: Garbage in, garbage out. The key to cooking, and therefore living well, is the best of ingredients.

French Women Don't Get Fat

"Bonjour Mesdames et Mesdemoiselles," the petite middle-aged woman greeted us the next morning in her cozy Paris apartment. "My name is Jacqueline Marceau," she said in her lilting French accent, "and I am the chef. Welcome to my home."

"Bonjour Madame Marceau," we said in unison like the twelve little girls in two straight lines.

"Please. Call me Jacqueline." She pronounced it *zhockleen*. She consulted a piece of paper in her hand. "Today we have Paige, Tess, Kailyn, Becca, Annette, and Chloe, *oui?*"

"Oui."

"I see we have some French names in the group." She smiled. "Perhaps you will have an advantage, *oui?*"

"I wish." A puff of air escaped my lips. "The only thing French about me is my name."

"Which is?"

"Oh, *pardon!*" I flushed. "*Je suis* Chloe Adams. And *je suis* terrible cook."

"*Bonjour*, Chloe. I am sure your cooking ability is not so terrible as you think."

"Oh, yes it is," Becca said. "I live with her. But then, I'm a lousy cook too. We pretty much live on takeout and TV dinners at home."

Paige dropped her head into her hands, and Jacqueline flinched almost imperceptibly. "And you are? Miss TV dinner?"

Becca stuck out her hand. "*Bonjour.* I'm Becca Daniels."

Jacqueline shook Becca's hand. A small smile played at the corners of her mouth. "Hopefully, by the time you return home, we will have supplanted at least a few of your TV dinners with some good French food."

"That's why we're here." Tess diverted attention from Becca's faux pas. "*Bonjour*, Jacqueline. *Je suis* Tess James. *Je suis l'agent de voyages.* Thank you for accepting us into your home. My client, Cara Hamilton, sends her compliments and says you're a marvelous chef. We look forward to learning from you."

"Ah. *Mon amie* Cara?" Jacqueline's eyes lit up. She and Tess chatted in rapid French for a few minutes while the rest of us enjoyed the sound of their musical dialogue.

"Don't you just love the French language?" Annette asked. "I wish I knew more than just hello, goodbye, and how to count to ten. Of course," she sent us a devilish smirk, "there is that song 'Lady Marmalade' from the seventies they used to play in the discos all the time, but it's a little naughty."

"And I'd like to thank you for not repeating it here," Kailyn said.

Tess and Jacqueline ended their conversation and the three remaining Paperback Girls introduced themselves to our teacher, who then handed each of us a snowy white apron and a copy of the recipe for the day in French, with English subtitles.

Jacqueline motioned us over to the kitchen.

And what a kitchen it was.

Big yet uncluttered and functional, with herbs hanging from a rafter and open metal shelving against the crisp white walls holding spices, oils, dry goods, and every size cooking pot imaginable.

I nudged Becca and pointed to a framed piece of calligraphy on the wall—in French, but with an English translation:

Animals feed; man eats; only a man of wit knows how to eat.

The Physiology of Taste,
Jean Anthelme Brillat-Savarin

"I think that's meant for philistines like me," Becca whispered.

Jacqueline had us pair off at shared work stations around a large butcher block island that took center stage: Tess and Paige, Annette and Kailyn, and Becca and I. The island held four cooktops and plenty of space for food preparation, which would include lots of chopping, as we were soon to learn.

"*Bon*. Shall we begin?" Jacqueline asked. "In France, food is a sensual experience, something to be savored and enjoyed with family and friends. And French cooking is all about fresh, *fraîche* ingredients. We go to the market, *le marchè* every day to select our food for the day—bread, cheese, *le fromage*, meat, fish. It is *très* important to buy locally produced ingredients."

She inclined her head to a bin of fresh vegetables in the center of the island. "Today, I have already been to *le marchè* so we could spend more time in the kitchen on the proper use of tools and utensils. The baby must crawl before he can walk, *n'est-ce pas?*" She smiled. "When we meet again on Wednesday, we go to *le marchè* first—be sure to wear comfortable shoes—and then I take you to Barthélémy, the most famous cheese shop in Paris, where you will learn the art of selection of *le fromage. D'accord?*"

We nodded.

Jacqueline began removing the vegetables from the bin. "Today we will make *le poulet* with rosemary and onion." She smacked her forehead with the palm of her hand. "*J'oublie.* I forget. Are there any vegetarians in the group?"

"No, she had to stay home for a triathlon," Becca said.

"Ah, *bien.*" Jacqueline picked up a yellow onion. "First, we start by chopping *l'oignon.*" She held up a sharp chef's knife. "You hold the knife like so."

Three hours later we pushed back from Jacqueline's glass-topped dining room table.

"*Merci*, Jacqueline. That was *très délicieuse*," I said.

"And not *difficile, oui?*"

"*Oui.*" Paige, Tess, and Annette chorused.

Becca held up her left index finger, which was sporting a small bandage. "Speak for yourselves."

"Speed comes with experience," Jacqueline said. "Faster is not always better—especially when you are first starting. Skill with the knife is *très* important in cooking. You must learn an economy of movement first, and then you will improve in the rate at which you can chop."

"Got that?" Kailyn sent Becca a triumphant look. "Economy of movement."

"Says the woman who spilled flour down the front of her apron."

Jacqueline tinkled a laugh. "When I first began cooking, I spilled everything all the time—like Julia Child. It is to be expected."

"That's for sure," Tess said. "In my newlywed days, my kitchen always looked like a disaster zone. My husband used to say he took his life in his hands every time he entered—never knowing what he might slip on." She smiled.

"On the subject of husbands," Annette sipped her coffee, "I can't wait to make that yummy *tarte tatin* for mine when I get home. He likes desserts that aren't as sweet."

"Not me." Paige smacked her lips. "The sweeter the better. That's why I can't wait to try out all the amazing pâtisseries and chocolate shops you have here."

"Ah, if you like sweets, you must stop at Ladurée on the Champs-Elysées and have one of their famous *macarons*," Jacqueline said.

"I don't like coconut."

Jacqueline looked puzzled. "Ah, you are thinking of the American macaroon, *non*? This is not the same at all."

Tess nodded. "Completely different. Not like the sticky cookies filled with coconut we're used to. These *macarons* are amazing." She and Jacqueline exchanged looks of foodie ecstasy.

"So what are they, exactly?" Kailyn asked.

"Two crunchy cookies joined together with butter cream or ganache filling in the middle," Tess explained. "They look almost like round mini-sandwiches, except they're sweet. They come in a ton of different flavors, but my favorite is hazelnut praline." She closed her eyes and expelled a sigh of pure bliss.

Jacqueline nodded. "*C'est délicieuse*. Although I prefer the *chocolat amer*, bittersweet chocolate."

"Stop." I held up my hand. "You're making my mouth water, and we just finished eating."

"Welcome to Paris," Jacqueline said. She turned to Tess. "And so, what are your plans for this afternoon?"

"Well, we want to go to the Arc de Triomphe, but after that, we're not quite sure." Tess lifted her shoulders. "We all have very different interests. Some want to visit more art museums, others want to shop, and still others"—she inclined her head to Becca—"want to go to Père Lachaise Cemetery and see Chopin's and Jim Morrison's graves."

"Ah, you are a music lover." Jacqueline smiled at Becca. "I hope you will pay homage to our Little Sparrow too?"

Becca ducked her head. "Sorry. I don't know who that is."

"Me either," Kailyn said. "Little Sparrow?"

"Edith Piaf," I said. "France's national treasure."

"Is that another one of your old singers?" Becca scrunched her eyes at me.

I ignored her. "Edith Piaf started out as a poor street singer in the thirties when she was just a teenager," I told Kailyn. "One of her most famous songs is 'La Vie en Rose,' which I happen to have on my iPod. They called her the Little Sparrow because she was so tiny—less than five feet tall. She's considered France's greatest popular singer."

"Bravo!" Jacqueline raised her wine glass and clinked it with mine. "Are you sure you are not a Parisienne?"

When we arrived at the west end of the Champs-Elysées, facing the Arc de Triomphe, Becca suggested we sprint across the intersection to get to the famous monument.

Traffic was insane.

There are no traffic signals at the Arc, and no one stops. Just twelve streets of cars coming together in a circle and sailing back out onto—hopefully—their desired streets. I'd read in my guidebook that insurance companies no longer argue about who's at fault when there's an accident there. They just split it fifty-fifty. I expected to see a couple of crashed cars on the side of the road and to hear the angry drivers yelling at each other in French.

"Are you out of your ever-lovin' mind?" Annette said. "I didn't come to Paris to wind up as roadkill on the Champs-Elysées."

"Especially since we haven't even had a chance yet to sample those amazing *macarons*," Paige added.

Instead, Tess led us through a pedestrian tunnel which brought us right up to the Arc, the symbol of French freedom.

We gazed up at the massive stone edifice.

It must have been at least twelve stories tall. And deeper than I'd imagined. I've always thought of it as mostly two-dimensional — like a couple square column legs supporting the arched top piece. But there were four legs. And the carvings. So detailed. People and plants and trees and reliefs of battle scenes and angels.

Becca let out a low whistle. "Way to make a person feel small and insignificant."

"And Napoleon never even got to see his brainchild completed," Tess said.

"No, but the Arc still stands today as a legacy of his men and their victories." Annette, our resident military expert, nodded to the voluminous list of names on the roof and interior walls. "Five hundred fifty-eight generals and one hundred twenty-eight victorious battles. Not bad."

"And today the Arc is a symbol of all things victorious in Paris," Kailyn read from a brochure. She looked up. "Hey, did you know this is where the Tour de France finish line is?"

"No, really?" Becca widened her eyes. "So that's why they

took all those pictures of Lance Armstrong here in his yellow jersey. I was wondering."

Kailyn stuck her tongue out.

"So who's game to climb all the way up to the top?" Tess asked.

"Isn't it about ten flights of stairs?" Paige flipped through her guidebook trying to find the exact amount.

"I think it's a little more than that," Becca said. "I read somewhere it's just over a hundred steps."

Annette blanched. "Don't they have an elevator?"

"Only for the disabled."

"You don't think middle-aged and overweight would qualify?"

"Somehow, I don't think so," Tess said. "But that's okay. I went up top years ago. I'll stay here with you while the young-sters scamper up all those steps. We can pay our respects at the Tomb of the Unknown Soldier."

Paige joined Tess and Annette. "I think I'd like to pay my respects too." She nodded at us. "You guys go right on ahead."

Kailyn and I glanced at the over-thirty contingent and then back to Becca, who was bouncing from one foot to the other. "Aw guys, come on," Becca wheedled. "Don't be wusses. Don't you want to see the killer view? It's supposed to be even better than from the Eiffel Tower. And"—she sent a knowing look to Kailyn—"there's a gift shop up there too."

"I thought you said it was only a hundred steps, Bec." I stopped to catch my breath again on the circular staircase leading to the top of the Arc de Triomphe.

"Yeah, you did," Kailyn said, stopping to rest two steps above me.

"No. What I said was it was *over* a hundred steps." Becca

continued up the stairs in her mountain goat way, leading the way to the top.

"How much over?" I craned my neck to look up the interminable spiral staircase that, like that old Energizer bunny, just seemed to keep going and going.

"I don't know."

Someone bumped into me from behind. "Oh, *excusez-moi*," said a very American, very male voice.

"That's okay." I turned around to shoot my—kind of cute—fellow tourist an apologetic smile. "I'm sorry. I shouldn't be blocking the stairs. I just didn't realize there were so many of them."

"Tell me about it." He grinned. "One site we googled said 232, another said 264."

"Two hundred something? Are you kidding?"

"Hey, are you okay?" He peered at me. "Your face went all white." He thrust a water bottle at me. "Here, have a drink."

"No thanks. I'm fine." I put one foot in front of the other and started climbing again. "I'm just going to have to kill a certain roommate of mine."

More than 150 stairs later—I stopped counting at 251—I finally made it to the top of the Arc, my calf muscles pounding like a sewing machine on speed, struggling to catch my breath.

Kailyn stumbled out onto the rooftop platform behind me, taking huge gulps of air, her long blonde hair plastered to her neck.

Becca raced over, not breathing hard at all. "Hey, you guys finally made it. Check out this view! It's incredible. Even better than the Eiffel Tower." She whipped out her camera. "Say stinky cheese!"

Kailyn glowered. "I just climbed over 280 steps. You say cheese."

"Aw c'mon. We're on top of the Arc de Triomphe looking out over the most beautiful city in the world. What could be better than that?"

"Throwing you over the edge?" I peered down at the melee of honking and speeding traffic on the roundabout below.

Kailyn joined me, looking down at the twelve avenues of cars, taxis, and buses radiating out from the Arc like spokes on a bicycle tire. "Those French drivers are crazy."

Becca was right. It was a killer panoramic view of the city. And since the Arc wasn't as high as the Eiffel Tower, I could actually identify the famous sights more easily as I walked around the rooftop—the Place de la Concorde, the obelisk, the Eiffel Tower, the Louvre.

Thankfully, going back down the steps was much easier.

Afterward, since Tess was salivating like Pavlov's dog, we took Jacqueline's suggestion and went to the famous Ladurée where we bought a couple boxes of mini-macarons to eat in a small park off the Champs-Elysées.

"Mmm. Can you say heaven?" Paige licked her fingers.

Annette scarfed down another *macaron*—this time, pistachio.

"My favorites are the chocolate ones." I stood up from the bench to brush crumbs off my coat and noticed the time in the process. "Hey, it's nearly three o'clock already. Shouldn't we figure out what we're doing the rest of the day?"

"I know what I'm doing." Kailyn opened her small travel journal with her list of Paris must-sees. "Mom and I are going to check out the haute couture shops along the rue du Faubourg Saint-Honoré and rue Montaigne. They have Dior, Yves Saint-Laurent, Hermès, and more! Can you believe it? You guys are welcome to join us."

"Please, oh please. Can I?" Becca asked. "Spending a thousand bucks on a shirt is something I've always dreamed of."

"Actually, there you'd probably spend closer to ten thousand."

"No way!" I gasped. "That's insane. Who could afford such a thing?"

"Oprah. Madonna. The Grimaldis of Monaco."

"Not in this girl's lifetime," Becca said.

"I can't afford it either," Kailyn admitted. "But it's fun to look. And when will I ever get the chance again?"

Tess and I decided to head to the Musée Rodin for some Sculpture 101. We asked Paige and Becca to join us, but they declined. Becca was museumed out after yesterday, she said. Secretly, I was relieved. I loved all the girls, but being with them 24/7 was a little much. And it would be nice to have Tess all to myself for a change.

Annette freshened her lipstick and fastened Becca with a gaze. "So what *are* you going to do then?"

"Whatever we feel like. Maybe we'll go to the cemetery and pay our respects to Jim and company, maybe we'll explore the catacombs, or walk along the Seine."

"Or just sit in a charming sidewalk café with a good glass of wine and people watch," Paige said. "That's always fun."

Less than an hour later Tess and I stood gazing at Rodin's *Le Penseur, The Thinker.* He looked different somehow in this Paris garden with shrubbery all around him.

More at home.

Serene.

A natural part of the surroundings.

The nearby gold dome of Les Invalides, home of Napoleon's Tomb, provided a striking background for the aged verdigris statue underneath an overcast sky. A trio of Japanese schoolgirls giggled as they clustered around the statue and struck the same philosophical pose in front of the world's most famous thoughtful man. "Would you like me to take your picture?" I offered.

"Yes, please." The shortest girl shyly handed me her camera.

After the giggling girls moved on, I held up my camera. "Okay, Tess. Your turn."

"You know, if you position yourself just right," she said, "you can line up three monuments in the same shot."

I looked through my viewfinder at my chic aunt in her red wool coat that matched her glasses. "You mean *The Thinker*, Les Invalides, and you?" I teased.

"I'm not old enough to qualify for monument status yet, thank you very much. No, if you move just a little to your left, I think you'll see what I'm talking about."

The Thinker, the gold dome of Les Invalides, and … oh! There was my beautiful Eiffel Tower in the distance. "Wow! This is going to be an amazing picture. Take mine next, please."

"Naturellement."

Tess and I strolled through the quiet gardens dotted with Rodin's larger-than-life bronze and marble sculptures. "I come here every time I'm in Paris," she said. "It's one of my favorite spots — although it's even nicer in the summer when all the flowers are in bloom."

"And it's a little warmer?" I tightened my wool scarf around my neck.

"Oui. I'll often grab a baguette, some cheese, and a small bottle of wine and picnic here on one of the benches where I can relax and admire Monsieur Rodin's genius at leisure."

I slowly circled around a bronze of three men that the little plaque identified as *The Three Shades*. "They're so real. I expect them to come to life at any moment."

"You can touch the sculpture, you know."

"Serious?"

She nodded. "You're not in the Louvre. This is an outdoor sculpture garden — the statues here are meant to be touched."

Now I knew I wasn't in Kansas anymore.

Tentatively I extended my hand to the joined hands of the trio. Their bronze fingers felt cold beneath mine, yet curiously warm at the same time. "How amazing to be able to create something glorious like this and to have it live on after you're gone."

I glanced around at the clusters of tourists from different countries oohing and aahing over all the statues. "And to touch so many people from all over the world."

"That's art."

We continued our stroll. "I seem to have a vague memory of you doing something with clay when I was a kid." I looked sideways at Tess. "In fact … come to think of it, didn't we try and make a bust of Dad for his birthday one year or something?"

"*Try* is the operative word." She chuckled. "That was my sculpture phase. I tried my hand at pottery first, but was lousy at it. And then I tried sculpting, where I was even lousier. That bust you're talking about actually came out looking like Yoda, which I didn't think your dad would appreciate, so I gave it to the boys instead."

"That's right. I remember now. Doesn't Tommy use it to hang his swimming medals on?"

"Yep. A telling commentary on your aunt's artistic abilities. That's why my art leanings are now confined to appreciating the work of real artists. *Et voila.*" She stopped and nodded to the bronze portal in front of us.

"What *is* that?" I stared in rapt fascination at the doors covered with despairing, tortured bodies, desperately intertwined and writhing in agony.

"The Gates of Hell—inspired by Dante's *Inferno."*

"Wow. What a graphic argument for belief."

"Mm. I know what you mean."

Inside, it felt more like we were in someone's home than a museum—a beautiful, spacious, two-story home that we learned had formerly been a hotel and Rodin's private residence, which he donated to France upon his death.

Slowly we wound our way through the rooms of sculpture, mesmerized. In one room, I was surprised to find some Impressionist works from Rodin's private collection—Monet, Renoir, and Van Gogh—traded, we learned, for sculpture.

The Kiss captivated me again as it had in San Francisco, but this time it didn't fill me with longing for Chris and love.

Instead, it made me long to create.

Be it true or false, what is said about men often has as much influence upon their lives, and especially upon their destinies, as what they do.

Les Misérables

"Hey, everyone, look what Mom got me for an early birthday present!" In the hotel lobby, Kailyn proudly fingered the colorful silk scarf at her neck. "It's *Hermès*! Isn't it gorgeous?"

"Beautiful."

"Exquisite."

"Love it!" We all took turns admiring the vibrant patterned scarf, which was unlike any I'd ever seen.

Maybe this was one of the scarves I needed to buy as souvenirs. I leaned over to Annette and whispered, "I might want to get one too. Do you mind my asking how much it cost?"

"Three hundred twenty-five dollars," she whispered back.

Maybe not.

Tess caught my eye as we left the hotel to walk to the

restaurant. "If you're looking for affordable gifts to take back home, we should check out the Monoprix chain. They have all kinds of goodies under one roof, including silk scarves at a fraction of the price."

"Sounds like my kind of store," Becca said. "Is it a cousin of our Target?" She gave the second syllable of her favorite store a French pronunciation: *zhe.*

"*Oui.* First cousin."

Tonight we'd decided to dine at Le Bosquet on the corner of avenue Bosquet and rue du Champ de Mars where I was delighted to see that the menu included an English translation.

I started with a yummy appetizer of goat cheese with caramelized sugar on top with a baguette, followed by a bowl of French onion soup.

And not just any French onion soup.

With my spoon, I broke through the one-inch layer of melted gruyere to scoop up a spoonful of cheese, onions, and croutons drenched in a delicious beefy broth. I stopped breathing and closed my eyes.

How can mere food be an experience of rapture?

"This is the most amazing soup I've ever had. Tess, you have to try this."

"And you should try a bite of my fish. *C'est délicieuse.*"

"Anyone want to try my pâté?" Paige held up a thin slice of bread slathered with duck liver.

Tess cut her eyes at Becca, who had started to make an exaggerated gagging noise. "No thanks, Paige," Becca said politely. "I'll just stick to my Brie."

Tess ordered a couple carafes of red wine for the table, which everyone tried except teetotaler Annette and me.

"I wish I could." I took a drink of my water. "But red wine always hurts going down. Gives me heartburn."

"That's because of the sulfites they have to add in the States," Tess explained. "They don't do that here."

"Really?" I took a cautious sip.

No burning. I raised my glass and clinked it with hers. *"Vive la France!"*

Annette had considered trying the steak tartare—raw minced steak with raw egg, onions, and capers—for dinner, but decided against it, much to our collective relief. Instead, she ordered steak frites.

"My stomach thanks you," Becca said. "Plus, how could we ever tell Jenna?

"What happens in Paris stays in Paris." Annette winked and ate one of her fries. "Yum. These are the best french fries I've ever had." She offered us each one and then directed her gaze to Becca. "So, what did you and Paige wind up doing today?"

"We strolled along the banks of the Seine, not realizing it was the romantic hotspot of the city. Everywhere we looked it seemed, people were making out—standing up, sitting down, sprawled all over each other. We started keeping count." Becca caught Paige's eye. "Did we wind up with seventeen or eighteen?"

"Nineteen, actually. We seemed to be the only pair along the river not holding hands." Paige giggled. "But even so, it was a great way to see the city. We walked over one of the pedestrian bridges from the Right Bank to the Left and thought of you guys as we wandered through the *bouquinistes*, the bookstalls that line the Seine.

"They had tons of great old books and magazines, vintage postcards, and souvenir posters. I could have browsed for hours, but someone"— she jerked her head at Becca—"had a date with the dead."

"Actually, the date was mostly on behalf of dark and twisted

Jenna." Becca swallowed a bite of her *salmon plat du jour.* "I asked her if I could bring her anything back from Paris, and she said a photo of Jim Morrison's grave. She's a huge Doors fan. So I dragged Paige along too, but she liked it. Right?"

Paige nodded. "I can see why Père Lachaise is called the world's most beautiful cemetery. The sculptures and monuments alone are spectacular works of art that could be in a museum. Did you know that Molière, Marcel Proust, and Oscar Wilde are all buried there?"

"Don't forget Chopin, Gertrude Stein, and Chloe's Little Sparrow."

Paige ticked off on her fingers. "*And* Sarah Bernhardt. *And* Isadora Duncan. *And* Héloïse and Abèlard, the famous lovers from the twelfth century! I had no idea so many famous people were buried there. We found out that the cemetery attracts hundreds of thousands of visitors a year."

Paige sent Becca a mischievous glance before continuing. "Guess who attracted a gorgeous admirer today amongst all those cemetery visitors?"

"Really?" Kailyn's eyes sparkled. "Tell all."

"There's nothing to tell." Becca blushed and concentrated on her salmon.

"C'mon, roomie, spill." I leaned forward. "We're all ears."

"Go on, Becca, give us the play-by-play," Annette said.

Becca frowned at Paige. "It was no big deal. Really. This Italian guy flirted with me. That's all."

"Italian? Ooh, they're supposed to be really romantic." Kailyn's eyes sparked. "What did he say? Did he ask you out? Are you going to see him again?"

"Now that's a first," Tess said. "Getting hit on in a cemetery."

Becca drained her wine. "He just flirted with me. No biggie."

Annette raised her eyebrows. "But was he cute?"

"Very cute," Paige said, since it was obvious Becca wasn't going to divulge any information. "Dark curly hair, soulful brown eyes ... actually, he reminded me a lot of Josh Groban—especially when he sang."

"He *sang*?" I stared at my roommate, whose natural olive skin had darkened to a ruddy flush. "In a *cemetery*?"

"Actually, he serenaded Becca out of the cemetery."

"Serious?" Kailyn's eyes grew even wider. "What did he sing?"

"Something in Italian that I didn't understand—other than the word *bellissima*."

"Doesn't that mean beautiful?" Annette asked.

"*Very* beautiful," Tess said.

Kailyn honed in on Becca. "So what was the problem? How come you're all shy and embarrassed over some gorgeous Italian guy singing to you? Most women would kill to have that happen to them on vacation. I know I would."

"Hear, hear," I said.

Tess raised her glass. "And not only on vacation."

Becca ignored us. "I think I'm going to have chocolate mousse for dessert. Or maybe that *île flottante* thing. I remember reading about that in our book. Floating island, right? What was it again, Paige?"

"A meringue steamed in milk with a thin custard sauce used as the 'ocean' around the island. Sounds delicious. I may have that too."

"Ooh, that does sound really good," Annette said. "Except ... I'm such a chocoholic, I may have to order the mousse. Could I try a bite of your floating island?"

"No problem." Becca was all magnanimity and generosity.

"Good try." Kailyn narrowed her eyes at Becca. "But I'm

not falling for it. You still haven't answered my question." She shifted her focus to Paige. "Don't let her distract you so easily. Now tell us the rest. What part of the Italian guy story are you leaving out?"

"Paige," Becca warned.

"I don't know why you're embarrassed. I think it's really sweet," Paige said. She lowered her voice. "Here's the thing: the gorgeous, curly-haired Italian with the soulful eyes and the beautiful voice is a little younger than the guys Becca usually dates."

"Aha! The tables are turned." I smirked at my roommate. "You didn't want us to know because you gave me such a hard time for falling for a guy five years younger than me. So how young is this Romeo? Nineteen? Twenty?"

Kailyn sent Becca a sly look. "Eighteen?"

"Eleven." Paige gave a low chuckle.

I choked on my water.

Becca scowled at Paige.

"Well, I've always heard Latin men have a great appreciation for women," Annette said. "I just didn't know they started so early. I wonder if there's a special school or somethin'."

Kailyn snickered. "Yeah. Flirting 101."

"No, I think it's called 'That's Amoré,'" Tess said.

Our entire table dissolved into giggles.

"Very funny." Becca shrugged. "What can I say? The kid has good taste."

"And you said *I* robbed the cradle."

"I didn't rob any cradle. The kid just sang to me."

"Well, we know what kind of day Paige and Becca had." Tess wiped at her eyes. "Kailyn? Annette? How was your afternoon?"

"Not as romantic as Becca's," Kailyn said. "But I'm *très*

happy with my beautiful Hermès scarf and perfume from Sephora."

"What's Sephora?" I shot her a curious look.

"Oh, honey, you really don't get out much, do you?" Kailyn said. "Oprah's included Sephora beauty products in her magazine as some of her favorite things. And there are stores all over the States—we even have one in Sacramento.

"The flagship store on the Champs-Elysées is a must-stop for every woman," she continued. "There's nothing like it anywhere. They have Juicy Couture, Stella McCartney, Badgley Mischka." Kailyn's eyes gleamed with unbridled designer lust. "It's the most amazing place, devoted exclusively to perfumes, cosmetics, and skin-care products."

"I never saw so many kinds of perfumes in my life," Annette said. "It's like a giant perfume department store—so glamorous! They have this fabulous wheel of scents in the center where they help you figure out what kind of scent you like—flowery, fruity, woody, spicy ... even chocolatey. Mmm." Annette closed her eyes. "I felt as if I'd died and been *scent* to heaven."

"Well, no problem guessing what flavor—I mean scent—you picked, Ms. Chocoholic," I said.

"You got that right." Annette's eyes flew open. "But get this! I don't know if y'all ran into this, but the thing we couldn't get over was all the fur we saw on the streets."

"Yeah." Kailyn swiveled her head toward me and Becca. "Even women *our* age. In fur coats. Have they not heard of PETA?"

"Good thing Jenna's not here," Becca said with an impish grin. "She'd have had a cow."

Paige rolled her eyes. Then she focused on me. "So how was the Musée Rodin?"

"Fabulous. You really need to go if you can. It's absolutely amazing. I'd go back in a heartbeat." I pushed my hair behind my ears. "If you think the sculpture at the cemetery was something, you ain't seen nothin' yet."

"Any polar bears?" Becca asked hopefully.

"No, but there was a great bust of Victor Hugo."

Tess tucked into her profiteroles. "So what does everyone want to do tomorrow?"

"I'd love to go to Versailles," Annette said. "I hear it's absolutely stunning—especially the Hall of Mirrors."

"Too much glitz and glitter for me." Becca scrunched up her nose. "I'd rather go to the catacombs."

I consulted my list of must-sees. "I'd like to explore Montmartre to see where Van Gogh and some of the other Impressionists had their studios. And then see Sacré Cœur. Or, go to the Orangerie to see Monet's water lilies, and afterward take a trip to Giverny to visit his actual gardens. Or check out the Latin Quarter." I looked up in delight at my book-loving friends. "That's where that famous bookstore Shakespeare and Company is located. Did you know they let writers stay there for free in exchange for helping out in the store?"

"I hate to break it to you," Tess said, "but Giverny is closed in the winter."

"You're kidding. I really wanted to see the place that inspired his water lilies."

"Me too," Annette said. "But I guess it makes sense since it's all about the gardens and not much would be blooming until spring."

"This gives you a good reason to return to Paris. But don't worry," Tess said, "there's still plenty of other things to see and do. I spent a whole month in Paris when I was eighteen, and I still didn't see all she has to offer. And every time I come back, I discover something new."

Tess zeroed in on Kailyn. "What about you? What did you want to do?"

"Well, I'd really like to see the Opéra Garnier at some point, but it doesn't have to be tomorrow. And the Moulin Rouge — *loved* Ewan McGregor in that movie. Who knew he could sing? And I'd like to do a little more shopping too, maybe at Bon Marché and Galleries Lafayette?"

Tess directed a look at Paige. "And you?"

She blushed. "Actually, mine's food-related. I'd really like to take another of Jacqueline's cooking classes. I may never have this opportunity again, and I want to learn as much as I can from her." Paige glanced at Becca, who gave her an encouraging nod.

"We talked about it earlier. Becca's not that interested in going to our next lesson, but she didn't want to short Jacqueline the fee. So we called and asked if I could take Becca's place some other day this week, and the only opening she had was tomorrow." Paige sent us anxious looks. "I hope you don't mind. I'll still have the rest of the week to spend with all of you."

"Why should we mind?" Annette said. "Just because you want to throw us over for some gourmet French cooking instructor. Doesn't bother me in the least. What about the rest of you girls?"

"That's okay." I expelled a heavy sigh. "I'm used to rejection."

"*Moi aussi.*" Tess jumped on the teasing bandwagon.

While the rest of the group gave Paige a hard time, I studied my roommate discreetly from beneath my bangs. I knew cooking had never been her thing, but somehow I had the feeling that her dropping out of our group class had more to do with the hundred-Euro price tag than anything else.

As I thought about it, I recalled that any time we went out to eat, Becca always ordered the least expensive item on the menu. And she hadn't stormed the gift shop at the Musée d'Orsay with the rest of us either.

Or any other shop for that matter.

Anyone could do that math. My roommate was broke.

Since there were so many different things we all wanted to see and do, we took a vote and agreed that we wanted to explore Montmartre, the Orangerie, and the literary Latin Quarter together, so we'd wait to do that until Paige was available.

Meanwhile, while Paige was taking her extra cooking class, Tess, Annette, and I decided we'd return to Île de la Cité. Annette really wanted to go back to Notre Dame so she could see a gargoyle up close and personal, and Tess said that if the weather cooperated, Sainte Chapelle and its exquisite stained glass was a must.

"Doesn't anyone want to go on the catacombs tour with me?" Becca asked, with a pout.

"I don't think so." I wrinkled my nose. "Skeletons aren't exactly my thing."

"Mine either," Annette said. "Plus, I'm a little claustrophobic, so that wouldn't be a good mix."

"Count me out," Tess said. "I choose stained glass and light over dark tunnels and piles of stacked skulls and bones."

"I'll go," Kailyn offered.

"Serious?" Our heads swiveled as one to the girliest girl in our group.

"Why are you so surprised? I'd like to see where Jean Valjean rescued Marius."

"Wrong place," Becca said. "That was the sewers of Paris; these are the catacombs."

"What's the difference?"

"Depth and smell."

That night while Tess and I were marveling anew at the

tower's dazzling light show from our window before turning in, there was a soft knock on our door.

I opened it to Becca, who thrust a paper bag at me.

"Hey, I found this today at one of those green bookstalls along the Seine and thought you might like it as a souvenir, especially since I messed up your other copy."

I opened the bag and pulled out a beautiful paperback edition of *Les Misérables*.

In French.

25

A faith is a necessity to man. Woe to him who believes nothing.

Les Misérables

Needing a little alone time, I got up early the next morning, slipped on my black pants, heaviest sweater, coat, and scarf and rode the tiny elevator down to the lobby.

"*Bonjour.*" I gave a smile and a quick nod to Arnaud at the front desk as I headed for the door.

I made my way to the pâtisserie, where I ogled the racks of tantalizing pastry in the glass display case. Millefeuilles mingled with macarons and meringues while cream puffs stood sentinel next to éclairs and a host of other delectable delights whose names I didn't know.

So many pastries, so not enough room in my stomach.

Finally, using my rudimentary French, I settled on an *amande*, a day-old croissant split down the center with a healthy dose of almond paste in the middle and powdered sugar on top.

I also bought two *éclairs au chocolat*, in case Tess and I found ourselves in the mood for a late-night snack.

Not for the first time was I grateful to my aunt for upgrading us to a room with a view—and a small refrigerator.

"Merci," I said to the clerk as she handed me my sweet-tooth bounty wrapped carefully in white paper and taped shut with a steepled effect.

Even a to-go container was an art form in Paris.

Walking briskly to keep the cold at bay, I set off for my early morning rendezvous.

One of the food trailers at the foot of the monument was just opening, so I ordered *chocolat chaud*. I stared, mesmerized, at the pot of melted dark chocolate that was calling my name. The vendor poured some of the rich chocolate from the pot into a to-go cup, added hot milk, and presented it to me with a flourish.

I sat on a bench in Parc du Champ-de-Mars sipping hot chocolate and munching my flaky croissant as I paid my daily respects to my fair iron lady. It was nice to have la Tour Eiffel all to myself for a change.

Well, not completely to myself.

At another bench a little farther down, an elderly man wearing an overcoat and black cap—not a beret—sat engrossed in his copy of *Le Monde*.

And two Mademoiselles—shop girls, perhaps?—who looked nineteen or twenty at the most, strode by with their arms linked, chattering softly in their black miniskirts, tights, high heels, and fitted jackets, with the ubiquitous scarves at their necks—one saffron, one cobalt.

A college student–looking guy in jeans and a thick chocolate brown sweater with a striped wool scarf wrapped around his neck and brushing against his scraggly goatee, gave the girls an appreciative glance as he bicycled by—perhaps on his way to the Sorbonne?

I always liked making up stories about the people that I people watch.

And people watching in Paris ranked right up there with seeing all the famous monuments.

Like the trim, fortyish, silvery blonde in a snug, expensive-looking black wool coat and black stiletto boots, with a scarlet scarf—probably cashmere—knotted stylishly at her throat, whose heels crunched the pea gravel beneath her feet in a hurry, as if she might be late to work.

She passed beneath the lacy ironwork tower without even glancing up once.

Now I knew she had to be on her way to work, clearly to some high-powered, high-stress job, if the tense set of her jaw and the lines around her mouth were any indication. Perhaps she was an editor at a high-end Paris fashion magazine, and she was on her way right now to fire some lowly assistant who'd gotten her morning café au lait order wrong one too many times.

Or maybe she was a buyer at one of the chichi designer stores that Paige and Annette had visited yesterday.

Or a curator at one of Paris's many museums.

More likely she was simply a well-dressed banker or accountant.

Happy not to have a high-stress job, but even happier still not to be at work at all, I continued munching on my croissant and enjoying the intoxicating view and the magical lure of the City of Lights.

Paris was like a drug. And I was addicted.

The city stirred my senses, opened my heart, and expanded my soul.

While I enjoyed my early morning solitude, my thoughts turned to Becca.

After she'd given me the lovely and unexpected book gift, I'd discussed my concerns about my roommate's precarious financial state with Tess.

"But how could she come to Paris without enough money?" Tess said. "She's the one who suggested the trip in the first place and said we'd have a year to save up for it."

"Becca's not really good at saving. Or with money in general for that matter." I thought of the couple of bounced rent checks she'd given me in the past.

But that was then. And this was now.

We put our heads together and agreed that I should find a discreet way to talk to Becca away from the rest of the group to see if I could discover just how bad things were. And figure out ways we could help.

"It would be better coming from you since you're closer to her age," Tess said. "Especially since she and I seem to butt heads so easily."

"That's just because you tell it like it is."

Tess chuckled. "With two teenage sons, you kind of have to."

I was a little concerned that Becca and I might butt heads too. I thought back to the time I had confronted her about her messy bathroom and dirty dishes. Conflict is not one of my favorite things. Would I be able to do it again, or would I lose my nerve?

"*Bonjour*," I said to Tess as I returned to our room of toile, divesting myself of my coat and scarf.

"*Bonjour* yourself." She popped her head out of the bathroom, where she was applying lipstick. "And where have you been with your cheeks all flushed and your eyes sparkling? Is there something you want to tell Aunt Tess?"

"Only that I've fallen head over heels in love."

"What?"

I stuck the éclairs in the fridge then plopped down on the far side of the bed and laced my hands behind my head as I stared at my tower in the distance.

"J'adore Paris."

A few minutes later I rode the elevator back down to the lobby and headed to Becca and Paige's room. In front of their door, I took a deep breath and knocked.

Paige opened the door with a sunny smile. *"Bonjour, mon amie. Comment allez-vous?"*

"Très bien, merci. Et vous?"

"Bien. Très bien."

"Can I talk to Becca?" I asked, having used up most of the French I knew.

"Sorry. You just missed her. She and Kailyn left about five minutes ago."

"Oh. Okay. I'll just talk to her at breakfast then."

"'Fraid not. She and Kailyn weren't hungry and decided to skip breakfast this morning. They wanted to do some more exploring of the city before they went to the catacombs and said they'd catch up with us in the lobby tonight before dinner."

A little relieved, I decided to head upstairs again and read until my two companions for the day were dressed and ready.

"How long ago was it that you were last here, Annette?" I asked as she, Tess, and I rode the Metro an hour later on our way to Île de la Cité.

"Thirty ... no, actually, it will be thirty-one years this summer. I was stationed in Germany with the Air Force at the time. My roommate Donna and I decided to come over for a three-day weekend in the summer. And we had a blast! Paris in the seventies when disco was king was quite a kick."

"I'll say." Tess's eyes gleamed behind her glasses. "I came

in the seventies my first time too. I was eighteen and fresh out of high school. My best friend Lana and I had saved up to spend the summer backpacking around Europe before we went to college in the fall. And we loved Paris so much we stayed a whole month."

"I wish I'd had the nerve to do something adventurous like that," I said. "Instead, I spent my last summer before college working in a bank. Very exciting."

Tess chuckled. "I remember that bank job. It was pretty borin — Hey!" Her head swiveled to Annette. "Wait a minute. I just realized that thirty-one years ago, I was eighteen."

"Very good," Annette said. "Eighteen plus thirty-one equals forty-nine. So you're a year younger than me. Don't rub it in."

"No. You don't understand. Don't you see? You said you came to Paris thirty-one years ago for a three-day weekend in the summer. Well, thirty-one years ago, I spent a month in Paris. *In the summer.*"

"Get out!"

"We could have passed each other on the street, or in the Louvre, or at a sidewalk café," Tess said.

"What month were you here?"

"July."

"That's when I was here too! And I remember it was hotter than blazes. We came for the Fourth of July weekend."

"Oh. We didn't get here until the middle of July."

"Ships in the night," Annette said.

"Did you go to that famous three-story discotheque that was really hot at the time?"

"Did we ever. And we stuck out like sore thumbs in our sweet all-American, girl-next-door sundresses. The women all had glitter on their faces and wore black leggings with long white T-shirts knotted at the hip."

"I remember it well." Tess slid her a wicked look. "I had one of those T-shirts knotted at the hip—only over jeans."

"Well, weren't you the queen of the fashion scene. Wait'll I tell Kailyn."

I pretended to lightly snore.

"Are we boring you with our trip down Memory Lane?"

"Whatever gave you that idea?"

"You okay, Annette?" I stopped at the top of the spiral staircase and called down to her. "You're almost there. Just another dozen steps or so."

"Fine," she gasped out. "Don't worry about me. I'll be there in a couple minutes."

"Atta girl," Tess said from a few steps beneath her. "That's the spirit."

When Annette finally reached the top, she struggled out of her heavy coat, red-faced, sweating, and puffing. "I sure hope these gargoyles are worth it."

They were.

So was the view of Paris and the Seine.

"Spectacular." Annette clicked away with her digital camera once she caught her breath. "You know, some of these gargoyles are pretty ugly. But they're so ugly, they're almost cute."

That wasn't exactly the word I'd have used to describe the frightening stone creatures. But they definitely left an impression.

After we left Notre Dame, Tess decided we needed a reward for making that long trek up the tower. "I'm going to introduce you to the best ice cream you've ever had," she promised.

"Ice cream in January?" Annette said. "What about a nice cup of tea in one of those salons du thés instead?"

"Later. But for now, onward to the most amazing ice cream and sorbets ever. Trust me. You're going to love it. And the lines shouldn't be too long either, not this time of year. In spring and summer they're absolutely insane — they stretch all the way around the block."

"Ooh, I read about this in my Paris research." I flipped through my notes in my small travel journal as we walked to Île Saint-Louis. "It's called Berthillon, right?"

"That's the place." Tess kissed her fingers. "And I recommend the *prune armagnac*."

"Prune ice cream?" Annette wrinkled her nose. "I've had garlic ice cream at the Gilroy Garlic Festival, but it was pretty awful."

"I can imagine it would be," Tess said. "But armagnac is completely different. It's sweet and flavorful. *C'est magnifique*. The pear sorbet and wild strawberry sorbet are also wonderful. And *marron glace*, chestnut ..."

"Don't they have plain chocolate?" Annette asked.

"Oh, they have chocolate. And it's anything but plain."

Except we weren't going to be able to put Tess's assertion to the test.

We stood as a trio in front of the closed and shuttered shop with the fancy *B*s beside the doors. Tess slapped her hand to her forehead. "I can't believe I forgot they were closed on Tuesdays."

"*Tant pis*," I said, "Don't worry about it. It's not the end of the world."

"Chloe, you're getting very good at the language," Annette said. "Before we leave, you'll be fluent."

I snorted. Softly. We were in Paris after all. During our exchange, Tess had stood there with her brow furrowed in thought. All at once her face lit up. "You're right. It's not the end of the world. We'll just have to enjoy some Berthillon at one of the restaurants in the area instead. There's a nice little café at the western end of Île Saint-Louis that carries it."

She looked up at the sky, where the sun had just come out from behind the clouds. "But now we must hurry to Sainte-Chapelle while the sun is shining."

Tess shepherded us back in the direction of Notre Dame so we could see her beloved chapel a few blocks away. "I know this is probably sacrilege," she said as we hurried along, "but I prefer Sainte-Chapelle over Notre Dame. Notre Dame's a bit too big and gloomy for me. But Sainte-Chapelle is this brilliant little jewel tucked away within the walls of the Palais de Justice. Louis IX had it built to house the crown of thorns that Jesus wore."

I stopped cold.

"Are you telling me we're going to get to see the crown of thorns that was on Jesus's head when he was crucified?"

"No," Tess said gently. "It's now kept in the Notre Dame treasury and shown only on Fridays during Lent. And it's not for sure that the relic is the real thing, but King Louis certainly thought so. He paid an enormous sum of money for it and then had Sainte-Chapelle created as a chapel that would be worthy of the sacred crown that had touched the skin of the Messiah."

"I can't wait to see it," Annette said. "I read somewhere that in medieval times, stained glass was like a book for the believers who couldn't read."

"That's right. Detailed scenes from the Bible were painstakingly crafted in glass to help teach the Bible stories to the illiterate faithful." Tess released a reverent sigh. "Just wait until you see the stained glass. It's the most beautiful I've ever seen."

She was right. Although, when we first entered the small stone church, I thought, *This is it? What's the big deal?*

Then she led us up a tiny spiral staircase to the main level, or upper chapel.

Annette and I gasped.

Walls of nearly solid glass held up the vaulted roof in the narrow room.

"It's like being surrounded by a curtain of stained glass," I whispered as myriad shades of sapphire, ruby, emerald, and topaz streamed in from every direction, illuminating the chapel.

"Exquisite," Annette breathed. "The others will be sorry they missed this."

I wasn't thinking about the others. I sank into one of the benches along the wall and stared silently at the glorious, jewel-colored windows telling the story of creation to redemption to Apocalypse. They say a picture is worth a thousand words, and as I gazed upon the vivid glass biblical pictures, I thought of the faithful who centuries before me had read in this very room without the benefit of words. And I thought of how much I cherished the written word.

Sometimes even words need a little accompaniment though.

I slowly reached in my pocket and pulled out my iPod.

Tess had told us there were often public concerts in this upper chapel—church services had stopped years ago—but today there was no concert, and I needed music.

And not just any music.

Discreetly I found the selection I wanted, stuck in my ear buds, and hit play.

Charlotte Church's pure, exquisite soprano filled my head as she sang "The Prayer." And moments later Josh Groban joined in. Singing in Italian, his glorious rich voice was a perfect counterpart to hers.

I stared at the stained glass windows, letting the music

and the sheer majesty of my Creator wash over me in that holy place.

And as the voices soared, my soul soared right along with them as I added my prayer to theirs in the same place where kings worshiped centuries ago.

Guide me with your grace, oh Lord. Fill me with your light.

26

When good Americans die, they go to Paris.

The Picture of Dorian Gray

For dinner that night, Tess and I suggested another neighborhood creperie as a lighter option instead of a heavy three- or four-course meal. The palpable relief in Becca's eyes at this less costly alternative confirmed our suspicions. Then, as we were tucking into our crepes, she up and said: "I think I'll quit my job and move to Paris."

We all looked up at once and said, "What?"

"I could live in this city in a heartbeat," she continued. "I'd quit Dunkeld's tomorrow and come live in Paris. It's such a cool city, and there's so much to do here."

"But what would you do for a *living*?" Annette asked.

"Work in a bookstore. Starve in a garret." She shrugged. "Whatever."

"Starving would be more likely," Tess said. "Paris is a pretty expensive place to live. Rents aren't cheap and getting work as a foreigner is next to impossible—especially for Americans."

"I thought you wanted to live in China," I reminded my roommate.

"I'm over China. Paris is more my style."

"What about the whole language thing?" Paige asked. "Your French is pretty nonexistent. And to work here you kind of need to know the language."

"Not necessarily." She flashed us a triumphant look. "Kailyn and I met this American girl in the catacombs today who lives and works here, and she said when she first came nearly a year ago, she could only speak a few phrases."

"That's a little different," Kailyn said. "Her husband works at the U.S. Embassy, and he got her a job there."

"Way to rain on my parade."

"Just trying to give you a reality check."

Annette sent a look of surprise to her daughter.

"What? That's what you always say to me."

"I know. But I didn't think you listened."

"Sometimes." Kailyn smiled sweetly at Annette.

Once again, my roommate was off on one of her spontaneous flights of fancy. It was getting to be par for the course. As was my practical intervention.

"Living in Paris is a nice fantasy, Bec, but apart from the obvious"—I ticked off on my fingers—"lack of a job, lack of a place to stay, lack of knowledge of the language, you couldn't move here at least for another month or so anyway."

"Why not?"

"Hmm. Let's see. There's all your stuff you'd have to pack up and put in storage—or get rid of, then you'd have to save up for another plane ticket, find a new home for your angel fish, give Dunkeld's a heads-up, oh, and then there's that little thirty-day notice thing you have to give your roommate so she's not stuck holding the full rent bag."

I smiled to show I wasn't being a nag. Sort of.

Becca smiled back.

"But most important of all," Tess interjected, "you're the fearless leader of the Paperback Girls. You can't abandon us. What would we do without your intrepid leadership? If it weren't for you, we wouldn't even be in Paris right now!"

"That's right," Annette said. "And I wouldn't have gotten to see my gargoyles, or tasted those yummy Ladurée macarons or Berthillon ice cream."

I nodded. "And I wouldn't have been able to see Sainte-Chapelle, the Eiffel Tower, or my woman with the green umbrella."

"Yeah, and I wouldn't have gotten my Hermès scarf."

"And I wouldn't be fulfilling the dream of learning French cooking from a Parisian chef."

"That's right!" Annette said. "What'd you learn to make in Jacqueline's class today, and did you bring us the recipe?"

"*Tarte au fromage de chèvre, bœuf bourguignon, and mousse au chocolat.*"

"Translation, please," Kailyn ordered. "All I got was the chocolate mousse."

"Goat cheese tart and beef burgundy, beef with red wine. And yes, I have the recipe. Jacqueline was kind enough to make each of you a copy." Paige pulled the papers from her purse and handed a copy to each of us.

Becca scanned hers and snorted. "Looks like a lot of time and work involved just to make lunch," she said. "I think I'll be sticking to my PB&J or grilled cheese and tomato soup."

"Julia Child said, 'Noncooks think it's silly to invest two hours' work in two minutes' enjoyment; but if cooking is evanescent, so is the ballet,'" Paige recited.

"What's evanescent?" Kailyn asked.

"Brief, fleeting."

"I wish that ballet I saw back home had been brief and fleeting."

"You're such a philistine, Becca," Annette said fondly.

"Yes, but she's our philistine. And if it weren't for our little philistine, we wouldn't be here in Paris celebrating everything that is nonphilistine." I raised my glass. "To Becca, our fearless leader."

The rest raised their glasses. "To Becca. *Santès!*"

That night we skipped the Nutella.

Kailyn groaned as she pushed back from the table. "I bet I've gained ten pounds since we've been here."

"Me too," Paige said. "And unlike you, I can't afford another ten."

"I think you'll be surprised," Tess said. "I'll bet when you get home you'll find you've lost weight instead of gained it."

Kailyn brightened. "Really? But how?"

"All the walking we've been doing."

"And all the climbing," I said. "I think I've climbed more steps here than in my entire life."

"And there's still more to come," Tess said brightly. "Just wait until we go to Sacré Cœur and Montmartre."

"I can hardly wait." Annette grimaced.

"We'll have to be sure and tell Jenna about the gym we found in Paris—the streets of the city," Becca said.

"Works for me. I could stand to lose my love handles," Paige said.

"You and me both," Annette told her. "There was no way I was going to diet in Paris, so it's a good thing we're getting this city workout."

We paid the bill—a fraction of last night's dinner—and walked out into the chilly night air. Kailyn, Annette, and Paige wanted to go up the Eiffel Tower since they'd missed out on that our first night, and although Tess had been several times before, she agreed to go along.

"Becca and I will meet you there," I said. "We need to do a roommate catch up."

"Do you know how to get there?" Kailyn asked.

I pointed to the sparkling tower a few blocks away. "She'll guide us."

As the others walked on ahead, Becca gave me a wary look. "Now what have I done?"

"That's actually what I'm wondering." I paused and screwed up my courage. "Are you out of money?"

Even in the night air I could see her face flush. "What makes you think that?"

"Oh, I don't know. Something about bailing out of the second cooking class, never buying any souvenirs, always ordering the cheapest item on the menu," I said gently. "Want to tell me what happened?"

Becca expelled a heavy sigh. "You know, the last thing I want to talk about in Paris is how bad I am with finances. Long story short, I found out just before we left that I'd maxed out my Visa, but I thought I had enough on my American Express to get me through the trip." She surrendered a wry smile. "Only it turns out I figured wrong, and our first day here I maxed out that card too."

"But don't you have any cash with you?"

"Some. Not a lot."

"What about in your checking account?"

"A whopping seven dollars and thirty-two cents until I get paid at the end of the month."

"Is this the same woman who just a couple hours ago announced that she wanted to move here?"

"Shut up. A girl can dream, can't she? What are we without

our dreams?" she said. "When you cease to dream, you cease to live."

"Hemingway?"

"Malcolm S. Forbes."

"Who in the world is that?"

"The head of *Forbes* magazine."

"You read *Forbes*?"

"Nah. I found it in one of my quote books."

I made Becca an offer she couldn't refuse. I told her I'd be happy to loan — even give — her money for the rest of the trip as long as she let me help her set up a budget when we returned home.

She agreed, but only to a loan.

The next day, after our final cooking lesson with Jacqueline, where she taught us to shop for and prepare *blanquette de veau* and *crème caramel*, we all trooped over to the Place de la Concorde area, where we took tons of pictures at "Kailyn's fountain."

We'd named it that because Kailyn couldn't stop gushing over it — like me and the Eiffel Tower.

Afterward, we walked over to the Orangerie, or Musée de l'Orangerie.

Tess told us a little of the history of the small museum on our walk. Initially built as a winter home to house fragile plants, Monet had rooms constructed at the Orangerie to house the immense lily paintings that were the culmination of his years of focus upon his water gardens at Giverny. He donated the final paintings of his life — painted as he was going blind — to France at the end of World War I.

We'd already seen one of the artist's beautiful *Water Lilies* in San Francisco, and I'd been entranced by the vibrant colors, peaceful scene, and use of light, so I was looking forward to more.

I followed Tess into the first gallery, reading the brochure about *Les Nympheas.* Then I looked up and gasped.

Color and light exploded from the curved walls of the large white oval room. Daylight streamed through the ceiling, offering a natural spotlight to the massive panels of ever-changing blues, greens, and lavenders.

I felt my jaw drop at the sheer size and magnificence.

Slowly, I moved around the room, drinking in the tranquil murals of the serene lily pond with its changing light and swirling color that looked like it went on into infinity.

"To think that he was able to create this even as he was going blind," I murmured, gazing at the swirling, evocative brush strokes.

Beside me, Tess said, "Someone once described this museum as 'the Sistine Chapel of Impressionism.' "

"I can see why."

After finishing our slow circle of the room, the others moved through the arched doorway into the next gallery, but I remained behind.

An oval bench in the center of the room beckoned me.

I sat staring for I don't know how long, at the peaceful, panoramic view in front of me. Then I walked to the other side of the oval bench that replicated the shape of the room so I could see the large panels behind me. I kept scooting to different places on the bench so I could take it all in.

There are moments in life when everything changes.

Sitting there on that bench in the Orangerie, something inside me shifted.

As I continued to gaze upon the soothing colors of the water scenes, I remembered the first of Monet's *Water Lilies* I'd seen many months before.

And I remembered, too, the painting of the peasant girl dressed in brown that I'd longed to pluck out of her drab surroundings and set in the middle of the lilies with her hair free from its dutiful bun and flowing down her back, her face turned to the sun, basking in the light.

I reached up and released my hair from its ponytail.

After our visit to the Orangerie—which included a *second* oval room of water lilies and the wonderful surprise of basement galleries of Renoirs, Cezannes, Picassos, and more, we went to the Opéra Garnier in search of the Phantom's underground lair for Kailyn and my mom and were surprised and delighted to find Marc Chagall on the ceiling as well.

I bought a small jar of opera house honey for my mom, courtesy of the bees that live on the roof—yes, at the Opéra Garnier. Go figure.

During the rest of our Paris stay, we visited Montmartre and had our pictures painted by street artists, climbed up myriad stairs to the Sacré Cœur for another beautiful view of the city, had lunch at Café de Flore in Saint-Germain-des-Prés where Hemingway, Picasso, and Truman Capote used to hang out, and squeezed between the bookshelves in Shakespeare and Company, where we bought used paperbacks for our next book club selections.

We walked and walked and walked.

We discovered small cafés off the beaten path where we had croque-monsieurs and onion soup, got lost, revisited Becca's bookstalls along the Seine, and shopped for souvenirs in the Rue de Rivoli, where Becca was delighted to find miniature Eiffel Towers for only one euro.

She bought five for friends and colleagues, and I bought one for Ryan.

In a nod to the absent Jenna, we visited the Conciergerie, Paris's oldest prison, where Marie Antoinette and others from the Revolution were incarcerated before being executed.

We also acquiesced to Tess and Annette and checked out Napoleon's tomb, a deep red sarcophagus inside Les Invalides with its grandiose frescoes and Corinthian columns. Then we paid our respects to Victor Hugo at the Panthéon, where he is entombed along with Voltaire and Rousseau.

One day we took the train to Versailles, and as Becca had thought, it was a lot of ritz and glitz at the Sun King's former palace, but we fell in love with the massive, well-manicured grounds.

Stunning. And probably even more so in the spring when everything would be in bloom.

Another time we went to le Grande Epicerie, the famous gourmet supermarket where we bought ham and pâté and three kinds of cheese, and baguettes, planning to picnic in the famed Bois de Boulogne. But it was way too cold, so we trundled back to the hotel and squeezed into our tiny room with a view and had a bedroom picnic instead, raising our glasses to La Tour Eiffel, which we could see out our window sparkling in all her nighttime finery.

Our final day, we enjoyed strolling through the city and picking up last-minute gifts and souvenirs. I bought silk scarves for my mom and Julia — not Hermès, but beautiful nonetheless — and a copy of *Madeline* for my niece; Paige went to Dehillerin, the famous kitchen supply store, and bought a madeleine pan and some cooking utensils; Kailyn haunted the "bowels boutique" in the Metro; and Annette returned to Ladurée for more delicious macarons.

While the rest of us were loading up with souvenirs, Becca asked Tess if she'd take her to Sainte-Chapelle.

As the sun was setting, I returned alone to the Musée d'Orsay to gaze upon my woman with the green umbrella once more and to say good-bye. Again, as before, there were artists-in-training practicing their painting in front of the Van Goghs, Renoirs, and Monets.

I stood and watched them awhile, aching for a brush of my own.

Finally though, it was time to go. Instead of saying au revoir, however, I murmured *à bientôt*.

See you later.

That night, my Eiffel Tower seemed to sparkle more brightly than ever, as if she knew we were leaving and was giving us a special farewell show.

> A man should hear a little music, read a little poetry,
> and see a fine picture every day of his life, in order that
> worldly cares may not obliterate the sense of the beautiful
> which God has implanted in the human soul.
>
> *Johann Wolfgang von Goethe*

This time when our plane took off, I didn't clench the armrests, and I skipped the Valium my doctor had prescribed. My fears had evaporated in the Paris mist.

Around me the Paperback Girls chattered happily.

"I can't wait to get home and see your daddy," Annette said to Kailyn. "I've missed that good-lookin' man! I'm going to plant a big wet kiss on him the minute I see him."

Kailyn adjusted her Hermès scarf. "I can't wait to show all the girls my new scarf. And I sure hope Daddy likes the black beret I got him."

"I wonder if my boys have destroyed the house in my absence," Tess said wryly.

"Oh, I'm sure there will be something still left standing," Becca said. "It's that sturdy California stucco, right?"

I turned my head to the window, hoping for one last glimpse of my iron lady silhouetted against the Paris sky. But the clouds hung too low.

Instead, I put in my ear buds, shut my eyes, and relived the memories of the past week. When "Do You Hear the People Sing?" from *Les Misérables* came on, I was cruising down the Seine again in a Bateau Mouche, passing the flying buttresses of Notre Dame. And when the Little Sparrow sang "La Vie en Rose," I was in every sidewalk café with my friends, eating *délicieuse* foods, laughing, and having a good time.

Then the Josh Groban – Charlotte Church duet of "The Prayer" came on, and I was transported back again to Sainte-Chapelle and its glorious stained glass.

The tears flowed.

"Chloe? Hello?"

"Huh?" I blinked and looked at my boss.

Bob grinned at me. "I think someone's still in Paris. They say it gets in your blood."

"That it does," I murmured. "There's nothing like it."

"Well I know where someone's going for vacation next year." He smiled. "Meanwhile though, we need to analyze this latest regulation."

I called Tess on my break and asked if we could meet for dinner after work. As I drove to our favorite Mexican restaurant, I stuck in the Joni Mitchell CD Tess had given me and sang loudly along with Joni to "Free Man in Paris."

Tess arrived ten minutes late, after I'd already scarfed down half the chips and salsa. She was flushed and out of breath, her cheeks pink beneath her red glasses.

"Sorry I'm late. James called from Chicago just as I was leaving work, and I lost track of time."

"No problem. I can see how you'd rather talk to the dashing widower instead of your favorite niece."

"That's not true," she protested, blushing. Then she saw my face. "Oh, you're teasing."

"Duh."

When Tess returned home from our trip, she had found that her boys, far from leaving her house a disaster, had cleaned it from top to bottom at the urging of and with the help of Clemmie, Tommy's now-girlfriend. Tess had been surprised and touched.

And delighted with the beautiful bouquet of long-stemmed yellow roses on the dining room table. Only the roses hadn't come from Timmy and Tommy.

James MacDonald, Annette's set-up from all those months ago, had called while Tess was in Paris. The twins told him when she was due back, and he sent a dozen roses and a card that read:

> Welcome home. Hope you had a wonderful time in Paris.
> Hoping also that you'll give me a second chance. *Bientôt*.
> James.

They'd had dinner a few nights later and then again the next night.

And the next.

He took her and the boys and Clemmie bowling — I tagged along as Timmy's "date" — and then skiing up at Lake Tahoe. The twins had pronounced him "cool" and were thrilled that at long last their mother had a man in her life.

I was too.

But at the moment that man was in Chicago on a business trip, so he and Tess were reduced to phone calls and emails.

Tess and I caught up on family stuff: Little Sophie was now two months old and doted upon by everyone in the family, particularly her grandparents; Julia and Justin had just bought their first house, so Mom and Julia were sewing up a storm, making curtains for all the windows; and Erica, the *enfant terrible*, had barfed all over her teacher after sneaking into the classroom during recess on Valentine's Day and gobbling up all the candy hearts.

And then I told Tess my plan and asked for her help.

"You're going to do *what*?" Becca said when I told her the next day.

"Go live in Paris," I repeated.

"By yourself? *You*?"

"Just me, myself, and I."

"But ... how?" she sputtered. "When?"

"I'm not sure exactly when yet — hopefully in the next month or so once I get everything set up."

Becca stared at me. "But what are you going to *do* there? You're the one who told me it was impossible for Americans to get jobs in Paris, remember?"

"To err is human. To loaf is Parisian," I said.

"Oscar Wilde?"

"Victor Hugo." I pushed my hair behind my ears. "And actually, I don't need a job. I've been setting aside money to buy a house ever since I was twelve, so I have a nice chunk of change in savings that will enable me to live there for a little while."

"Which brings up the question, *where* are you going to live?"

I shrugged my shoulders. "I'm not exactly sure yet. I've gone on the Internet and looked at apartment rentals, and there are a few that look promising. I emailed Jacqueline, and she's going to check them out for me in person. Otherwise,

Tess has a flight attendant friend based there who's gone a lot, and she thought I might be able to stay in her place. She emailed her, and we're waiting to hear back.

"I'm not worried. It will all work out." I grinned at my roommate. "Sometimes you just have to go for it and step out in faith."

"I can't believe you're quitting your state job. Not sensible, practical Chloe."

"Who says I'm quitting my job? I'm simply taking a leave of absence from it. It will be here waiting for me when I come back."

Becca snorted. "Yeah, like you're really going to want to go back to that boring job after living in Paris."

"You never know. It's just always good to have a back-up."

"Well, it's nice to see you haven't thrown off all of the old Chloe." She tilted her head and looked at me curiously. "So if you're not going to work, what *are* you going to do over there? You're not a party girl, so I know you won't be knockin' back the absinthe and painting Montmartre red."

"No, but I will be painting. I'm actually hoping to take some art classes, along with some French language classes to help me get around." My eyes sought my lady with the green umbrella that I'd framed and hung on the living room wall. "More than anything, I want to go sit in the Musée d'Orsay and just paint. I have no delusions about becoming an artist. I simply want to pick up a paintbrush again and feel the canvas beneath my hand."

"Then you should go for it," Becca said. "Carpe diem, baby!"

All at once she realized the implications of my decision. "Hey, what about me? I can't afford this place all by myself. Where am I going to live?"

"I figured you could find another roommate, and I could sublet the place to her. Kailyn's been wanting to move out from her folks', and we already know she loves the condo."

"*Kailyn* as a roommate?" Becca gaped. "You must be joking. We'd kill each other."

"We didn't."

"That's because you're not a ditzy blonde clothesaholic. Kailyn and I have absolutely nothing in common."

"You have book club. And I thought you guys bonded at the catacombs?"

"I guess," she said grudgingly. "A little."

When I told the Paperback Girls my Paris plans at our next book club meeting, they couldn't believe it either.

"Serious?" Kailyn said. "You?"

"Why does everyone keep saying that?"

"Well I think it's great," Annette said. "If I were young and single, I'd probably do the same thing." She grinned. "Oh wait—I already did that when I joined the Air Force right after high school."

"I'm thrilled for you, Chloe, but I'm also jealous," Paige said. "I'd love to spend a couple months in Paris studying cooking."

"Or shopping." Kailyn's eyes glittered. "How fabulous would that be?"

Jenna frowned. "I just don't get it, I guess. You're doing this again, why?"

"Because."

"Because why?"

"Because," I said simply, "it feeds my soul."

Julia and my folks had responded the same way. At least initially. But once I explained it all, they understood.

Sort of.

"I don't know," Mom worried. "A young girl going to Paris

all by herself? Are you sure it's safe? I've heard they have white slavers over there in Europe just waiting to pounce on pretty young girls and do who knows what to them."

"I'm not eighteen, Mom. I'm twenty-nine. And believe it or not, I do know how to take care of myself."

"Of course you do," Dad said. He squeezed my mom's shoulder. "Don't worry, honey. Chloe's got a good, steady head on her shoulders. She'll be just fine."

Julia winked. "Yeah, and by the time she gets back, Sophie might be walking and talking."

Ryan was the only one who got it right away.

"That's great!" he said, giving me a huge hug when I told him. "Good for you. It's nice to see that the timid butterfly has at last shed her cocoon. I knew it was just a matter of time." He grinned. "Now I have an even more compelling reason to visit Paris. If I come over, will you be my tour guide?"

"As long as you come within the next few months. I can only stay in Paris ninety days without a visa."

"Oh, I'll be over." He sent me a slow smile full of promise. "You can count on it."

A month later, early on a cool spring morning, I sat on a bench in Parc du Champ-de-Mars munching on a *pain au chocolat* and gazing at my iron lady before all the hordes of tourists descended for the day.

I thought back over the past year and all that had happened since Chris's fateful text message — a message that, at the time, I was sure had destroyed all my happily-ever-after dreams. I thought of all the adventures with the Paperback Girls and how they had led me to this point.

Then I thought about my family and how my relationships with them had changed. Especially my sister.

And I realized that I had changed too.

I wasn't Julia the Perfect, Becca the Adventurous, or Tess the Wise.

I was just Chloe, and that was enough.

My happily ever after was just beginning, and I couldn't wait to see what tomorrow would bring.

> The good ended happily, and the bad unhappily. That is what Fiction means.
>
> *The Importance of Being Earnest*

BOOK SELECTIONS IN DARING CHLOE

The Adventures of Huckleberry Finn, Mark Twain, 2005 (originally published in 1884).

Coming Home, Rosamunde Pilcher, 1996.

Dove, Robin Graham, 1991 (originally published in 1972).

Emma, Jane Austen, 2003 (originally published in 1816).

French Women Don't Get Fat, Mireille Guiliano, 2007.

From the Mixed-Up Files of Mrs. Basil E. Frankweiler, E. L. Konigsburg, 1998 (originally published in 1967).

Heidi, Johanna Spyri, 2002 (originally published in 1880).

Les Misérables, Victor Hugo, 1987 (originally published in 1862).

Little Women, Louisa May Alcott, 2004 (originally published in 1868).

Marjorie Morningstar, Herman Wouk, copyright 1992 (originally published in 1955).

Murder on the Orient Express, Agatha Christie, 2004 (originally published in 1934).

A Walk in the Woods, Bill Bryson, 1999.

ACKNOWLEDGMENTS

Reading is to the mind what exercise is to the body.

Sir Richard Steele

Thanks must first go to my fabulous and *très* cute agent, Beth Jusino, who helped me brainstorm Chloe and the Paperback Girls and also find the perfect home for them at Zondervan. Thanks for your encouragement (and the glasses tips too).

To my editor, Andy Meisenheimer, thank you for your enthusiasm, your availability, and your expertise, and for helping me to grow as a writer. Your insights made Chloe even stronger.

Thanks also are due to Becky Shingledecker and the creative and hardworking team at Zondervan.

A huge *merci beaucoup* to the talented and well-traveled Siri Mitchell for reading the Paris chapters to ensure I didn't make some dreadful faux pas. Thanks, also, for correcting my extremely limited French. Any errors are mine.

A big thank you to Shannon Holme and Karen Tubbs for being my twenty-something eyes and ears. You guys rock!

For the snorkeling expertise, thanks are due Jamie Topper, Andi Davis, Beth Jusino, Cindy Martinusen, and Sean Gaffney, with a special nod to Jamie, the nurse-shark lover for the rule of thumb about sharks. I won't test your theory.

Thank you to Mary Ann Adams for her foodie help in some French cooking choices.

My lasting gratitude also goes to writer friends Cindy Martinusen and Sean Gaffney for their loving act of kindness and selflessness during a difficult and frightening time. Also, to Jon Drury and the Redwood Chapel Christian Writers conference for his servant's heart and for their understanding and prayers.

I am blessed to have amazing friends who love and support me and encourage me in my writing.

Ginormous thanks to Dave and Dale Meurer for spoiling me again on my Redding getaway and for feeding my meat-starved stomach, with extra thanks to Dave for the brainstorming and editing advice on the camping chapters. Notice however, my funny friend, that the words *Gitmo* and *Husqvarna* appear nowhere in this novel—and will never appear in any of my novels.

Say it with me again, Dave: "This is a chick book."

For providing encouragement, reading support, and crucial feedback when I needed it, my sincere gratitude goes to: Lisa Cook, Sheri Jameson, Jennie Damron, Katie Young, and Shane Galloway, with special thanks to Anne Peterson who's always so willing and available to be my first reader. Anne, I appreciate your enthusiasm and feedback.

Deepest gratitude to my sweet writer friends Annette Smith and Cathy Elliott, who are always ready to read chapters and offer loving encouragement and support across the miles, as well as the occasional—and necessary—reality slap up the side of the head when I get too neurotic.

Last, but never least, to Michael, my beloved, best friend, and life's traveling companion: Thank you for helping breathe life into some of Chloe's adventures, especially those on or around water, and for keeping such a meticulous travel journal. Thanks, too, for refreshing my "mentalpause" memory in the Paris chapters and correcting my mistakes. Without you, I couldn't do this. *J'adore, mon amour.* I can't wait to return to Paris with you!

Meanwhile, we'll always have the Musée d'Orsay.

Share Your Thoughts

With the Author: Your comments will be forwarded to the author when you send them to *zauthor@zondervan.com*.

With Zondervan: Submit your review of this book by writing to *zreview@zondervan.com*.

Free Online Resources at
www.zondervan.com/hello

 Zondervan AuthorTracker: Be notified whenever your favorite authors publish new books, go on tour, or post an update about what's happening in their lives.

 Daily Bible Verses and Devotions: Enrich your life with daily Bible verses or devotions that help you start every morning focused on God.

 Free Email Publications: Sign up for newsletters on fiction, Christian living, church ministry, parenting, and more.

 Zondervan Bible Search: Find and compare Bible passages in a variety of translations at www.zondervanbiblesearch.com.

 Other Benefits: Register yourself to receive online benefits like coupons and special offers, or to participate in research.